backwards *the drowned* go dreaming

by CARL WATSON

SENSITIVE SKIN BOOKS

BACKWARDS THE DROWNED GO DREAMING
Copyright 2012 Carl Watson
All rights reserved.

Cover Photograph: Hal Hirshorn
Book Design: Bernard Meisler

Published in the United States by **SENSITIVE SKIN BOOKS**.

First Edition 2012 **SENSITIVE SKIN BOOKS**

ISBN-13: 978-0983927143
ISBN-10: 0983927146

address any questions or comments to:
info@sensitiveskinmagazine.com

find us on the web:
www.sensitiveskinmagazine.com

ACKNOWLEDGEMENTS

Early versions and sections of some chapters have previously appeared in the following publications:

flashback/tombstone appeared in *Milk* (The Poetry Project 1993)
Chapters 1–3 appeared in *The Reading Room* (Great Marsh Press 2000)
Chapter 9 appeared in *The Unbearables Big Book of Sex* (Autonomedia 2011)
Chapters 22–23 appeared in *Sensitive Skin Magazine* (Sensitive Skin 2011)

Special thanks to Ron Kolm and B. Kold for editorial insight, Rob Hardin for line editing and T. Cho for proofing and excellent suggestions.

Contents

Part 1
falling off the edge of time

(1)

IT WAS MAYBE 10:30 PM, EARLY OCTOBER, 1974, A TIME OF profound spiritual dislocation and emotional collapse. Only scientists had computers. Television had not yet begun dictating public behavior. Some people even lived without phones. The level of dialogue on the street was less confined. There were three eggs frying in a pan along with some leftover Chinese rice. Half of a bottle of Jim Beam was waiting on the window ledge when Tanya McCoy climbed into that window on the southwest side of Portland, Oregon. It was my window, but she was looking for somebody else.

She knocked the Beam bottle off the ledge and I heard it break in the alley below just as I cranked up the volume on the radio. The song was Janis Joplin's "Piece of My Heart." I should have thought it meant something, but I wasn't thinking anything. I began singing along in a theatrical manner. I used such music as a purgative. Get drunk, go through my repertoire of gut-wrenching facial expressions. Wring my heart like a rag of tears. Usually I felt better in the morning.

But if I looked stupid doing it, she looked ridiculous watching—dressed in a stocking hat, railroad overalls, strapped and buckled square-toed Frye boots. She was packing a bottle of Gallo Tawny Port and a joint of Vietnamese bozo weed. She said "All right," as if she could identify with my folly. She apologized for the loss of the whisky as she twisted the cap off the port for a toast. Within hours, we had sewn the seeds of our middle-class discontent and would spend the next three years running toward or away from our separate demons.

Think Heloise and Abelard, Dante and Beatrice, Hammett and Hellman, Humbert and Lolita Hayes. This wasn't one of the great love stories of the ages, though. To tell the truth, I'm not even sure it was a love story. I'm not sure love stories exist other than as models for emotional oppression. Concrete walls erected by tiny romantic sadists in our minds to batter our souls against, like bags of broken toys. But if it wasn't the stuff of legend, it *was* a story of passive obsession and two people who thought they could turn their ennui into religion.

Romantic fatalism aside, we would be travelers in strange times. The previous heady decade had degenerated into some sort of collective entertainment anxiety. Individualism was about to become a disease rather than a cure. People were dropping like flies from various vague illnesses.

One guy I knew went crazy from the "Fun," a term he used to describe the ominous evil out there, manipulating him, turning him into a party animal against his will. This "Fun" looked like a clown, or a punk from a nightclub, or a babe from a beer ad. Sometimes it looked like his own face in a hotel mirror. Another guy died from what was later called "Denial." Actually it was the same guy. Then there was the "Fear," but that's been around a long time, under different names. Some called it the "Horror." Others knew it as the face in the mirror.

So that's pretty much it—Kurtz and Bozo, hand-in-hand, walking through the collective psyche in bell-bottoms and running shoes. Of course these days those days seem like a veritable renaissance. But you can't go back. So this is how my story begins—the story of Frank Payne and Tanya McCoy. It begins with fried eggs and whisky in my Portland, Oregon kitchen, and Janis Joplin.

&

BUT WE DIDN'T stay in Portland. We didn't stay in Ogden or Denver either. In fact, we didn't stay anywhere. We stopped in Chicago briefly for a drink, but we didn't stay there. Within weeks we were headed down to New Orleans. We got a ride in a school bus headed for Normal, by way of Peoria. The driver, whose name was Doug, had a bag full of porn magazines, some righteous pot and what seemed to be a trained dog. The way the dog used his tongue was a clue. We didn't really want to know any more than that. It was too early in the morning.

Outside Normal, we got ride with a family of glassy-eyed kids heading to some Tennessee commune by way of Evansville and Bowling Green. They had invisible TV sets tuned to a better world glued to their eyes. They asked us to join them, but we declined. There would be other such offers of companionship, lifestyle choices. We avoided the possibilities these parallel universes offered. We were going somewhere.

We had to backtrack on 40 through Memphis because we had gone out of the way. Next, some half-pint-sucking, crumpled-hat hillbilly with one eyebrow and a hidden agenda gave us a tour of the local back roads which I mostly remember as a black-and-white film of rapidly approaching tree trunks looming in front of the windshield. He dumped us at some god-forsaken intersection in northern Mississippi, and we were happy to be there in one piece.

Next we got picked up by a country-western band, and that's when we met Mary Stone, aka Jessica James, a runaway, a kid really, but a clever one. Mary became our friend. She would go the rest of the way with us to New Orleans. Mary Stone was a seasoned hobo and knew all the hobo ways of being in the world, especially that tactic of disappearing and not being seen again for days, weeks, months, or ever. This happened in New Orleans. We didn't see her again for weeks.

There's always that part of your life you spend chasing clichés. And New Orleans is nothing if not a road-dog cliché. You have to pass through there if you want any credibility. So the road-dogs say. It's a town where the smell of alcohol and Spanish moss blends into a murky bouquet that soaks into your skin, lungs and liver until you feel like you're living in some soft-focus nostalgic version of your own life. Some say the city makes you mean and lazy. Some say it makes you think you know something that you don't. Either way, it's dangerous.

&

ME AND TANYA got a cheap three-room joint in a mostly black part of town just upriver of the Quarter. We rented the back room hourly to horny couples in exchange for drugs. But we made the greater part of our money selling flowers on the street—dyed carnations, roses, and some sticky, carnal, orchid-style number that smelled like old sweat and soap. We ate crawfish and fried oysters. We drank all day and pretended we still had a thing. Tanya got involved with a band for a while, but they never played anywhere. The rehearsals were just excuses to get high.

We knew everybody on the street and they knew us. There was the Chicken Man, Clyde, Sal the Money-Man Mazolowski, and Raul the Candy Man. There was Charlie the Lucky Dog Man, too, and a runaway adding-machine heiress who called herself Antoinette, or "Andi" Salmon. It was a good life. It was almost as if we belonged somewhere.

We had a few people living with us—and off us—on and off. An emancipated stripper named Sheyly, a waiter/hustler named Smiling Bob, a half-Cherokee pot dealer who was called Steven Long Claw and his pregnant Italian wife, Sofia Cenci. There were two others I don't remember well—two thieves who snuck out one night with half our stuff. They were all fakes, but then we were, too, so we couldn't call them on it.

We loved the fringe people, the freaks. Unfortunately, these fringe people, these freaks, didn't like each other as much as we thought they should. One day Steven Long Claw hit Smiling Bob with a length of motorcycle chain. I can still see the way it snickered out of his pocket—an articulated steel-link snake with a voice like a whining cat that snaps back into a cry. Bob was suddenly bleeding from the link marks on his cheek. For a second it looked like red quarter notes dripping from a red music staff. He had two smiles, Bob did. Both red.

As usual the fight was over a woman—something she said, or, more likely, showed. Sheyly thrived on trouble—a genuine glow-in-the-dark blonde, flaunting her teenage sex up and down St. Bernard Avenue. like it was a prize. Maybe it was. Her friends were mostly Harley riders. Heavy-weight guys with bad posture and testosterone problems that rubbed off on others. Even Smiling Bob took to practicing nunchuck poses in the front yard. Road-Kill Pete did Buck knife tricks. It wasn't exactly a welcome-to-the-neighborhood sign. And they were doing dope all the time, too. I was glad when they finally left, but I would have been gladder to be the one leaving.

(2)

MEMORY CAN BE A TRICKY THING, EVEN A TACKY thing. it uses you. You might remember killing someone when you didn't do it. Many people do. They say the bedroom is the most dangerous room on earth. Police know it. Emergency room workers can tell you. I wish I could say such passion was mine to regret. But reconstruction is hard. They say it's in my head, my sin. Apparently this is true.

"There are already enough people who have as their mission in life the extinction of the fire." I read that once. Simone de Beauvoir. It's a nice thought—that the soul is not immortal by nature—it can only become so if fed. So I guess the road is more food than geometry—more consumption than myth. In fact the modern road story is the opposite of myth. There are no heroes. There are barely any actors. There are only observers and what might be called events, or non-events. As time goes on you move less and less.

No one feels they make anything happen, except maybe by bumping into things, moving through life as a means of making contact with the world. But the harder you look, the further it recedes: there's the fourteen-year-old girl you loved as a child, or the stepfather who sent you into a psychological tailspin. They dissipate, mutate and reconjugate. The effect redefines the cause. A car and its driver traveling down the highway might think they're fighting fate when they're really only illustrating the second law of thermodynamics. The White Queen bandages her finger, then begins to bleed—then comes the act that wounds. Backwards is the direction of order. Without punctuation the sentence can't mean anything. The mistake you made is the last thing you see.

There's a way to beat the system, though, to trick God and chaos. You punctuate your life—you tag emotions, connect them to senses, smells, sounds. In fact the whole of experience is a trackless web that begs to be labeled. I think there's a term for it—transubstantiation, transfixation, transference neurosis, something like that—the intense codependent association of particular sensations and events in memory.

For example, take a song from the 60s—"The Lion Sleeps Tonight," by the Tokens. Because of the conditions under which I first heard it, it will always remind me of a neighborhood girl, Beatrice, who looked like a figure in a surrealist painting by De Chirico or Magritte. Then there's

"Daniel," by Elton John—the song he wrote about his blind brother. I always associate it with the sight of a writhing dying dog, hit by a car during shift change traffic on US 20 as I drove toward the Gary Mill gates. The sulfurous air, the anticipation of the bone-deadening job: I'm placed right there in the driver's seat every time. "California Dreaming," by the Mamas and Papas will forever be associated with the fork in I-80 where it goes north or south. I had decided to leave the land of steel mills. Me and Eddie Mercury sat there in a '69 Opel Cadet. I flipped a coin. We headed north to Portland, Oregon. That was the song on the radio. We did the opposite. The next thing I remember was Patsy Cline's "Walking after Midnight," on the jukebox in a Boise, Idaho Bar, while two women circled each other with bloody pool balls in their hands, a crowd of truck-driving drunks egging them on. That's how the system works. The image is pinned to the bulletin board of the brain by the song.

&

ANOTHER INSTANCE IS "Pusher Man," from Easy Rider. But I didn't associate it so much with the movie as with the smell of US 30 dragstrip. I went with my brother's friend, Roy Latoure. The motorcycle is the connection here. Roy had one. So did Dennis Hopper. Roy Latoure was a displaced Texas biker hippie with an eye patch. He lived with my brother in a basement pad in Hammond, Indiana. He was from Beaumont, not far from Port Arthur where Janis Joplin was born. He was the same age as Janis. He might have drunk in the same bars, or met her at a high school party, or even seen her sing in an Austin cafe. Being outcasts, they might have been thrown together like that. I didn't connect any of this at the time.

Roy was skinny as a stick. But he had this 200-lb. girlfriend named Ginny-Lynn, a gal very much like Tanya, and who was also an aspiring country-western singer, although she might have been a little better. I don't remember. She could have been worse. They used to come to the burger joint where I worked over on Highway 41 and I'd fix them up with a sack of burgers for the price of a cold drink.

Roy was tuned in. He had traveled, and he always had something new lying around. *The Chicago Seed.* Acid Rock albums. *Surrealistic Pillow,* by Jefferson Airplane, and *Cheap Thrills,* by Big Brother. I remember the grainy picture of Janis on the inside cover. I remember the exultation in her face.

Roy rode a Triumph Tiger 650. It was really a rat bike, but he tricked it out with odd parts. I used to hang out at his garage while he worked on it. Since then I've always had a predilection for the British machines. It was Roy, in fact, who turned me on to my first bike—a BSA 440 Victor. I got it at Molnar's in Hammond. It was fun and fast but hard to start, so I sold it. Then there was the Triumph Tiger 500. It didn't run very well. But it ran until I wrecked it. I jumped it into a ditch to avoid eating the grill of a Mack truck. After that, it never ran at all. It looked good sitting in my front yard, though. I sold that one to this guy, Jerry, who paid me by taking money out of his girlfriend's purse while she was passed out.

&

SIX YEARS LATER, Tanya and I were wondering how not to be in New Orleans, when, one day, I was walking down Rampart past the Mr. Acropolis used car lot. The song "Pusher Man" was playing on someone's radio nearby. Then I saw it—a 1969 BSA Lightning. Smiling Bob dared us to buy it. The bank cashier knew I was locked in a self-fulfilling prophecy and had no intention of straightening my life out. She probably didn't care either. And Mr. Acropolis didn't care as he counted out our cash on the metal desk. He knew the bike wouldn't make it to the edge of town.

In fact I had to walk it home because the brakes didn't work. It wouldn't start either and the kickstand was broke. But that's the great thing about machines—unlike people, they can be fixed. And Tanya wasn't one of those women who stalk the outskirts of a broken-down scene bitching. She never gave a thought to any physical, financial or chronological impossibilities. To her it made no difference that the bike didn't work. We would make it work. She didn't mind if we spent the better part of our lives making it work. We were gonna ride the Beezer to LA and then up the coast on Highway 1. We had a couple hundred dollars between us. No problem.

Tanya called around to some friends of hers in LA, making sure we would have places to hang. One of her old boyfriends, Reggie, called back. He told us to hook up with Elaine when we got to town. Elaine would know. Tanya said Reggie seemed hyper, over-alert. There was no reason to think anything was wrong, though, because he was always like that when he wasn't high.

Tanya quit the "band." We said goodbye to our "friends" and left New Orleans before noon on May 3. I remember sleeping out near a bayou access road that night. We caught some blue gills in a backwater at dusk and burned them into the bottom of an aluminum pan. We chased the seared flesh with cans of Dixie. The night was murky but there were some Van Gogh-style stars to be had. The intense call-and-response rhythm of the insects was like a million African fiddle players hidden in the trees. There were soft breezes and clouds of blood-sucking mosquitoes to keep me awake. When I finally did fall asleep, I had a dream of having my head bitten off by a praying mantis.

&

THE RAINBOW BRIDGE over the Neches River between Louisiana and Texas was a kind of Wagnerian passage to Valhalla. For some, at least, I suppose it is. For us, the crossing meant we were in Janis Joplin's hometown. It was exactly as I pictured it—oil derricks, oil fields, great pumping cranes, burn-off stacks—it was like a southern version of Whiting, Indiana, but more spread out, more humid. We stopped at the first liquor store we found and bought a bottle of Southern Comfort, most of which we drank in the parking lot of a laundromat. Then some guy came and chased us out of the parking lot. I guess Port Arthur is not so much like Whiting after all. In Whiting, Indiana, you could drink in the parking lot. I think you were supposed to.

They say machines are an extension of the body. One thing's for sure: a motorcycle makes you hyper-aware of every nuance—flowers, dead animals, wind and humidity, and the cold odor of tires, oil, road dust and gas. I liked the motion of the springs, the way the headlights cut a tunnel in the dark, the guttural pipes, and how, if you were slightly drunk, the asphalt winding out ahead of you could seem like your guts being rolled onto a spool somewhere in the future, as if you were being disemboweled by your dreams.

We lit out for the long crossing: Texas, Arizona, New Mexico, California. We drove over white mountains and red deserts, romantic wastelands and ravaged pastorals. We crossed fields of sunflowers like the yellow eyes of old men, reptilian and tired. Morbid one moment, elated the next, we drove and drove. But while we should have been experiencing some incredible lightness of the road, that freedom from emotions and home, we were actually more attuned to its opposite—a heaviness we didn't want to admit to, a sluggish cosmic humidity that made everything somehow sinister, like we were under an intolerable curse and had to keep moving to stay free of it. And we felt this weight, this density, in states of awareness that should have been the most subtle—the trembling of water in a roadside ditch, the vibration of a flower petal.

There were times when the bike actually seemed out of control, racing along an asphalt swell, and the progression of images, the beauty that flashed along either side, often seemed lost on us, even as we enthused about the grandeur. Still, with Tanya's hands upon my shoulders or in the pockets of my insubstantial jacket, one might say we were looking for trials, tests of mettle. But we were just drifting, buoyed up on a sea of

Port Arthur oil products—road tar, rubber, gas—all churned out from the distilled energy of an ancient sun, a thick soup of flesh and circumstance, which we, as sacks of sentient chemicals, were part of. And no amount of mechanical clairvoyance or intuition would save us. Life was always elsewhere. Further back. Farther ahead.

Janis Joplin wasn't going to save us, either—that raw voice of hers like sandpaper and motor-oil—but we heard it anyway, in our heads as we drove. We pretty much drove straight to LA, stopping briefly for drinks in Houston, Tucson, San Diego, Nogales, Tijuana, El Paso. We passed through Salinas, the artichoke capital of the world. Tanya loved artichokes. She was the only person I ever met who did.

We took the little roads when we could, the blue highways, the diner-lined routes, the 66s and the 77s. There were scorpions in our boots in the morning, skies salted with stars, trucks like giant glowing grasshoppers in the night, naked drunks screaming in small town gas stations. But we had no flat tires and only one actual engine problem—from time to time the bike would cut out erratically. I thought it was the carburetor. She said vapor-lock. We were both wrong. Loose battery cables.

(3)

TANYA HAD FRIENDS IN LA. SOME WERE "WEEKEND warriors" and some were full-time. Reggie was full-time. It took nearly half a day to find him. He changed addresses every couple of months. Sometimes he changed names. We spent a lot of time running down false leads. LA is all stop lights and telephone wires. It's hard to know where you are in the first place—forget about finding anything. Nobody is sitting on their stoops to help you either, because of the carbon monoxide.

Santa Monica had some tacky sections back then. We found them. We got to Elaine's house first. Elaine Robinson was a friend of Connie who was living in Colorado with another biker dude named Bobby Jesse, or Jesse Bobby. He had two first names. Jesse Bobby was a friend of Reggie's from the old jail days. Connie was Tanya's friend from different old days, partly in jail, partly in the golden light of a free and righteous life.

Elaine's mother, Camille, answered the door. "Well . . . Tan, been a few years . . . you clean?" This was a woman having no fun in life and she wasn't trying to hide it. Her face had that California pancake-colored-mud-slide-frozen-in-time look that lets you know.

"Been clean for a while, living in Oregon now," Tanya said, as if that were proof, like you couldn't be dirty in Oregon, even though we hadn't been living in Oregon. Camille opened the door to let us in. Whatever coated the furniture and the windows in that house was soon coating our skin.

"How's Naomi?"

"She's cool. Living in North Africa, Tunisia I think."

"Cool," said Camille. The word seemed a odd coming out of her mouth, like she was too old to say "cool," but she had to say it in order to communicate with the kids. Then I realized she was mocking us. I felt appropriately embarrassed.

&

EVERYBODY ASKED ABOUT Tanya's mom. Naomi was a legendary figure among Tanya's less-than-legendary crowd. They called her Naomi, too—using her first name as a way bringing themselves closer to her legendary status. If they were asked to describe her they always said that Tanya's

13

mom was "cool, man, really cool." She was simply a very cool person.

By all accounts Naomi O'Connell had had an eclectic career. She ran around the country collecting kicks with the beats. Supposedly she was one of the characters in *Howl* and *On the Road,* but no one knew which one. She had been in the SDS. She had been at Woodstock; someone said they had seen her in the movie. I never did. She was an existentialist, an early hippie, a mystic, an anarchist and an intellectual. She worked with Dorothy Day and Dr. King. She knew Steinman and Mailer. Lived in a squat in Paris with Sartre and Beauvoir. She'd hung out with the abstract expressionists and the Golden Dawn. She worked as an activist and organized labor, was a major anti-Vietnam protester and a proto-feminist.

There were many stories about Tanya's mom—too many for them to be true. She'd have to be 150 years old and have the ability to travel in space. She'd simply done way too much in too short of a life. Still, her myth was out there, mutating, attracting inconsistencies. Nobody pushed it, because they needed it, especially Tanya. The myth served her sense of inadequacy. By maintaining an image of Naomi that was more than she could ever live up to, Tanya could justify her lifestyle as an underachiever and a drug addict.

At first it seemed odd to me that Tanya hadn't changed her name to follow suit with her mother. Years ago, Naomi had traded McCoy for O'Connell, perhaps to avoid the hillbilly connotations. Back in the '50s there was a TV show called *The Real McCoys*. Understandably, Naomi wanted to avoid any association. Even though she hung with a liberal crowd, no one liked hillbillies; they were the same as rednecks to most northerners—the cause of segregation and war. The name O'Connell preserved her Scotch/Irish identity while dropping the negative traits. Tanya, however, sought to reclaim the adjective *real* that clung to McCoy like an appendix. It suited her career aspirations and her personality. It also severed the nominal umbilical cord. Tanya needed to have control over the use of her mother's legend, and not being immediately identifiable as Naomi's daughter helped. It provided some distance and let her weigh her options.

People often used the idea of Naomi to bolster their own obsessions. I think it was Reggie who once told me Tanya's mom had been one of the first women to take birth control pills, before government approval. They'd been smuggled in from Europe and passed around like candy amongst the hippest people. Supposedly Naomi's crowd was all taking them and screwing all the time. According to Reggie, Naomi was a party girl and she and her friends had virtually invented orgies.

At first I assumed he was only into the prurient aspects, but as time went on his agenda became clear. Reggie knew that while Tanya *thought* Harry Sandman was her real father, the fact was she didn't know. This subliminal doubt was one reason she was crazy or depressed, and in Reggie's acute mind, that doubt was his trump card—a key to some Pandora's box of demons in Tanya's psyche. Thus the flexibility of Naomi's myth gave him a leg up. It fed his sense of power. Like I said, it was in his mind. But for most people the mind is no different from what is real.

I myself pictured Mother Naomi as both vixen and scholar—obviously something to do with my own Greek tragedy. Truth be known, proximity to her legend gave my life a sort of roguish intellectual quality that it didn't really have in those years, as if I was drifting for a "reason" as opposed to simple laziness or cowardice. However, since I had never actually met Naomi I had no way of knowing what she was like or by what right I could lay claim to my fantasies of her.

There was also a dark side to the woman that no one talked about, something beyond the name-dropping and history-making. There was Naomi the absent mother, Naomi the tyrannical control-freak, Naomi the reckless libertine, Naomi the unbalanced moral compass, and Naomi the alcoholic whose scrapes with the law often had little to do with leftist idealism. These traits were seldom elaborated on, however, since they were of little use to anyone.

&

"HAVE A SEAT, Lainy's upstairs. She just got out of jail last week—big bust down in Venice, but I guess you heard."

We hadn't.

"Hey Lainy, your *old friend* Tanya's here!" The words *old friend* were uttered with a measure of sarcasm. Camille returned to her lounge chair, and her vodka and lemonade. There had been some music, but the needle was merely skipping around the center of the record now.

"Reg around?" Tanya asked.

"Not much," Camille answered indifferently.

Elaine came downstairs. She looked dull and under a lot of strain. She and Tanya hugged each other lightly as if they had forgotten exactly why they were friends and found little interest in rekindling the memories. Distrust was like some horror-movie goo coating them, gluing them together in the worst sort of way.

"You clean?" Elaine asked, glancing nervously toward the kitchen.

"Yeah," Tanya said. "I don't do that stuff anymore, livin' in Oregon now. Where's Reg?"

"Staying in Venice, in that old building Tom Parker was in. Got himself this white woman, Redondo Beach. They've even got a kid, someone says. He calls himself Rolando, at least when he's with her."

We heard a door close out in the kitchen. Elaine seemed to relax a little.

"Rolando?" They laughed. A car started. A large cockroach crawled across the wall. I smacked it. A glass broke somewhere.

"What an ass." Tanya laughed.

Apparently it was Roland for a while. Then Rodrigo. He finally settled on Rolando as the credible alternative—given that it was California. Reggie was one-eighth Mexican, which to his way of thinking gave him a diluted version of Andalusian blood. Apparently he had taken to wearing scarves tied around his neck, sporting Spanish berets, and affecting a roguish swagger to pick up chicks. Rich chicks. Why bother, otherwise? It was something you could do in California.

"The white woman, she likes the danger," injected Camille, sarcastically, with a put-on accent, swirling the ice cubes in her glass as a form of punctuation. Most people couldn't pull off such an obvious cliché. Camille could. You got the feeling she invented it. Then for a second I saw her face go completely slack, as if she had just seen death walk through the door with a box of candy. It was hard to tell whether this distortion was due to thorazine side-effects, simple boredom or some other primal force working its geological will under her skin. It was fun to watch, though—a pleasant distraction.

She took another drink and managed to reign her muscles back to their holding pattern—the perpetual smirk of the fallen debutante, the has-been actress with a pill problem, a woman with so much past that it all canceled out and you could pretty much attribute anything to her you wanted. But I'm being too harsh. Maybe she *was* a cipher. And she didn't deserve my judgment. Still, I couldn't imagine the woman ever being seductive. Someone must have. There was a daughter to prove it. And here was the daughter now—talking. She was talking to Tanya, and they were snickering at some inside joke. I reached out and tried to join in. I wanted to laugh, too.

Apparently, in the argot of this crowd, "white woman" referred to that middle-class, clean, secretarial type who was really looking for a wallet but went sucker for an outlaw. They got pregnant or gave away their money. Then they went home. This one was pregnant. Rolando was milking her.

"More power to him," said Tanya. The way she figured it, anybody could do anything they wanted.

"Family's the most important thing," Camille added, scratching her thigh.

Camille knew she was no Naomi, and she resented Tanya for that, as if the mere existence of Tanya's mother had turned Elaine against her own mother. Apparently she couldn't see herself in the mirror of her daughter's eyes. But then how could Camille keep it together when she had this wild child making her life miserable, drugging and drinking and seducing her boyfriends? Camille couldn't compete. Elaine resented her mother for being a whore. The two of them were teaching each other a lesson, one that was going to take years.

Tanya and Elaine seemed unable to speak above a whisper for awhile, and I caught little fragments like "Yeah, me too," and "Yeah, right, okay." Then I took a seat and talked to Camille until the crank ran down and she passed out.

&

AT SOME POINT we replaced beer with tomato juice and vodka. As I stared into the thick drink I heard a train whistle far off in my head. As a kid at night I used to love the sound of distant train whistles, imagining gaunt skeletal men hanging off those boxcars, their hollowed eyes gone dead from the overload of speed and booze, playing their harmonicas and banjos and beckoning me like bad father figures to a life on the road. And I was afraid—afraid that I too might one day live in those gondolas. But then, maybe that was better than a trailer home. Of course, I *was* in a trailer home already, at least the emotional equivalent. The more things change, the more they become the same. TV was proving the point over and over again. So I watched the TV for comfort. Train robbers. Prairie dust. Gunfire. I started to doze. But I woke myself up. Things seemed a little too well synced-up. Someone shouted, "Fuck you" out in the kitchen. It sounded like Elaine. I heard a glass break. A cowboy on TV said, "Try new Rodeo Deodorant Soap. You'll feel fresh as a Montana morning. R-O-D-E-O. Ya-hoo."

It was a minor relief when Ben, Camille's boyfriend, showed up. He stepped through the door like an angry actor coming on stage after weeks of bad reviews, knowing the audience hates him, and it's going to be real hard to get another job. His real name was Ben Pantone. Italian, Irish, Jewish—a nervous mix. Ben seemed to have a carburetor in his neck that jerked his head around in sudden small bursts of paranoia, augmenting his chosen role as the ideal antidote for whatever tranquilizer you were on—simply because you just couldn't help being irritated by the guy.

He was about fifteen years younger than Camille and proportionately louder and drunker. They started fighting as soon as she came to. Ben was one of those guys who are always going to get job the next day. He's got an interview or a deal lined up and he just needs a little more time, a couple more bucks. For the time being he was living off Elaine's mother's money. She took advantage of the audience to let him know what she thought.

"Get a job yet, Benny, baby?"

"Going downtown tomorrow, Cam," (he called her Cam). "I got a line on a gig selling real estate in the valley."

"Okay baby," she said. "Now make me a drink."

Ben picked up the can off the tray table, poured some juice in a glass, threw in some ice, added the vodka. "Here's your drink."

"Turn that shit off. Put on some Patsy, will you, baby?" Ben turned off the radio and picked out a record. He put the disk on the turntable and lowered the needle without saying anything.

"You like Patsy?" she asked.

"Everybody loves Patsy," I said.

"You talk about failed love. Patsy knew about failed love. Men treated her like shit. Walked all over her. Daddy always listened to Patsy."

There it was. I had been waiting for the father to show up. The decor demanded it. I also knew there was a photograph in a drawer somewhere that explained all this. Maybe it was the man she really loved, years ago, the one who let her down. Dad. The boyfriend who went to Nam. Maybe Dad was the boyfriend. I wasn't going to ask.

"It's just that her music makes me sad," I said. I lifted my glass to commiserate.

"Life is sad," Cam said.

"Sad and crazy," I replied.

The song was "Crazy." Apropos or not, I laughed. It was an ugly loose laugh. It scared me because I was starting to fit in.

Suddenly out of nowhere Ben threw a beer can across the room and broke a candy dish full of cigarette butts. The girls came out from the kitchen. We started in on bourbon and Seven-Up. I was adventuring in the American night, or rather a thickening Santa Monica afternoon version of it.

"I need some smokes. Bring me my purse, Benny."

"I'm putting your purse by the door, Cam."

"No, bring it in here." He didn't.

We heard the door slam. Ben was off to enjoy himself.

In the meantime, the room seemed to fill with heavy water as if seeking to preserve us as evidence. We were no different than those mutants in formaldehyde-filled jars one sees at Wisconsin county fairs. I even thought I heard a barker outside the house, offering an admission discount to decent folks who might want to witness the frailty of the human condition.

It was time to go. They did the embracing thing, then Elaine looked at me and said "Nice meeting you, come back again some time, any time."

"Sure," I said, trying to get out before I drowned.

We decided to leave most of our stuff at Elaine's until we knew where we'd be. Tanya was bringing it into the house. I crossed paths with Ben on the front porch. "Looks like you need a refill." He pulled out a pint bottle of Early Times. I declined. We stood there, silent, man-to-man. He took a dirty toothpick from his pocket and stuck it in his mouth. Then he snuck a sidelong glance at Elaine's ass and said "If she's anything like her mother, she's a pistol." He started rolling his hips in that vulgar gesture men use to indicate they're getting some, and by God they know what to do with it.

"Hot today," I said.

"This is a hot town," he said, wiping the back of his hand on his forehead. But it wasn't that hot. He was probably just worked up from his recent act of virtual intercourse.

"Well, we gotta get . . ." I said. But he wouldn't let it go.

"Nope. Best reason to love the mother is to get a foot in the daughter's house, if you know what I mean. The daughter *is* the mother only 20 years younger, and you can't go wrong, going back in time like that." He grabbed his crotch as if the volume and weight of his manhood was a bother to him, as I'm sure it was.

But I was already on the sidewalk. I started the bike, wobbling a bit on the foot-pegs. The thick currents were pushing me one way, then another. I called Tanya, because if we didn't move soon we would be stuck forever in this aquarium of angst and anger.

Maybe I asked way too much of life—I wanted it to be easy and it only got harder. But I followed leads and sometimes amazing consequences came from them. And here was one consequence now, coming into focus, emerging from the house looking wilted. Tanya carried her baggage with a certain grace as she came down the sidewalk even under the weight of the liquor. She mounted the bike and we pulled away.

I'd ridden drunk before. I was about to do it again. Maybe I would live through the day. It was slow going at first—the air had gotten so heavy. I wondered if we would make it. My face in the rearview mirror had circles under the eyes. I needed a shave. Then I could see Ben, standing there, surveying the street in both directions, rolling his hips and drinking, pointing his finger at me in the mirror. And he was still like that when we turned at the end of the block, bound for the Santa Monica

Freeway, shimmering like the grey tines of a six-lane forklift jammed in the mouth of Mother Earth and making her feel the pain.

4

WE PULLED UP IN FRONT OF A WHITE WOOD-FRAME building about ten blocks from the beach. The door was unlocked. A woman was just leaving the communal bathroom on the second floor. She smelled like Herbal Rainforest shampoo. The aftermath of a bad Chinese meal filled the hall. Floral wall decorations added to the glamour. Tanya asked if she knew Reggie Morales.

Reggie lived in number 3, with Anzo and his girlfriend, she said. We knocked on door number 3.

"Who is it?"

"Uh . . . I don't know." Tanya, chuckled, thinking they would recognize her voice.

They didn't.

"Who is it?" came the mechanical reply.

"It's Tanya." The door cracked. An eye appeared. Whoever owned the eye then stood out of the way, opening the door a little more, so whoever was on the bed could see who it was at the door. Then whoever it was undid the chain. A bottle-blonde stared blankly back at me. I waited for her thoughts to focus but that wasn't going to happen. I smiled but she wasn't in the mood.

"Remember me?" asked Tanya.

She turned her head toward Tanya slowly while the abused bearings of some ancient human machining complained in her neck. You couldn't hear them but you knew. Whatever emotions once oiled those bearings were gone. Still she spoke.

"Of course. How are you doing? You haven't been around in a long time."

"It's Tanya."

She didn't seem to know who Tanya was. She looked back to Anzo on the bed to be sure that at least he knew who Tanya was. But Anzo was watching TV. A good-looking young man in bell-bottoms. No shirt. No shoes. This *was* California. And junky California of top of it. Eventually, we managed to get through the door.

"Where have you been, Tan?" asked Anzo, without moving his eyes.

"Oregon."

"Oh." They didn't seem to know each other that well either.

"Where's Reggie?"

"Redondo Beach. Probably be back tonight, he doesn't like to stay there. Got any beer?"

Tanya and Anzo tried to talk old times, but they seemed to remember different old times, so they talked about the big bust instead, and about Venice and what a hot town it was. Tanya was saying how she could not wait to see Reggie—it had been so long.

"It's been so long," Anzo repeated, happy to have something to agree with.

We went out and got some beer and came back and watched TV.

There was a show on about the Taj Mahal and how it was a great monument to romantic love. The vultures perched on the minarets were screaming. A sigh passed through the room, a sigh followed by political commentary because, apparently, "the builders of such public burdens walked on the backs of the poor. In fact, at bottom, everything is nothing but oppression and population control, you know what I'm talking about?"

I looked to the source of the voice—a woman, Suzanne. She was wearing a beret. She could have been a young Naomi. Or at least Naomi could have prefigured numerous women like her—a young radical with no energy to manifest her values. There were fewer and fewer of her type around.

Anzo's girlfriend, Doris, wasn't taking sides. She sat slowly turning the pages of a magazine. *True Romance,* I think it was. Her dried green eye-shadow was beginning to scale off and there was a fine dark powder on one of her cheeks that she mechanically smeared with numbed hands. Doris could have passed for a young Camille. Perhaps Camille had prefigured numerous women like her. Some bored little Egyptian goddess, miffed at being transplanted to this fallen place. There *were* more and more of her type around.

&

THE ROOM WAS over-lit with fluorescent bulbs which gave it the aura of a porno movie set or an emergency room, as if the relationship between the erotic and the pornographic and even the traumatic for that matter could be boiled down to nothing more than the light level. Somehow the religious figured in there, too. God, headlights, floodlights, flash, fame, ecstasy. There was a connection, but you wouldn't find it if you looked for it. Still, the artificial light in the room made the actual sunlight seem thin and tired, as if it had been late afternoon for an excruciating amount of time and the natural light just couldn't justify itself anymore.

I looked around. People talked. I should have been interested but

I wasn't. I decided reading magazines was the exciting thing to do in this case. In a magazine about country home decorating, there was an article about folksingers, and the folk revival in America and how that was influencing home decorating. Then there was a picture of a family who lived in a home decorated the way folk singers might decorate their homes, except the home in the magazine was clean. Then there were some pictures of old guys who still really were folk singers in some small town in Appalachia. Apparently they just sang for fun and didn't care about money. They had a certain authenticity. In the article they were reminiscing about their days on the road, singing folk songs. Funny thing, then they started moving—the pictures, that is. At least the lips in the pictures. The old folksingers were telling me to get out of town and hit the road. They said the answer was "blowin' in the wind" and I oughta be "choogglin on down the highway."

I didn't like being told what to do, so I picked up a copy of *Big Bike World*. There were women in *Big Bike World*—stressed-out, white-trash women draped over motorcycles like some kind of bikini-clad fungus. One photo showed a naked woman soaping down a guy's Harley beside a country stream while he relaxed nearby drinking beer and reading *Big Bike World*, showing little surprise that his woman was also in the magazine washing his Harley. He knew something lewd would take place soon. His faith went all the way back to the industrial revolution—the great Victorian bellows, the giant Jules Verne pistons and churning camshafts deep inside some immense sweating motorcycle engine of the universe. In fact, if you tried, you could extrapolate all of thermodynamics from this simple scenario of impending biker sex. These magazines could take you straight to the heart of the cosmos without you even knowing it. Orgasm and production. Capital and decay. Cosmic truths and biker bitches.

I didn't have a big bike. I had a BSA. I was wondering if they would even let me into the heaven of Big Bike World with a BSA after I died. I developed an inferiority complex about it. Then, just as fast, I didn't care at all. Then again, I did. I wondered if Big Bike World was a good place to live. It seemed to be. Nobody spoke in Big Bike World. Nobody knocked on your door the way they did here in Venice, California at the beginning of the last quarter of the century, which was also the beginning of the end of the industrial age.

&

IT WAS 6:30. There was a knock on the door.

"Who is it?"

"Mark and Joanne."

23

Doris got up. It was the exact same scene as five hours earlier only this time I was on the inside. I put a blank stare on my face. I wanted to fit in. Doris went back to her magazine. The polish on her nails was like paint peeling off a humid wall. She pulled at the little strips with her teeth. I wondered if polish was poisonous.

The Taj Mahal show had changed to a show about tagging giraffes in Africa. Every so often the picture would go haywire. The giraffes would appear to burn with soft black flames. Then Marlin Perkins would interrupt the fire, explaining how we humans, just like the giraffes, can never be secure and that is why we need Mutual of Omaha insurance. Then Marlin's head burned away too. Then a show about insects taking over the earth took over.

I think it was Walter Cronkite who said the cacophony of insects was nature's opera in which the *sturm und drang* of life and death could be heard. They played Vivaldi's *Four Seasons* while they showed a female praying mantis eating her mate's head. Walter said that just like the male praying mantis, you couldn't know when your head too will be bitten off by some ungrateful female.

Then there was another knock on the door. By this time, Tanya was pretty sure it must be Reggie, so she jumped.

"Who is it?"

It was Reggie.

He was good-looking and had a mustache. In fact he looked a lot like Anzo. Everyone in California was good-looking. They all looked like Anzo and Reggie. Some of them had mustaches. This started to bug me. Where I came from everyone was ugly and wore dirty blue clothes. Still, Reggie was Tanya's ex-old man and though they had split a couple years ago, they were close. He'd started her on heroin, given her hepatitis, gotten her arrested and nearly disowned. So of course, she was crazy about him.

"We went to jail together," Tanya said.

Their enthusiasm seemed to rub off on the others and for a while the room became a party. Everyone talked, and everyone appeared to understand. Anzo had, somewhere along the line, changed channels yet again. It was not Marlin or Walter anymore. It was some other guy, Mike Walleye. Tanya and Reggie finally left the room about midnight and didn't come back. But the shows kept coming. You couldn't stop them.

&

I GOT UP early and went down to the beach. Nothing much was going on. A bleary-eyed drunk stumbling around in the sand. The waves rolled in with a steady thud, as if driven by some dark undersea engine. Some guy at a sandwich truck called me over. He wanted to give me a free sandwich. He must have figured I was out of luck. He swore up and down there was nothing wrong with the free sandwich and that he was just trying to be a helpful guy. He had a black beard and looked a little like Charles Manson, but without the swastika tattooed on his forehead.

"There's nothing wrong with it, man, it's totally cool," he said.

I sat down on the curb, tore off the cellophane and ate it, trying to position myself so he could see me eating. I didn't want to hurt his feelings. After an appropriate amount of time I figured I might as well go back to the apartment. Tanya was there. She was awake and it was too early for her to be awake. Of course, Reggie was awake too.

The three of us had breakfast in a sidewalk cafe called The Celebrity Cafe, a place where movie stars ate famous omelets. Reggie pronounced some movie star names. He liked the way the star name sounds rolled around in his mouth like little massage balls. I felt sorry for him. He was from the coast and didn't know better. East Coast, West Coast, it doesn't matter. They enjoy their debt to celebrity. I suppose people have to feel inadequate about something. Midwesterners have our own devils. We don't need celebrities to berate us.

And so our conversation rambled. Tanya's mom. Los Angeles. Some new movie. Mostly Venice. Reggie loved Venice. He thought it was just about the hippest place in the world. He said it was built by and for movie stars so that movie stars could think they lived in Venice. Reggie thought it looked just like the original.

"It looks just like Europe, man. Don't you think?"

He took us on a tour, pointing his finger at places, saying: Jim Morrison was a drunk there. Janis Joplin was a junky there. Charles Bukowski fucked whores there. Someone else lived over there. Raymond Chandler drove down that street. And there were stores that sold T-shirts that proved all this was valid in case you didn't believe it.

I said Janis was a hippie and hippies lived in San Francisco. But Reggie said no, the hippies started in Venice and I didn't know what I was talking about. He said all cool things started in LA. Then he said he would show me the Landmark Hotel where Janis died if I wanted. I was embarrassed, but I said that would be fun. We never made it. He did show us an apartment building he had robbed once. Him and his partner tied up the occupants. They pissed on the rug and made a lot of long-distance phone calls. In fact, that's where they were the night he called Tanya, back in New Orleans. Then I looked at Tanya, but she looked somewhere else. So I looked where she looked, but there wasn't anything there.

We went to a hipster thrift store called the Fallen Angel. While I looked at the leather jackets, Tanya went through a bin of old clothes. She bought a red-fringed dress for two dollars. Half cowboy, half flapper. She said it would be a great stage dress. I didn't think it would fit her.

Later, around 3 o'clock, I drove the bike over to some obscure intersection in Ghost Town. A white Camaro was sitting at the curb in front of a record store. Inside there was a guy named Toby, his wife Elsa, and three small kids alternately screaming and laughing. Elsa took four tight little balloon bags out of her mouth and gave them to Tanya and she gave her 80 dollars.

&

AROUND 5:30 ME and Anzo went over to Hot-Jo's sandwich shop and bought steak sandwiches with cheese. I wasn't hungry so I gave half of mine to a guy on the beach who looked like me. I swore up and down there was nothing wrong with it. He took it anyway.

"If you see the Buddha on the road, kill him, man, kill the motherfucker," he said, and stumbled off. I guess it was his way of thanking me.

I spent the rest of the afternoon looking at a magazine. It was getting to be a habit. The woman to my left was slowly nailing a syringe into the back of her hand. When that didn't work, she tried her foot. She kept at it, as if trying to pin herself to something. But there was only nothing, and that nothing wouldn't let her be an ornament. It was depressing.

I soon became aware of a cord of flesh wrapping around my spine and stomach—a thickening sensation, as if that flesh were a sponge filling with black blood. The deadening follows, the deadening that feels like a better life, a more empathetic life. I gave myself over to the joy of sliding subtly down that thin, sharp wire between all opposing concepts. Life was a toy. Death was a toy. I had two toys, and I didn't care about either one.

Tanya was modeling her red dress. At first it looked kind of cute, but then she just sort of collapsed. People continued to knock on the door. One friend of Anzo brought another toy—a cheap little 9mm from some Asian country, the kind punk teens carry on their first stick-ups. A few people looked at it, held it, acted familiar with it, but nobody wanted to buy it, not for 25 dollars anyway. Tanya just looked away. She said she did not approve of guns at all.

Later that night, with everyone passed out, the lights on bright and the TV still going, Tanya wanted to do it. But I couldn't muster the blood pressure. So she went to sleep and I watched TV—a movie about the dead coming back to life, a guy eating another guy's face. The last scene I remember was giant grasshoppers taking over the Manhattan—different movie, probably.

26

&

THE NEXT DAY was very much like the one before, except the weekend warriors were also rousing themselves to action, flexing their soft muscles. The room was full of the odor of sulfur. Reggie threw me a sidewise glance. "We should be careful, we don't want Frank to go out on us," he said as he struck a match. I knew what he was up to, though, and it wasn't going to work. They weren't going to get my taste.

Meanwhile Anzo was absent-mindedly strumming a guitar. Either he didn't know how to play, or he was just fucked up. He was trying to remember some lyrics to go with the chords. A song he heard from a bum on the beach. A guy from Portland, he said.

The day I was born they told me I was dead
Everything blue turned out to be red
Whatever was worst was the best they said
And they planted them devils in the back of my head
Them devils lived out on the road

&

HIS REAL NAME was Manzoni. Anzo was a nickname. His father had a rep as some kind of con. Reggie said he was a major fence and a gambler. Tanya said he was a salesman with some vague connection to her father, Harry. Someone else said he had a crystal meth factory in the valley. I made a mental note to ask Tanya more about it.

Then some suburban girls came by. Missy and Carol and Brenda, all fresh from volleyball. Bronze, blonde, bleached teeth—in fifteen years they'd be filling the gaps in their character with skin spackle. But they were fun girls for the time. Young and careless and not nearly as loose as they wanted to pretend. The low-life experience was on their agenda and they were willing to spend daddy's allowance money on heroin for the gang. Nobody objected but somebody would have to make another run.

"Don't look at me, I'm wasted," I said.

Roger passed around a picture of his three-month old daughter. We took turns making pleasant faces. She was so cute. Everyone said so. She deserved a good home. Hopefully the adoption agency would find one. Not to be outdone, Tanya claimed that if her mother hadn't left her alone in that hippie commune with all the perverts, she might never have become a junky. But she was gonna make it as a singer. Everyone agreed that she would make it. She had soul.

One of the girls had a copy of *On the Road*. We all laughed along with her.

I was starting to feel a little self-conscious. The room grew oppressive.

Suddenly everybody in the room seemed to have duct tape over their mouths. They were strapped to their chairs like hostages who hadn't seen the sun in days. I decided to take a walk. I asked Tanya if she wanted to come along.

"No, I'll stay here," she said, sitting on the floor, stoop-shouldered and cross-legged, her eyes receding.

I nodded to the motorcycle as I walked out the door, but the motorcycle ignored me. It seemed to have copped an attitude. Still, it was mine—I owned it. I could go anywhere I wanted, with or without it. I wanted to go to Venice Beach. I walked. On the beach I saw a lot of healthy people on roller skates and some winos. Apparently there were also a lot of other people who used to hang out with famous people, but now they were just hanging out on Venice beach. Just as I was wondering if I would run into Charles Bukowski, a beachfront fortune-teller grabbed my arm.

"You're going on a trip," she said. I said nothing. She stared at me a little longer. "Leave the girl, she's trouble. Two dollars." Still I didn't reply. "Don't be a saint. It doesn't suit you."

"Leave me alone."

"Two dollars."

"Get lost."

"You're going to meet someone," she said. "You're going on a trip. Two dollars." She was getting desperate.

She was right about one thing, though. I did meet someone. I sat down to drink white port with the guy, a has-been musician with an expansiveness problem. He had played with Janis Joplin and Jimi Hendrix. But not on the same day. I was not surprised to learn that he knew Bob Dylan, too. I didn't believe a word. His name was Johnny Ray. He said, "Anytime you're down at the beach just ask for Johnny Ray, everybody knows who I am."

I was sure it was true—he had a familiar face. He had been the bleary-eyed drunk stumbling down the beach the previous morning. Probably coming back from a wild party with some rock stars.

5

I HAD ABOUT FIFTY EXTRA BUCKS I KEPT IN MY BELT FOR emergencies. In case we woke up in a flood, or a tornado stole our stuff, or Tanya took the keys and ran off with a wild man. It had happened before. And it happened again. This time the wild man was Officer Willie Perez, head of the narcotics division in Venice. I never met him, but I'd heard stories. Reggie. Anzo. Some of the others. Perez saw himself as a one-man clean-up squad for the middle-class vice that was ruining the town. He wanted nothing to do with the Morrisons and the Joplins and their wake of freaks. He saw Venice the way it was supposed to be—swimming pools, movie stars, rich folk holding hands on bridges over canals. Personally, I never saw a canal.

Before I knew about Tanya's date with Perez, I took that money and bought a brown leather jacket at the Fallen Angel thrift store. The same store where Tanya had bought her cowboy dress. The jacket was classic JC Penny—more Kerouac than Brando, or one could say London with a dash of Crumb. It was slightly small, but it would be cold in the mountains and at night on the coast and I needed a better jacket, even though I was paying at least double what it cost when it was new, which would have been at least twenty years ago.

"We don't bargain," the hip little proto-punk mannequin said as she palmed my cash. Her gaze was fixed beyond me, over my shoulder, on some future where bums like me wouldn't bother her and she would be every bit as important as she already thought she was. I turned and looked that direction. It did look nice, like a party you're not invited to—cold and pretty.

I hoped my purchase might be interpreted by Tanya as a hint—it was time to go. But when I got back to Anzo's on Sunset, there was nobody around to hint to. They had already gone. The whole floor was vacant. I went downstairs, and sat on top of a concrete fence next door. I waited about an hour, then a girl came by—a California girl.

"Are you Tanya's friend?" she asked.

I said I was.

"I'm Gloria. Billy and them got busted."

"You mean Reggie?"

"Who's Reggie?"

"Rolando, Rodrigo." I was fishing.

"Billy?"

"Who?"

"Never mind. Anyway, Tanya's with them. I was with them too but they let me go. They might let her go later—it depends."

I knew I was riding solo to Portland. Gloria knew it too. She was cut from similar cloth as Tanya—cute, tough. Irish-Mexican maybe. The suburban debutante wrestled with the ancient street punk over her soul. Neither one was winning.

"Call the police station. Maybe you can visit her. 19th precinct, I think."

Apparently she was familiar with the terrain. Then she forced a smile, flouncing her hair around in that tired imitation of a Clairol commercial so many women like to use. I think there actually was a Clairol ad at the bus stop nearby. Maybe that was her cue. Still, it wasn't working. No one was paying any attention. So she stopped.

"Thanks," I said, "I wonder what I'm going to do now. I don't know anybody." She refused to fill my pregnant pause with any invitation, so I hammed it up. "Man, I don't know anybody around here. I have nowhere to stay." I threw my arms up in the air in a frustrated way and waited. Suddenly, it was as if she'd read my mind.

"If you need a place to stay you can come to my house later on." She said the address fast without enunciating or waiting for me to write it down. She walked off without asking if I had a pen.

I spent the rest of the day and evening wandering the streets and beach. I bought a large bottle of pineapple coconut milk. It was healthy and reasonably expensive. Someone out there was looking after me, and knew I would feel better if I spent some money. About 9 o'clock I called the Venice police. They put me in touch with Woman's Detention. No one knew who Tanya was. They gave me another number. I called it. They knew who she was but said her case hadn't come before the judge yet. Then I called somebody else who said it had. They told me she was already gone. They were watching something on TV and joking about it. Probably eating donuts, too. I called another number and they said she wasn't there. Call back next shift.

At 11 o'clock, I knocked at the Indiana Ave. number Gloria had given me. Wrong address. But it was close enough. Somebody in the room knew who I was talking about. They sent me around the corner to a red house on Indiana Ct. I knocked.

"Who is it?" It was a man's voice.

"Frank. I'm a friend of Tanya and Anzo. Gloria said I could come by."

"I don't know you man. I don't know any Gloria either."

"C'mon. Is Gloria there?" I asked. I heard him talking to someone further back in the room. Then for a while there was no sound. I was about to knock again.

"She doesn't know you, man—better go away."

I went to Elaine's house. They knew me but they acted nervous anyway, a gratuitous sort of nervousness based on TV cop shows. They said, "too bad about everything, but that's how it goes, you know."

"Listen, why don't you take her stuff with you?" Elaine said.

"I don't have room."

"You brought it here," she insisted.

"No I didn't. What stuff?"

"Her blanket, and clothes and all that kitchen shit and . . ."

"No, that must have been here from before. All we left were our saddlebags."

"Well we don't have room for this crap either. What are we, a storage garage for people in jail?"

I heard someone laugh in the living room. I shrugged. Apparently this was an old argument.

"Take the radio at least." She stuck it in one of the bags as she handed them to me. "It gets lonely on the road. It's good to have a radio."

Then I heard some glass breaking upstairs. Then she said I could sleep in the backyard if I wanted. I slept on the beach, using my brown leather jacket for a pillow. At least it was quiet and I didn't have to worry about the police breaking the door down.

&

THE NEXT MORNING I went out to Lynwood, the Women's Detention Center. Tanya was tough all right. She didn't seem to give a damn. I gave a little bit of a damn. I cared about the trip. Maybe I cared about her, too. I don't know. She didn't care about me, though. At least, that's what I thought as we spoke through bulletproof glass. Tanya was puffed around the eyes, and drawn at the mouth. She looked like she'd aged a couple years in the last twelve hours. She told me her PD was cool, though, and would try to get her off, but she had to get some papers together, character references, letters of recommendation, and it would take a week or so. And, no, I couldn't help.

Months later it occurred to me that she probably could have gotten out, but wasn't trying. After all, she wasn't holding, and she knew nothing about the dealing. Her friends would back her up because they had no reason not to. It would be good for them to have a friend outside too, maybe accumulate some karma. They all needed it. But Tanya wasn't even

31

going to even try to beat it. She knew her sentence would be short and a stint in the pen would teach her mother a lesson. It would teach us all.

"Don't tell my mother anything," she said.

I understood. If Naomi knew, she might have come to rescue Tanya by paying a lawyer or posting bail or some such thing. Or then again Naomi might do nothing at all, and this would be the worst scenario. So Tanya figured why test it—safer to do her time than to find out what course of action Naomi might take. Or, maybe it was reverse psychology. Maybe she really wanted her mother to know, she just didn't have any way of delivering the news, except through me. If she asked me not to, she must have thought I would. But that was wrong because she could have just called her dad to get the number. I didn't know where Naomi was. Tangier, Tunisia, Tulsa—I couldn't look it up in the phone book. Maybe Tanya was just outright scared of what her mother might think. Naomi was a liberal after all, but she was definitely down on narcotics.

There was no way to second-guess this one. Tanya herself created the image of her mother to fit the situation, whether it was to gain points, or to rationalize some otherwise dubious activity. For instance, if she were trying to justify her gravitational attraction to low-life, Tanya would claim she spent too much time with pretentious existential artists when she was young because her mother was a *poseur*. If Tanya wanted to justify watching TV, it's because her father, Harry, wouldn't let her, and Naomi was never around. If she longed for life on the farm with a dog, well obviously, as a child, she traveled too much. If she needed to justify traveling, she cited her mother's rebellion against inflexible 50s role-playing. If Tanya was a capitalist it's because Naomi was communist. If Tanya was a pacifist it's because her mother was a terrorist. And if Tanya was now in jail, it was, of course, by some circuitous reasoning, Naomi's fault. And to top it off, she had inherited the drinking gene from her. So she drank.

"Maybe I can get bail." I said. "It's not that much."

"You can't."

"I'll try." I was lying. "Anyway, what about your friends?"

"Friends?" She laughed. I was pretty naive, I guess.

"Don't try to be a saint. It doesn't suit you. Just go. I'll catch up later. Remember, it's only three months, man. And probably a lot less."

Funny, that was what the fortune-teller had said, how sainthood did not suit me. "Keep working on the PD." I added. "That's their job, to help you."

"Yeah. Yeah. I will."

I knew she wouldn't. "You've got to try, anyway," I said. "Why would you want to be here, if you didn't have to be?"

"Hey, ever think maybe this is what you want? That's why you're with me. I'm a loser. Or maybe you're sick of me."

"What a weird thing to say." It was. It came from nowhere.

"Why did you leave anyway, yesterday? My friends think you're a rat."

"Fuck them. I don't . . . Look, let's drop it," I said. Anyway, it seemed a little ridiculous to get into an argument about failure in jail.

"I'm sorry. I'm sorry."

"It's okay, take it easy." I could see my face reflected in the protective glass.

Then Tanya put her mouth close to the mic and began to sing in a low voice, that old blues "Ball and Chain." "That's my new song." She laughed. It wasn't funny. She thought it was. "Listen, if you're going to ball any chicks, just don't tell me about it, all right. I don't want to know."

I couldn't tell if she was being liberal or trying to hurt me. She was only really ever sarcastic when she was drunk. But you can't drink in lock-up.

&

THE GNOSTICS HAD the idea that to eradicate evil from the world, you indulged it, you wore it out. It follows that to alleviate suffering, you wallowed in it, made it work for you. You could pretend you cared excessively about the world, and it hurt. In the hard-boiled code of life, which apparently I was living, you had to keep a notebook with you at all times. A catalog of bitter sayings that you could practice like a mantra, as if life was just a collection of different ways of being battered and beaten and coming out of it with a tale to pass off as truth. But I was over-reacting, exaggerating my sorrow with unnecessary metaphors.

The afternoon was wearing on, and I was still in LA, with a busted girlfriend and an old motorcycle that could break down any second. It may sound corny, but I suppose that was part of it; you know the girl will go bad and the bike will break, you just don't know when. That was part of the thrill—the doubt, the tension. A cloud of unknowing hovers above every mile. You imagine you live in that same devil-may-care dimension inhabited by tight-rope walkers, criminals and bums.

But we had faith in those days. Faith and arrogance. We'd bought the BSA on a dare and maybe rode it all of twenty miles before beginning a cross-country trip. Arrogance may be the opposite of modesty, but it is a religious force in its own right. It's a form of Karma. Inanimate objects are aware of it. Arrogance can make engines run with blown valves. It can squeeze forty miles out of a thimbleful of gas. I never had enough—I had to borrow mine from Tanya.

So far we had been lucky. But *we* were over. It was just me now. I was on the Coast Highway in rush hour when arrogance failed and the clutch cable broke. I left the bike at a gas station. I had to run three miles back to town, before the parts store closed. It's part of the thrill of owning a British bike.

As I replaced the cable in the deepening Pacific evening, blondes drove by. Hair like waves. Their lipstick left lurid streaks in the velvet air. Their teeth flashed then stretched into bolts of white. Even the fading laughter hurt, that small town har-de-har pumped up and reshaped to sound sophisticated, or at least condescending. These were the fun people with their fun things—convertibles, sunglasses. The sons and daughters of imagined celebrity, and all of them racing through life, trying to stay ahead of the game, trying to stay ahead of the hour they were in. And the weird thing was it made sense to want to do that, because moving faster increases the noise, which increases the possibilities, which, ironically, makes each one less likely, creating a kind of relief from the world of definitions and the decisions they demand.

Amongst the oil fumes and the briny dinge of the sea, greasy, tired, frustrated, I had a flash. Suddenly, I had it all figured out—the psychology of despots and CEOs. I figured that in order for civilization to exist, people have to stay in one place, and so it seems somehow natural that the evolution of society would be to create an *illusion* of motion where none exists. Faster cars. Faster editing. Increased sensory stimulation. But all the while we are actually sitting more and more still. The population is placated by the feeling of progress, when in reality they are imprisoned. Even if we feel or strive to be utterly irresponsible, we're still somehow doing our job.

I saw a future in which speed was the new religion, and I wanted to be a part of it. I wanted to hasten the return of Tanya. To leap across these endless hours of thinking and decision-making. I wanted to hasten everything. I had my church. My wheels. Anybody could buy into it. Everything was for sale. All we had to do was eclipse all those dreary hours of actually living.

&

LATER, OUT ON the road, on a poorly-muffled, push-rod driven, 650 Lightning Special, for the time being, I was more primal than the saps, more in touch. I wove my way through the traffic. I didn't even laugh because I didn't care. And eventually the highway opened for me, a white rushing tunnel carved by my headlights in the fog. The asphalt unwound like a typewriter ribbon through the Santa Monica mountains but I couldn't see what was ahead. I could hear a story being written, but I didn't know what it said. There was only the rhythm, the staccato pumping of the exhaust, which was way faster than any human heart. More like that of a bird about to be crushed in a fist.

(6)

Y OU DEVELOP A PARTICULARLY CLOSE PHYSICAL RELATION-
ship with a bike, especially an older one. You get to know
its moves, eccentricities and limitations. Mechanical quirks
can translate into physical effects—sore shoulder muscles
or a stiff neck from trying to keep your head straight at
4500 rpm in fourth and a front-end shimmy, or a kidney about to blow
from the vibration of a badly tuned engine or worn shocks. You wonder
why you put up with the discomfort. It becomes a challenge. Then you
wonder why you need the challenge. You turn in upon yourself to examine
the issue. After a certain amount of time on the road, you might even
begin feel an inhuman loneliness, like a bit of sentient flotsam being
hurled through the universe toward some glass Oz you would like to
believe in. There is no radio, no conversation, only the motor's drone and
the endless hours of your own voice in your head chattering away about
some past grudge or girlfriend. Things come back that you'd thought you'd
forgotten, simply to fill the vacuum in your mind caused by speed.

&

HER NAME WAS Dolores. But she was "Beatrice Magee" in her mind. She
was the goofy girl at the end of the block, the daughter of the dad who
listened to opera while staring out the window on weekends, and the dead
mother. And she was sister to the brother who made mutant insects out
of erector sets and animal bones. She was the bird girl with the popsicle-
colored lips and the butterfly net in hand, standing in her red jumper on a
bridge down by the dirty river. I must have been around nine when I first
saw her. She wanted to be a pilot. I wanted to be a poet.

She was the first person I ever knew who traveled in outer space. She
and I used to climb to the hayloft of the great white barn off in the field
across the drainage canal, and listen to her transistor radio while we gazed
at the empty fields, and still further to the apartment projects being built
at the end of the township that would eventually cover those fields, and
in our own way we talked about the progression of matter across the void
and our own eventual deaths and what it would be like to live as pure
energy, like some force or broadcast, and how maybe that's what the dead
were—just patterns in the air, and nothing more.

We were atom-bomb babies, raised to search the sky for mushroom clouds. Our memories were formed by the transistor radios under our pillows, the Exciting News Flashes, the possibility of Martian Invasions, Tuesday Morning Air Raid Drills, the paranoid thrill of The End of the World. She disappeared from my life when I was fourteen—they took her to an institution in another state. The last time I saw her was from a distance. She was wearing a white hospital robe. Years later I would hear her laughter in the crowds of foreign cities. And it's true there might never have been a Tanya without her, although Tanya was nothing like her.

&

AND SO I was about 100 miles from LA when I finally made camp on a bluff just north of Santa Barbara. I was older and more paranoid than I had been 48 hours before. It was starting to rain. I tuned the radio to an oldies station, stuff from the late 50s, early 60s. The rain was causing some static. The DJ segued from Brenda Lee's "Johnny One-Time" to Dolly Parton's "Lonely Coming Down". "Can you stand the heartache?" the DJ cried. "Well there's a lot more coming, right after this word from our sponsors." But the station faded before the sponsors could make their needs known.

When I was a kid, the only female singers of significance in my psychological landscape had been Brenda Lee, Patsy Cline, Dolly Parton, and Billie Holiday. Smoldering or brilliant women whose voices, thin and clear as wine, or thick and thigh-shaped, contained a sexuality beyond my years. Brenda Lee had undercurrent and innuendo; Patsy was clear, polished, chrome-plated and arrogant; Dolly was more like hobo wine drunk around a campfire; Billie Holiday, on the other hand, only made me sad. As I had these thoughts, the clouds broke for a moment and the stars became visible over the ocean. And there on the horizon, I saw a new constellation: a dinner party of all the sad singers—a genuine martyr's table of whining women whose men should have loved them better. The Greeks never saw it—they never saw Dolly and Billie rising like a female yin-yang sign. They never saw Brenda Lee in the sky with her liquor glass either. But I did.

But speaking of atom bombs, I figured if you exploded an atom bomb inside the head of a Brenda or a Patsy you might get a Janis Joplin. When I first heard it, I guess I felt that mushroom cloud. And so, I suppose, Janis Joplin *was* to become my Patsy Cline, in that I associated both with the decline of social standards in the shadow of mass destruction. Perhaps the clue lies in the rumor that she was not a good singer and didn't care. But the point wasn't whether she could sing or not. It was the presentation

38

of emotion. One didn't need to separate words, for the same reason that opera is only moving when it is sung in a foreign language. The words are stupid. You actually don't want to understand them. Words trivialize emotion the way photos trivialize memories. The vacation never looks as exciting when you get it back from Photo-Mart. In the same vein, some say the narration trivializes the event. Others say myth is not the worst disease of language—reality is. I do feel, however, there is something to be gained from the obliteration of meaning. And in the case of Janis, it was the vocal overkill, the desire to mop the factory floor with the song, to wring every last drop out of it, to strangle it with a rapidly depleting bagful of mannerisms. Maybe it *is* exorcism—I always had the feeling of being robbed after I heard her. Not by the voice, but by the life.

But why was I even thinking about Janis Joplin? I guess because I was thinking about Tanya and they were somehow related. Tanya had insisted on the radio. Our little transistor job might have been blood red, but it was the direct descendant of those brown Bakelite art deco boxes that ran on tubes and lived in Norman Rockwell paintings, with jazz notes hovering around them. That traveling salesman lying in the small town hotel room didn't know he was living on the cusp of a new age, when all men in hotel rooms everywhere would be connected by common riffs and melodies, the way all men who look at the moon are connected. It was the birth of the collective unconscious of a different magnitude. And even though I don't listen much to my subconscious anymore, much less my unconscious, and even though Freud and Jung may very well go bowling nightly in my skull with medicine balls, and entropy may show itself to be nothing more than divine cynicism, I believe it is no accident that psychotherapy increased in the general population with the advent of mass media.

Because of the weather the country-western station faded out. I ran around the dial in search of something else. What I found was Wagnerian Opera, *Tristan and Isolde*. Talk about gut-wrenching angst. In some countries, I think you can actually use it as a legal defense for murder. Chromaticism mingled with the static and I couldn't tell one from the other. I watched, through the wind and mist, the rough waves crash slowly on the sand like the combs of insane roosters. The swelling music merged with the sound of the ocean in a great maternal swallowing. Then the clouds rolled in. And I suppose at some point I slept, because I had a dream of a mushroom cloud hovering over the western horizon. Communists had blown up LA. I knew that I could trust no one from that point forward.

I woke up still aware of the ocean. The rain had stopped, but the radio maintained its Wagnerian static. I crawled out from under my lean-to of green plastic. The scenery was misty, spectacular. It seemed to be sweating light. But the place I was camped was no romantic bluff-top hideaway, but rather a muddy construction site—the future home of the Surf & Turf condo development. I packed up all my gear and started my engine. It ran like hell for a few minutes but smoothed out once it warmed up and dried out. Workers were arriving in pick-up trucks. Some waved to me as I rolled off their land.

&

A MOTORCYCLE CAN be like a lonely-hearts club on wheels. People will talk to you just because you're on it. You can meet new people in small towns because of a bad gasket, a short, a blown oil seal, out-of-sync carbs. I'd only gone about a hundred miles; it was still morning, but I was having some kind of trouble up by Cambria. I was tinkering with my battery cables when Peter and Jane pulled up behind me in their station wagon. "Hey man, follow us." We had tuna sandwiches and coffee for lunch. They swore there was nothing wrong with the food even though they had got it at a salvage store. We listened to the Eagles and the Doors as Peter swept his hand across the yard at the three broken-down cars, the Honda and the Harley that didn't run. This was as far as they got, he said, on a trip to India.

I drove by Big Sur and passed Point Lobos in heavy traffic—those places we read about in the travel sections of Sunday papers. Just north of Santa Cruz I decided to make camp around Davenport. There was a bluff to my left. I knew the ocean was over there and it looked like I could get a view of it if I crossed some railroad tracks and climbed a path up to what looked like a plateau. I almost ran into somebody's tent—Richie and Margaret, brother and sister. They'd been in a crash and were camped here going on two weeks. They survived on food they stole from the 7-11. They paid for the wine and anything else too big to fit in the pockets of their field jackets. They didn't like people who were in a hurry, so I slowed down and drank with them. I talked about my troubled mind, my broken heart. I was starting to sound like a country-western song when Richie, fed up, cut me off. "You don't know shit," he said, pointing to the skid marks and the broken glass on the road, "cause that's a broken heart." My friends gave me a compass and a pocket screwdriver for luck when I left. "True north and tight screws," Richie said. I used the screwdriver to balance my carburetors. I never used the compass.

When I got to San Francisco, I discovered my brakes were inadequate. I found the Haight area and parked in front of a hippie boutique. In the shop window was an old poster for a Janis Joplin concert at the Fillmore. The Hell's Angels were going to be there. That is, they were going to be there in 1967. I bought a pack of rolling papers. The shop keeper, Patty, talked about the way San Francisco used to be, about how great it once was, and wasn't now. "I'm going to write a book about it," she said.

"Cool," I said.

We empathized a little about the decay of the world, then I asked the woman if she'd keep an eye on my bike while I checked out the neighborhood. "It'll be cool, man," she said. I was gone two days. When I went to get my bike, the store was closed but my stuff was still there. I rode across the Golden Gate through Marin County. That night I stopped in the redwood forest on yet another rocky bluff overlooking the sea. There seemed to be a lot of these rocky bluffs around. They all reminded me of paintings. In fact, everything seemed to be imitating something that was imitating it—San Francisco, the landscape, even me. So I combed my hair in the rearview mirror, packed up my gear and started out again. I was imitating restlessness. Besides, I figured I could put in another hundred miles before camp. Somewhere in those hundred miles I passed a guy who looked exactly like an old friend of mine from New York. Actually more like an Edward Munch screaming-man version of that friend caught in my headlight, out there in the redwood darkness.

&

SOMETIMES YOU FORGET about the wind. Especially if you don't ride for a few days. But the wind is always waiting for you. Never mind about airplanes and weather patterns, chaos and butterflies flapping their wings in China. One does not experience turbulence anywhere as much as on a motorcycle in the wind. The curves, curlicues, whistles, howls and groans—they seem to find every available curve and cove inside your skull. You might hear: Mozart, Beethoven, Zappa, Ravi Shankar, the Mahavishnu Orchestra from Mt. Abora. It's all there in the whirlpools of white noise. The selection is based on predisposition. Nature vs. nurture. Pleasure vs. paranoia.

But it's definitely the paranoia which detects the subtle rhythm of the inevitable engine malfunction—some frame part that is surely shaking loose as you lean into that curve, or a newly broken sprocket tooth rattling around in the transmission that will soon seize up at 60 mph, or that carburetor screw you should have tightened back at the last gas station about to be ingested by an overheated cylinder. If the scenarios often point to death, the wind wants to help in that cause. It buddies up with the speedometer to slowly coax your hands off the grips. "C'mon, just for a second, c'mon, let go, embrace us," they plead.

I didn't give in. I crossed the border into Oregon, passed through Ashville and kept going. But my mechanical problems were only partially in my head. The clutch was slipping. So I decided to stop in Corvallis before heading into Portland. I had made the trip in little over a week. But since I had planned on spending the whole summer there, I was a little disappointed by my impatience.

Part II
tales of Burnside

(7)

I ROLLED UP TO FIND MY OLD BUDDY NEIL AND HIS SHINY NEW wife sitting on their front porch. Healthy young adults, each coming out of some passage or trial they thought should be their last. Him out of the army. Her out of EST. They didn't want to mess around anymore and marriage seemed the way to stop, which might be why they acted glad to see me. I probably short-circuited their next argument. And I know well how that can be mistaken for pleasure.

Neil had a chip on his shoulder the origin of which could not be traced. Kimberly was the demure kind of low-spoken woman such men search for, and she was possessed of an unwarranted sense of duty that might make a man happy, but would always make her sad.

"Where's Tanya?" Neil asked politely.

"In jail," I said.

"Oh." He smoked. He could have shown a little more interest.

"What's up with her mother, what's her name, Nanette? Nancy? The righteous Nan?"

"Naomi." I said.

"Yeah, how's Naomi?" Neil liked to make fun of Tanya when she wasn't around. He, himself, had no need of heroes.

"She's in jail, too," I said, joking.

He was staring at something as we talked. Somewhere along the line he'd managed to buy a Triumph Bonneville, a nice machine, with money he'd borrowed with no intention of paying back. It fulfilled two fantasies. It made the bike seem free, and also like he had worked hard to get it. I parked right beside it. We cracked open the Jim Beam and lit cigarettes and started where we had left off years earlier.

I was reading Woody Guthrie's *Bound for Glory* at the time. I said I thought the American road was fading as a metaphor for freedom and that in modern life the quintessential western narrative was no longer the "road story" but rather the mystery, if only because paranoia and deception were rampant. The process of detection seemed the obvious way to conduct one's life. Even if the revelations lead to repression, hell, at least it was living. Neil thought the road was nothing but shopping anymore and that the homogenization of the world was just beginning. I had to agree.

When the talk got tired, we looked at our motorcycles like they were dogs or babies or something, one of those conversational crutches people use to fill dead space. Still, he was grateful for some money I had lent him which he never paid back, which of course led to a slight tinge of obligation, which bred resentment along with a need for revenge, which then bred further mendicancy, which I suppose is why he decided this would be a good opportunity to try to borrow even more money. His Triumph needed a rear view mirror, he was short on the rent and he wanted to get something nice for the wife. She was in Corvallis, after all, studying sociology or social psychology or something like that. Neil was living off her. He felt bad.

I said I was strapped. The trip from New Orleans up the coast had chewed my clutch plates. The battery cables were shot. I needed a rear tire and a place to live. I was running low on cash. So I turned the tables and asked if I could stow the Beezer under his awning while I got a job in Portland and got some money together to fix the bike. It was a stand-off.

"What are you gonna do, be a bum in Portland?" Kimberly said, pretending it was a joke. It wasn't. She thought I *was* a bum, or should be.

It's like telling a kid he's dumb. He believes it, and so he becomes it. Parents and teachers sow the seeds of failure in their children so they have someone to blame later on for not living up to their expectations. It also allows them to feel better about their own lives. Kim was a closet mom, and she wanted me out of Neil's life. And she had that kind of low pinched voice that gets in your head like a bug and lodges somewhere behind your right ear. It can even reach you from the grave. I left just to stay ahead of it.

&

I ARRIVED ON Burnside before eleven, still in time for the breakfast special. I drank seven cups of coffee, ate my pancakes, then took a walk on skid row. I'd been there before. I was there again. But this time, all I seemed to notice were the bums. They were like popcorn or Chia pets or instant orchids. It was as if some kind of philosophical/spiritual convention were going on, no formal invites needed.

It was just like Kimberly had suggested. With a few words, she had somehow focused the lens of my anxiety. She had tagged something, the way women do, hit some nail in the male head that makes us squirm. It's easy for them. They learn it early and use it often. They can make it happen with a raised eyebrow, a twitch of the mouth. Suddenly you're in a slide from which it may take thirty years to recover.

Still, I couldn't really blame her. She'd only spotted a pre-existing tendency. You couldn't call it a good thing, but skid row, at least the idea of it, well, it was like home to me—clean, but not too clean. Styrofoam cups and old potato chip bags were jammed between the grimy pane and the window screen that faced the brick wall of an air chute. Five years of dust was packed in the sashes. Outside, it was a land as big, open and beery smelling as your mama's lap. And if it is true that a disease of society eventually becomes a disease of the personality, then it may well be an Oedipal fact that more than one hard-time generation has internalized skid row to the point that, even if investment capital manages to obliterate it, it will continue to exist in some Twilight Zone, a grey street way down in the lower east side of consciousness that acts as a magnet for everything that is tired, pessimistic or beaten down in a person.

I took a room at the Freeway Hotel. The name was due to the fact that it was right next to the freeway. I could have thrown beer cans at the cars that roared below my window. The room was carpeted. There was a bed, a chest of drawers and a chair. There was a radio built into the wall and a faint smell of death. Acme Extra Strength Carpet Cleaning Powder apparently never got rid of it. Neither did Mr. Clean. I never opened the closet for fear of what it might reveal.

The desk clerk was a prematurely-aged, mid-life eccentric who was so stoned most of the time he could barely count out change for the cigarettes and bags of chips he sold. He liked to tell people it was shell-shock from the war but he was really just perpetually high. He spent a lot of time in the bathroom, and the exhaust fan in there needed oil. You could listen to it squeal while you sat around on the lobby furniture watching the public TV.

I slept for an hour or so, took a shower, threw on my existential overcoat and hit the street. Skid row, bum town, me and Tanya's old stomping grounds. I went into a bar we used to go to. There was a woman there—receptive, aggressive— but I wasn't ready for her. It was too sudden. But she didn't care what I was ready for.

"Stop feeling sorry for yourself. You're nothing special, don't start believing that you are," she said.

"I really just want a drink," I said.

"Whew," she said grinning, then added sarcastically, "I see—a cynic. Very well. Perhaps the indifference of our cold hearts will save this meeting from mediocrity."

"Huh?"

"Forgive me if join you. Let's drink to forgiveness." She raised her glass. I was entranced by the Victorian mannerisms, forced as they might have been. I was also surprised that I was entranced. I responded in kind.

"Without blame there is no need for forgiveness."

"What?" She laughed.

Then I laughed. Then we dropped the farce.

"My name's Elizabeth. Call me Liz. Liz Sid."

"Sid?"

"Short for Siddal."

"I'm Frank but you can call me Luc," I said.

"Buy me a drink, Frank."

She ordered Southern Comfort. So did I. It should have been a clue. Instead I let myself believe my luck had changed—that I was going to get laid by a beautiful woman without any aggressive act on my part. But Liz Sid split, stealing my money off the bar when I went to the bathroom. That was too bad. I had assumed her embellished speech patterns indicated some romantic notion about life. Actually they did; the next morning I heard she died from an overdose—probably with my money. The world did seem to revolve around me in those days, and everyone knew it. But then everybody knows everything about everybody down on Burnside.

(8)

THE FREEWAY HOTEL WAS TOP OF THE LINE FOR THE AREA. there were plenty of others with more religious-sounding names like the Providence, the Heaven's Gate or the Rising Sun. Tags heavy with intimations of fate and redemption. In those days, the Burnside district seemed like a great medieval neighborhood airlifted into the modern world—dark and damp, and driven in its pinball intricacies by rituals involving alcohol, intoxicants and sad sexual intercourse. Merchants from foreign cities barked orders at shoppers. Broken-toothed peasants wandered through the tableau, looking both lost and found, as if they'd been trucked in by some Anachronisms Anonymous Anti-Segregation league. And there was always this sense that you were at the wretched bottom of everything, traveling through some murky reflection of a greater reality you couldn't see. Searching for the holy cup of coffee, the sacred bottle of wine. Inns and bawdy houses announced themselves with intense Twilight Zone-style neon signs, mocking continuity and narrative structure for the sake of a tiny profit. People approached you in the street, brandishing trinkets overloaded with significance.

As the summer clawed on, I grew into "the life" like a kid grows into his older sibling's clothes. I became a familiar face in my corner of town. I was known at Alice's All-Nite Cafe. I was known at The Fool's Paradise, at The Caribou Club, at Morrison's and especially at The Seven Seas. The bartender there called me "Bud." He said "Good morning, Bud ... What'll it be, Bud? ... Closing time, Bud. Drink up."

There was an odd sense of familiarity. People would see me in the street and they would think they knew me. Sometimes I'd look in the mirror and not be sure where I came from. Some swamp, a European forest, maybe. But if I felt I'd lived before, it wasn't my fault. It's common enough: children, mystics, monks, saints, Hindus, schizophrenics. We are all simply, suddenly here, but with a nagging inkling of an elsewhere. Elaborate stories weave themselves in and around the doubt. Some, like myself, believed we were delivered by flying saucers. Others are sure they are the result of biological experiments. As a kid I was sure those people who were supposed to be my parents were really government-appointed caretakers. I'm told there are ways to prove the continuity of existence without resorting to paranoia, but I don't know them.

JUST ABOUT EVERYBODY on Burnside thought they could have been something once. One guy had been a limo driver for rodeo stars. Another had been a genius at adultery. There were Jake and Joey—a has-been lingerie model and one-time inventor of the lamb shank-deboning machine—they were a cute couple. And then there was The Mayor of Burnside, a used-to-be politician voted into and out of office by booze. For the time being, I was happy to be a voyeur.

I needed an identity so I adopted the one I was already using, the disenfranchised post-war American male. I spoke in clipped terse phrases and kept to myself in order to dramatize my presence, hoping at the same time to promote a sense of mystery. People will mistake silence for judgment. It makes them nervous. They may even mistake solitude for nobility. Or else they assume you're dangerous. Someone once said, "You don't always know who lives next door, or even in your own room." And that's where the whole thing starts really.

I often asked the reflection in the mirror who I was, trying to get a statement. I did the good cop/bad cop routine. Laurel and Hardy. Friday and Romero. The self-induced schizophrenia really didn't help, though. It becomes too easy, and, of course, you never get as high as the first time. Soon, it's a habit. After a certain number of drinks, the rubber face comes as a relief. The future goes to work on your bone structure. The face in the mirror begins to fit in nicely with the men who lined the 3rd Street sidewalk, the men who slept under moldy blankets in front of the Salvation Army, the 5 a.m. men waiting for the buses to take them out to the fields with whisky and soda in their canteens and bleeding gums, the men sitting on the edges of their beds, in humid rooms, their shirts on hangers, and all their possessions jammed into a 7 x 9-foot human mini-storage, hostages in a war waged outside their sphere of influence. Economic dislocation is what the university hot-shots were calling it. It was like panning for gold or separating the wheat from the chaff— you placed society on a screen and shook it and these were the people that fell through. Men whose wives had left them, or been driven away, men whose children turned to crime, whose friends had turned against them or turned their backs; especially after their government had fucked them, and they lost their jobs and their houses and their self-respect to swindlers and two-timers, etc.

You could even make a movie about it, call it *Men without Women*. I could see the marquees in my mind. Burt Lancaster as the *Birdman of Burnside*. Kirk Douglas as *Johnny Burnside*. Jimmy Cagney in *Big House on Burnside*. Elvis does *Burnside Rock*. Johnny Cash "Live at the Providence

Hotel." Debates might be held about the meaning or the outcome. But for those who really lived here it was a world without time or telephones, where, in the privacy offered by a 40-watt bulb and a quart of malt liquor they could contemplate the warrior and the lover and the male mother. But in the end they could not avoid the truth that, too often, the male mother looks too much like the hobo caught in the headlights of a fugitive car. Two faces became one, the driver and the hitch-hiker, separated by nothing more than ten or twenty years. And that face was like a contagion, a virus; it passed in handshakes of recognition between men in bars and drop-in centers. Suggestion alone was the carrier, like a subtle itch behind the left ear.

&

OF COURSE MOST of these men didn't have regular jobs, but I did. I went around town with money in my pocket. I spent my off-hours drinking and shooting pool to a background score of jukebox tunes which quickly became the themes of my life, although I can't remember any of the specific songs like you're supposed to. I worked on the railroad for about two weeks. Then I got fired. I dug ditches, toted boulders, laid hot roofs—I had four jobs in six weeks. I finally settled in at the Goodwill, dumping people's discarded lives on a conveyor belt so they could be sorted into categories: electronics, toys, clothes. The Goodwill people had a philosophy. It all had to do with the redistribution of possessions and how the belief in those possessions had caused the plight of the people who worked there.

The place was alive with epileptics and post-traumatic stress disorder victims—colorful characters, if you're not one of them. There was Philip, who thought he worked for a detective agency. He wore a white trench coat and he had a business card with an eyeball crayoned on it. "I got an eye on you," he would say with a conspiratorial wink. There was Lew, the ghost hunter, who spend his off hours searching through the dusty corners of his rooming house for the source of the voices of the dead he heard nightly. There was Sam, who invented the game "Clue," and sold it to the corporations, so he claimed. His cure for insomnia was two quarts of cold Columbia beer, which he never hesitated to ask me to buy for him.

One day I was sitting in Washington Park. I was watching some loving couple humping under blankets off in the distance. They couldn't watch me watching. Or if they could, they didn't care. I was the pervert in their story. But I didn't feel like a pervert. Just a guy eating a sandwich. Then Chopper, a guy I knew from the Seven Seas, pulled up in a blue truck painted with a silhouette of a buxom black woman and the words

'Soul Food' in fluid rock & roll style letters.

"Hey Bud, what you watching, Wild Kingdom?" Chopper asked.

"I love nature," I said.

"Wish you had some nature, huh?"

"I got the flowers, the clean air, the pure fresh water. It will have to do."

"Tell you what. Wanna buy a piece?" he asked, holding out a brown paper bag with a revolver butt sticking out. "Put you out of your misery."

"No, but you can give me a ride back to town. Leastways then I won't have to torture myself with the joy of others."

"What?" Chopper looked confused.

"Give me a ride back the Seven Seas. You going by there?"

"Sure, c'mon. Wild Kingdom?" he asked again, offering the gun butt one more time. "Always hard. Always hot. Women can't resist."

"No thanks."

He had some beers in the truck so I drank one as we took the winding road down into the neighborhood, where he dropped me off. I went into the bar and immediately someone asked, "What are you hanging out with Chopper for? You got some ugly friends, chum."

I soon got the lowdown on Chopper, or Toby, his other name. He was a substance abuser who lived in another hotel just up the street. There was some long drawn out explanation of a deal he facilitated for Jimmy T, the night clerk from the Providence. The piece was one of the perks.

The story was mildly interesting but my mind soon wandered. I began thinking of gorgeous, solvent, socially well-placed women, who might be drawn to me by the very act of my thinking of them. This is the kind of thing one thinks about in bars. But all it did was make me hungry.

&

IT IS SAID that memory is a construction not a xerox: Prodigious? Maybe. Pathological? Definitely. A physical event composed of the passage of a few electrons moving at approximately the speed of light through some grey chemical-charged mud. Bias is inherent. Skewed perceptions too. The process produces heat. Heat, in turn, increases entropy. Strange things happen over and over. Sometimes everything seems new, even if it's really old. Or everything seems old, but it's really new. Time can go backwards, and you don't know it, because you're going backwards with it. If you think things are getting better, starting to coagulate and make some sense, you're wrong, though it is quite probable the universe *was* once as perfect as an egg and not crazy, but that was once upon a time, when answers were obvious and sensation was kin to reason.

I look at old photographs, and bells ring at the back of my mind, the sound of black water lapping a stony beach in the brain. Melodies come too: recordings, reproductions, broadcasts caught at opportune times like something heard on the radio on a mountain road. There's that affinity I feel for places I supposedly "remember." Places I've never been: Paris, Antwerp, Bordeaux, Benares, Barstow, West Virginia. We see people in photographs or travel books and we identify with them. A child by a tributary of the Amazon. A blackened Welsh mine worker at the turn of the century. A Lucknow washerwoman. It's like a museum of stray remembrances out there.

Photography propagates this illusion of collective memory, something private yet available to the public. We might see there some great purpose, a journey we are all on. Some religions prohibit representation because if one can characterize God, one may come to believe oneself similar to God, and at that point in human history people begin killing for sport. Polymorphous religions like Hinduism have another answer—mutation, deferral, renewal. 20th century consumerism is based on this process—something for everyone: "Here we made this car just for you. Have it your way. Now shut up."

Colors, locations, calendars—they all add up, but the sum is never everything we think. Because the secret is always the same: that the joke is on you, not with you. It's part of the insidious nature of representation, the appropriation of time by images, the reduction of life to voyeurism. The mind expands to imprison the world, causing one to question the very heart of wanderlust. There's a confusion between the active and passive principles. Traveling may relieve you of responsibility, but when it's over there's no where to go that you haven't been already—why not just sit home? Today, many people do.

&

I WALKED OVER to Morrison's Cafe for an SOS. A girl with a pocked sad face, sweet and breezy, served me. Her name was Francie. I played the jukebox for her. I played Janis for Francie. I played Patsy. I fell to pieces, then I fell in love—with Francie the waitress in the Burnside dive. In fact, I put quotation marks around the idea of her. I imagined being upstairs with her, in a tiny room, peeling off that rough habit, only to find a blinding purity revealed. But my soul was not pure and I could not comply, even as a whole life of "caring" spread out ahead of us toward that better world where no one was lonely. Then I heard the bell ring. Someone's order was up. A burger with fries and gravy.

Several times I imagined Francie tried to catch my eye. I searched for confirmation, but there was nothing. A vast glacial moraine. A deserted speedway. I took offense at her indifference. But then who did I think I was? My halo grew heavy, more like iron than light, and I grew depressed and lonley. Lonely people make passionate lovers, I told myself. Actually, I never found this to be true. Awkward lovers, maybe. I returned to my room, alone and awkward.

They say part of the attraction of skid row hotels is that they are like the welcoming unkempt houses of our childhood, not swept so clean in the corners but good to come home to. There's something maternal about them. But it's the bad-mother sort of maternal, the cigarette-smoking mom with the gin bottle on the ironing board who knows she isn't quite raising you right, but then life is tough, and you're always welcome to come home but don't stay too long. And don't bring that bitch with you either.

BEING ON THE ROAD CAUSED ME TO MISS MOST OF THE major social and so-called youth movements of my day, preoccupied as I was. As compensation this "skid row" world was about to provide me with my own alternative "Summer of Love." But it would be depressants—alcohol, barbiturates and heroin—that would fuel my mini-revolution, and not the hallucinogenics and good vibes of the free love generation. No tie-die. No beads. No Woodstock Nation. I wanted to forget about Tanya, and the "Little Death" was one way of doing it.

I met Patsy Little Death at the bar. That wasn't her name. I never knew her name. I don't know if she had one. Patsy Barfly maybe. I walked in the bar because I heard a song on the jukebox—"Summertime." It's interesting how banal the pivots of our lives can be.

I ordered the shot-and-a-beer special because it was still happy hour. I was minding my business, watching a television show about insects taking over the world. A couple of red ants were killing some black ants, when this pale, baked redhead in blue jeans walked in and grabbed the elbow of my black jacket. "Doesn't all that killing depress you?"

This didn't seem like a pick-up line so I said, "What?"

"Never mind. Listen, could you give me a hand a second? I got a problem."

Apparently one of her friends was getting beat up by one of her other friends and she didn't know how to interfere without showing favoritism. She needed some passer-by with no personal interest. I was that passer-by, even though I was sitting perfectly still. "Of course, I mean you don't have to, if you're not feeling up to it. But I really would appreciate it," she said, unsubtly brushing my leg. My sense of "duty" was fueled by the vague promise of "intimacy" on down the line.

The fight was half a block away. We broke it up simply by screaming at the same decibel level as the participants. Then we went to Patsy's place where, as she had hinted, I was to do as I pleased. I guess that was my reward. I doubt if it was hers. She went about the task mechanically then offered me her back. I let some time pass just to be polite—at least five minutes—before leaving. She thumbed a magazine while I pulled on my pants. She started cooking a fix while I laced my shoes. She lit a cigarette with great intent as the door closed behind me.

I did see her again, though. In the same bar on a different day. I said hello. "Do I know you?" she replied with little conviction.

"No," I said, somewhat relieved, but also embarrassed because she probably thought I was trying to pick her up. But then I doubt it. She was listening to the men in the Seven Seas. Seemed like weeks had passed. Days at least. And they were still talking—talking about a gun. They had circumstances, facts, figures. It was so many millimeters. It was German, not Japanese. Probably cost so many dollars once. And the kid was a loose cannon. But the gun was also to blame. Apparently it was one of those guns that did things on its own. The people who held it often had no responsibility for their actions. It robbed people. Made men treat their women mean. Just having it on the table could cause a fight. A gun, a girl—little things, big events.

I thought back to the previous night. Perhaps my presence may have been what stopped an act of violence. It was arrogant to think so. But it turns out that Toby, the guy with the gun, was the husband of the woman who had been in the fight. He was recently out of jail and pissed. She'd been the one fucking the guy up in the park. Toby had gone up there to scare her. Or threaten her. Or him. Or so he claimed. The guy happened to be Patsy's ex-boyfriend. This was no secret. And now it was quite possible he knew that I had screwed Patsy too, even if it didn't mean anything. The net was tightening. My neck seemed to be in the way. Everything's connected, they say. The universe is a seamless web. Or maybe just a seamy web.

When we'd had enough to drink we went out and yelled at some people. It was like starting the relationship all over—no baggage. We were young, dumb, belligerent and dumped on. Owed and angry. We went to her place again. She got high straight away, not bothering to wait this time. She knew there was nothing to wait for. Certainly not desire. In fact, I don't think we even wanted to do it, just following a script, some scenario written in some time immemorial by some lonely scribe—an act of joy rendered as an act of attrition. Millions of men and women in bars across the country are forced to end their evenings with sexual intercourse, no matter how useless and empty they know it's going to be. They see the little bead of a human skull in the clown gallery in the back of their minds and they have to shoot at it with something. Knock one down and prolong your life for a second, or a day, or a year. It's a carnival game. The ancient gene engineers and the modern dramatists had got together on it. There was nothing anyone could do.

"Are you done?" she asked.

She went to the bathroom. I stared out the window. A man standing under a streetlamp, smoking hard, stared back. Smoke hovered around his head like a cloud. I heard the toilet flush. "There go my children," I thought. A tear came to my eye as a tugboat cruised up the Willamette River, crossing under the Burnside Bridge.

Then the door opened. "There you go again. Stop feeling sorry for yourself," Patsy said, and with that, she walked back to the mattress and passed out. I gazed lovingly at the passed-out woman, and thought how delicate and vulnerable she must have been, once. Then I poked around some more: a cat-o-nine tails hanging on the wall, medieval headgear. She made me feel like a kid. Down the dark hallway of her building I thought I heard a bottle break. I heard a muffled argument in another room. It was starting to rain. I felt a slow, dull rhythm building up in my brain. I went to the bathroom, too. There was a picture of a little boy stuck in the mirror frame. A little boy on a truck-tire swing. No doubt Patsy Little-Death stared at this picture every day with a touch of remorse.

&

MY SUMMER OF love continued. I was shooting pool with this Japanese guy who called himself Yazoo Nokami. We were headed from one bar to the next when this chick grabbed my arm outside the Silver Moon on 19th. I called her a chick, but she was probably 35 years old. We went back to her apartment.

"What's your name, Baby," she said.

"Frank."

She said hers was Sherri, Sherri White Flower. Something like that. Her boyfriend worked nights.

"Boyfriend?"

"Yes . . . oh, but it's okay, he's at work. If he comes home early, though, he'll kill us for sure."

"Yeah?"

"Yeah probably. But I don't think he will."

"What? Kill us?"

"No. Come home early." She chuckled sardonically to herself. But the strain split me in two. I became two people—one watching the door and windows, the other watching her. I also watched myself make a bad decision. I felt light and heavy. Totally alive and dead at the same time. Only women and fear can do this. And certain chemicals.

Sherri released the snap on her bra, as she continued. Apparently, Sammy, her boyfriend, had been in jail on and off for years on battery and manslaughter charges and was a jealous man, etc., etc., etc. Once Sammy had found her screwing a friend of his. He beat the guy so bad he was in the hospital for a week. And that was a friend.

"C'mon, we better hurry." She was ready. I balked. "Nervous?" she said, watching the clock and scratching her thigh.

"Why should I be?" I lied.

"Well then let's get it on, Daddy. We ain't got all night."

I found it interesting that she would use the word "daddy," when she had called me "baby" a few minutes earlier. I began to think her plan was simply to poison the womb of her enemy—her husband. She'd get pregnant. He would kill me and end up in jail where she could taunt him daily with a white man's child. It was a savage plan, and a bad movie plot. But this was the real world and it probably *would* happen. Or, he would kill her. I wouldn't say anything. I might not even know. There would be a mention in the paper. Actually, I would be a major suspect. I hadn't thought of that. But whatever she wanted, she was out of luck. The giant picture of Tanya floating in front of my face was choking the blood-flow to my loins.

Tanya had said after all, "I just don't want to know about it." But she *would know* about this if it made the papers after the murder. But maybe I wanted her to know. Maybe I was getting back at Tanya for her infidelities with Reggie and other suspects. Much of the sex drive is based on revenge. You not only gain power over the person you screw but power over those who know about it. Of course, they must actually know. You could hope they divine it. Or you could brag about it. You could try reverse psychology—say nothing, be subtle. But subtlety is really just a way of screaming at certain people. Or you could act suspiciously. But in cases of revenge sex, suspicion doesn't always cut it. Tanya wouldn't know unless I told her. But she could suspect, and that might drive her crazy. A sort of delicious persecution. But then I knew she knew already. She was in the room, watching me in the mirror. "You're not hurting me you know. I'm in jail," she said, "So I hope this is fun for you."

I didn't know if it was fun. I guessed it probably wasn't. But then why go on with it? I looked at the woman below me on the bed. All that was lacking was the frame of reference. Maybe we *were* all gravitating toward some iconographic degree zero, based in self-disgust. Sherri seemed nonplussed, if a little miffed by my remoteness. I hadn't even realized that we had started, that I was already doing her. Suddenly, the baby started crying. Sherri unplugged and left the bed to check on it. I was sure, for a second, that I heard a key slide in the lock. But just for a second. She came out with the kid at her breast. The kid's name was Billy.

"You better go now," she said. "I'm sorry." But I was already on my way out. I had just seen what I swore was a man's shadow outside the window.

A week later I saw Sherri again at the Silver Moon. She was crawling up the chest of a 300-lb., 7-ft 3-in. one-eyed thug with a Buck knife on his concha-studded belt and a tattoo that read "San Quentin '72." We exchanged a few words, during which I noticed a tall grim figure standing outside under a street lamp on 19th, smoking a cigarette. It was the same damn guy, waiting for me to join him. I ordered another beer. Somebody put a quarter in the jukebox. "Summertime," again.

&

ANOTHER NIGHT WHEN I was walking down Burnside, a beautiful woman came out of a bar and took my arm. She was slim and fairly healthy looking. She was carrying a book-bag and she had a highball glass in her hand. "I've seen you before," she said. I hadn't seen her, but it didn't matter—it was the '70s. She led me to an alley and then to a kind of bower between buildings where we lay down in the ferns and flowers. After a brief attempt at foreplay, she said, "C'mon, let's do it." Almost immediately she began making noises, but they were noises from a darker universe than ours.

As the proceedings moved along, I looked to the side and noticed to my surprise, a male version of The Wicked Witch from Oz. But he wasn't riding a broomstick, he was smoking a cigarette and riding a bunch of bones loosely resembling a horse. I couldn't tell if he was mocking my carnality or living it, vicariously, through me. He called me "cowboy." But he took the title back right away. "You're no cowboy," he said. He accused me of fraud and cowardice. He said I had forsaken spiritual hardship for the pleasures of the flesh. I said he was mistaken—that it was no comfort, and barely pleasure. He puffed himself up like some Roy Rogers from hell. "Tell, me, is it empathy or pity, or pure spite you're feeling right now?"

"Leave me alone," I whined.

He wouldn't. "You better be careful, cowboy. Where do you think you're going anyway? No. Don't bother answering. I'll tell you."

"Please don't. You're ruining the moment," I said.

He laughed. "You think it's that easy. You think you do it enough, you break on through, you exhaust this world of matter and memory and somehow come out clean. Well, you're wrong."

"Maybe. Maybe I need to learn by experience."

"Maybe you are not the man you thought you were." He slapped his skeletal horse's ass and yelled "Ya-hoo!"

"But I never was anyway. And besides there is no end to justify the means," I replied. I felt a brief flush of pride at my insight, but then I just felt stupid.

He said nothing. No reaction. There was only the wind whistling through the bones of his mount. That was enough. I had to defend myself. "You don't know me. You don't know who I am, or why I think these things," I said out loud.

The woman beneath me turned her sweaty, intoxicated face toward mine and asked, "What is it, doll?" I liked being called "doll."

"Nothing," I said.

"Then hurry up, I have to get to work."

That hurt. I could hear Janis Joplin music coming from one of the apartment windows above us. "Summertime." It seemed like everybody in Portland was playing that record back then.

The woman looked back again to smile. But this time it was my mother's wrinkled face on the lithe sweating little body of the drunk. I didn't like it one bit.

"Harder, son. Harder." she said.

"What?"

"What are you doing, Frank? You used to be such a good boy."

"Look Ma, I'm just doing what I thought I was supposed to do."

"Yeah, well. Come on, Baby."

"Oh shit."

"You know you want to."

It was an awkward position. I couldn't refuse her because I was already inside her. And what can you do anyway when it's your mother's spine writhing like the white line down the center of your erotic highway. I didn't say any of this. But I finally had to stop. Maybe I was a moral guy after all. Maybe that was the test.

"What's wrong?"

"I don't know. I thought you were in a hurry."

"Yeah. Yeah. Well . . ." She seemed pissed. "I am now." She pulled her jeans back on.

We had time, however, to get a drink. Her name was Gretta Trevi. She was Polish, Italian and Greek. Black hair. Thin face. She told me all about her ex-old man who was in jail—a musician. They weren't in love, but they *were* soul mates. He was buying hashish when the bust went down. But he was a good guy, a choir boy. They all were. Never brutes, but always proud men backed against the wall. Just like the victims you read about in the morning news, little saints who happened to step in the way of gunfire.

I began to feel stigmatized, as if I had become a magnet for the lonely mates of incarcerated men. Of course, I had an old lady in jail. I just never mentioned it.

Gretta played the jukebox. She had good taste. And she liked to sing along drunkenly in the soft-focus jukebox mist. She could do a great Patsy Cline, albeit with an accent. She liked Dylan and the Morrisons, Jim and Van. She played "Light My Fire." Then she played "Brown-Eyed Girl." She sang along. *"Sha la la la la la la la . . ."*

Apparently this woman was more than just an easy lay. She was a Reed College student slumming. She said she wanted to be a writer and she was writing things down in a notebook as she said it. She said if Keats had been born in our day he would have been a rock star. She said her brother went insane reading the poet, Arthur Rimbaud. Lost his job, joined the Navy, went to 'Nam. Then his wife left him. Gretta hadn't heard a thing in years.

I checked the time. I asked Gretta Trevi why she wasn't going to work. "I was kidding. You just never know when the police are going to come." We both laughed. But we were laughing at different jokes. While we were laughing I looked outside for the smoking man and he was there. He was wearing a cowboy hat, standing on the street corner, and he was laughing with us.

&

MARSHALL MCLUHAN MIGHT have said the highway is the ideal indication of potency for our industrial age, in which case a road story would be nothing more than the quantification of that potency—miles driven, towns breezed through, number of chicks made, number of strokes delivered, number of orgasms, all lost eventually, like trees falling in the forest unheard. They say passion is popular precisely because it obliterates time. And that's the "too-real" reality of the Little Death. It can make one intensely, intolerably happy for the shortest possible duration. But for the lonely awkward people of the world it doesn't work. It only elongates time and makes life sad.

I went to Morrison's Cafe to eat. I was comfortable there. I was no longer surprised by my reflection in the mirror there. I watched the cook as he reached into the dishwater and pulled out a carving knife. There was blood on it. A blind man with a red-tipped cane walked in. The waitress passed me by with a plate. I didn't ask. There was a fishing show on TV. Three men in a boat. The special of the day was duck. I ordered chicken-fried steak and mashed potatoes. The potatoes stared me down. I went to pay my bill. Above the cashier hung an old sword and a dusty stag's head.

I BELIEVE EINSTEIN said time is a neighborhood of space. But I think time and space are separate. Time you can waste. There is nothing do be done about it anyway. Space has to be overcome. Life can be seen as a progression of images to that end. Sometimes you see them before they get to you. They might determine your actions. Sometimes you don't see them until years after these actions have taken their toll.

Anyway, that was the end of my summer of love.

(10)

IT WAS ALONG ABOUT MID-AFTERNOON. I WAS AT MORRISON'S. I was half-asleep, sitting in a booth thinking about Roy Latoure. In my head was an image of Roy riding down some Indiana road on that green, one-eyed Triumph. That road became a ribbon which rose and formed a coil and then the coil formed a drome, a motorcycle drome at a county fair, and Roy was going around inside it, going around in circles fast, like he was caught in a record groove, spiraling down that groove toward the center. It was a carnival and everything was running in circles.

Then I had a flash that somewhere beneath me was a great whirlpool, and something was disappearing down that whirlpool and I couldn't put my finger on it. It wasn't color or sense impressions. These things still existed. And it wasn't emotions, because people still seemed to have them. Whatever it was, it was being drawn off down a funnel—perhaps into another universe, a universe that was just then forming. A young jealous universe—if inanimate things can be jealous, which I believe they can be. But I'm not Pantheist. I'm not a Buddhist either. And I don't define the world in negatives—by what it's not. I mean, I might explain myself that way. Cynicism is a modern kind of Buddhism. And I am a cynic. I'm not a Neo-Platonist, though. I don't see everything as a degraded reflection.

&

I WAS FEELING funny. I turned to the TV because I didn't want to think about Roy or Platonism or Pantheism or degraded reflections. I needed some reality. Giraffes on TV were running through a burning forest. But the picture started rolling and then the channel changed. The air in the bar changed too. The air had been thick, greenish and oppressive. It opened up a little. I detected a hint of the smell of a familiar place. What was it? Ogden, Utah, canned sardines, white wine, lemon juice.?Yes, that was it. Then I heard someone talking in a close voice.

"As I walked through the wilderness of this world, I lighted on a certain place." It was a gruff voice, a voice of someone who gargles with glass.

"Hey Roscoe, two pitchers over here," another man called, further away.

"And I laid me down in that place to sleep; and as I slept I dreamed me a dream."

On the TV there was a documentary about American hobos during the '40s. At first I couldn't tell if the voice I heard was part of the narration, or some disembodied narrative assembling itself out of the muddle of bar conversation, as often happens in the minds of the dispossessed.

"Might I rest my dogs for a spell by your campfire, friend."

"Hey, man, I need you to shut the fuck up," I said, "I'm trying to think."

"Maybe you think too much, Rubberman. Lighten up."

But I couldn't lighten up. That smell of Ogden, Utah. It was in his clothes. I tried not to pay attention. I crushed the butt of my smoke out in the steel ashtray. He kept talking.

"I've hung from crosses too, my friend. You can see a lot from up there, but you can't do anything about it, can you? No sir. Better to climb down and join the world. You're nobody special. Don't start thinking that you are."

The bartender was still flicking channels. There was a show on about some rich and famous people sitting around the side of a pool in Palm Springs talking about themselves. It seemed they were trying to convince themselves that they were more than just images on TV. The channel changed again. A female praying mantis devouring the head of her mate. I took a drink. Then Marlin Perkins came on. He was talking about insects that imitate poisonous plants. Suddenly I had the taste of heroin in my throat. Another ancient memory. Marlin Perkins must have kicked that off. It tasted good. But it went away.

&

THEN THE GUY just sat down. He didn't ask my permission. At first I thought he looked a little like Marlin, but I was wrong. He looked more like Roy Latoure, the guy I had just been thinking about earlier. Then I wondered how he even knew Roy. Maybe he didn't, maybe he had simply taken Roy's image as a way of worming into my confidence. Shit, I thought. I began to feel violated, paranoid, invaded. Every time I sat down or relaxed it seemed someone appeared. Someone I didn't want to see. But maybe this *was* Roy. Maybe he had come back from the dead to warn me of impending world cataclysm. But that was improbable. Cataclysm wasn't impending. And Roy was no Messiah.

Okay, so the guy didn't look like Roy so much. He merely embodied some of his mannerisms. Or maybe I just wanted to see those mannerisms. I had been thinking about Roy after all, transposing my daydream onto my surroundings. It's called transference. Everybody does it.

The guy sitting next to me wore a black stocking cap and had a black beard. He was trying to look older than he was. But he was old enough. He had ten, maybe fifteen, years on me. But then I was young. Now, I feel I was actually older then. But that's a cliché. But so was he. The guy wore green lizard cowboy boots and a red-checked flannel vest—a backwoods kind of Christmas party look. He had an old cane, the pommel carved with a cynical clown's head. His left eye seemed particularly clear, glittering in a way, like a spark from a departing train wheel or a welder's bead, and it fixed me.

"What's up?" I asked, a common courtesy in these bars.

"In distant countries I have been, friend, and seldom have I seen a healthy man weep in the public roads alone."

"You talking about me? Do I seem to be weeping? Do I seem sad?"

"I think so. I think I'm talking about you." He pointed to my glass. "Riding that liquid pony on down to your personal Slough of Despond. That's no progress, Pilgrim, that's sadness and sadness ain't sainthood. There ain't no shrine in pain."

His name was Walker Birdsong. He let me know right away. We had a sizing-up party on the spot. I assumed he was a drunk or a con and prepared myself to dismiss him. For his part he couldn't have known if I was a tough guy or a shmuck. He might have thought I was a fake, that I didn't belong in this milieu, and it was his job to show me the door. But he didn't. He said he'd just got into town from Ogden, Utah. Rode the rails in. I didn't like it. Coincidence makes me nervous.

"You know sometimes I have premonitions. I think I just had one. I passed through Ogden on my way from Chicago, once, and . . . just now I . . ."

He cut me off. "Aren't you lucky. Living in two worlds like that."

"Funny, I'm sometimes called Lucky," I said, trying not to lose a beat.

"That your name?"

"Name's Luc. I'm only Lucky rarely. It's an old nickname."

"Maybe you are an arrogant man then. Yes, maybe that's what you are."

"Actually I'm Frank. That's my real name."

"Well, I guess I'll call you Pilgrim then. So listen, Pilgrim. You don't know anything. Don't act like you do."

"Last time I heard someone say that," I said, "it was a woman, in this very bar, and she was dead three hours later, one of those romantic types," I stared at my empty glass all melancholy-like.

He didn't think it was funny. "Don't let the statistics get you down, though. Look, I'll tell you what, buy me a beer, I'll tell you a story. A happy story, something to ease your pain."

"Maybe I don't want to hear a story, and who says I'm in pain."

"We all want to hear stories, bro, keeps the wheels turnin'." He was looking at the wall.

"I don't. I'm watching TV."

He must have sussed out what I was thinking because all of a sudden he got reallly helpful. "I got some advice for you, if you want it."

"Wait," I said.

"What?"

"Let me get out my notebook. My memory's not so good."

"You've got a smart mouth for a Pilgrim. You should humble up some, pal."

There was a pause while he waited for my reaction. I didn't give him one. The pause got longer. Finally it broke. Like a plate of water on a tile floor—it just went everywhere. "Sorry," I said.

"Like rock and roll?" He put a shopping bag on the table—seven, maybe ten albums in it. I didn't remember him carrying those in, but then I didn't see him come in. "You buy one, then I get my own beer. Okay? You're off the hook. And I'm started on a brand new drunk."

"I don't have a record player."

"Don't need one. Just for looking, see." He took one out of the bag and started looking at it with one eye closed, all intense.

I looked through the rest: *The Doors, Surrealistic Pillow, Cheap Thrills.* More coincidence. I bought a couple for the hell of it. Fifty cents apiece. That was three beers for Walker Birdsong. Actually two, because first he got a bowl of mashed potatoes with chicken-gizzard gravy from the cafe. "I like the sweet meats," he said, "You know what I mean?"

&

AS I STARED at his food my mind wandered. Then I thought: What if this was the same copy of *Cheap Thrills* that Roy Latoure had owned back in '69? What if it had passed from him to others, then through several thrift stores and finally into a garbage bin, from whence it ended in Walker Birdsong's shopping bag?

Walker stirred his potatoes and gravy. "Let me tell you that story," he repeated.

"You keep saying that."

"I know I do. And I surely will. But you'll want to hear it. It's about you."

I settled in, against my better judgment. I don't like to hear about myself. Self-knowledge is usually bad news. But then the funniest thing happened. Walker didn't talk about me at all. He talked about himself: The Walker Birdsong Story—One Chapter One.

Apparently Walker was no fruit picker. No, sir. He was adamant about that. Blackfoot, Irish, Romanian Gypsy, Jew. He was not above using the occasional alias either, and probably didn't remember some of them. I figured he was lying. I waited for the punch line.

"I'll tell you one goddam thing, though. Don't trust me," he said, trying to earn my trust.

"I thought this was supposed to be about me," I said.

"Okay, okay. Where you from? What's your name?" He asked with such enthusiasm, I thought he might really want to know.

"I already told you my name."

"Yes. Yes you did. Stranger. And you came here from Chicago, once upon a time, long ago, back in the old days."

"How did you know that?"

"You told me. Remember?"

"Huh?"

"Now . . . what happened to the woman?"

"What woman?"

"There's always a woman."

"All right. There was. I lost her."

"Living the wild life?"

"I guess. Now I'm . . ."—I searched for words—"just sitting here."

"Talking to barflies like me. Sad end, ain't it?"

"If you already know how it ends, why do you ask?"

"I been in Chicago, asshole. New York, too." He pounded his cane on the floor. "Frisco. Tulsa. New Orleans. Up and down the line," he said, staring off toward the TV. "I done everything, knew all them people. Most of them were assholes. Just like you. You go back in time if you want. You ask about Walker Birdsong. They'll tell you. I'm the real thing, Pilgrim. You don't know, but you will."

"What I don't *know* is what you're talking about."

He took the *Cheap Thrills* album out of my hand and started thumping it. "There was some shit going on in Madison. My old lady went up there. I had something working in the city. I met her then, '64, I think. Friend of my buddy, Nick."

"Who?"

"Janis," he said pointing to the album. "Now that was one fucked-up bitch."

"I guess."

He studied me a second. Then his face changed. "Sad broad, really."

"Uh-huh." I didn't want to show interest because it could lead to trouble.

"She gave it away, you know. It was all for free. And there was never nothing in it for anybody." He handed the album back.

"Apparently." I began looking at the album like a newspaper, studying the cartoons. No matter where you looked, your eye gravitated to the ball and chain in the middle.

"So what are you doing here, what's your story?"

"Looking for someone," I said.

"Who'd that be?"

"You wouldn't know."

"I'm sure you're right. Still . . ." he rolled his fingers on the table. "I'm dry."

"Let me buy you another drink," I said, and started to get up.

"Sit down a second. Let me tell you something, Pilgrim. I don't want your damn money. It's your ear I need."

&

HE WENT ON with his biography. This movement, that movement. White-cross-fueled 60-hr. coastal driving jags. Tijuana, Seattle, New York. The migrant labor trail. He said he was a man of the people and that he believed in Justice and Communism, and that everybody was the same and different at the same time. But his egalitarianism had failed him somewhere along the road. "It's what I call picking up a thorn," he said. And now he wasn't going to get any more pleasure out of this life unless he fucked with people—the fakers and the fashion fucks. So he was fucking with me, and I could tell it was making him feel good.

He knew Grace Slick, Country Joe. And Dylan of course. He never met Woody Guthrie, but he had written a song with Doc Boggs once. And that was another thing. He was a songwriter, singing about freedom. But the freedom drove him to the mental hospital, then to jail. First Willamette, then San Diego County. He met Manson on a transport bus on his way to Quentin.

"Aren't guys like you supposed to have guitars?" I said, refusing to be impressed.

"Quit that shit." He spoke indignantly, soft and close to my face. "It would be playing their game." Instead of a guitar he had a notebook full of songs and poems about social injustice and hypocrisy. Then he got disillusioned and started writing songs about disillusionment. Eventually he was just writing songs about writing songs, so he gave it up. "There's enough things to bow before. No new idols needed, sir. You listening, Pilgrim?"

I was. But I was also thinking about Tanya. I could do that back then. I could think about two different things at once. "I'm thinking about my old lady," I said.

"I had an old lady once. We were partners. Then I found out she was screwing some guy while I was inside. They're all whores. But you know that right? Least you should . . . by now."

"Sure. What were you in for?"

"Bringing a load across the border."

"A load of what?"

"Weed, two kilos. Want me to apologize? Somebody dropped a dime on my ass. That's how it is. That's how it was and always will be. Watch your back. Always watch your back." He paused. "You like poetry?"

"No."

He sat up straight and began to recite. "I have planted a false oath in the earth, it has brought forth a poison tree; I have chosen the serpent for a counselor, the dog for a schoolmaster, and taught the thief a secret path into the house of the just. Along the broad highway I have traveled among men unknown, in lands beyond the sea."

"What's that?"

"Well it ain't *Leaves of Grass*. But I do think it might be Bill Blake. You ought to know about it. Call yourself a road dog. Road dogs read."

"It's all right. And I didn't call myself anything."

"Yeah? Listen, my liver's shot and my dick is limper than a dishrag. The docs say I got bone cancer. Old lady said it's my bad attitude. I say it's you, you and all the cynical assholes just like you. You know this used to be a hell of a good country. I don't understand what went wrong. People just got plain afraid, I guess. Now they see a free man and they wet their pants."

A dog fight had started in the street. "Listen. Hear them howling? It's foolish love drives them dogs. Drives a man too—insane." He drew out the last five words as if they were lascivious.

"What's that?"

"Ever pack a gun for a woman? Go a week without sleep? Quit your job and ride across country just to see she's screwing your best friend?"

"What for? Why would anyone do that?"

"*L'amour fou*, my man. Clown love." He nodded to his cane leaning in the corner of the booth. "Like when you got the chattering clowns in your head, and some men just can't stop drinking about it, and I'm damned if I'm not one." He raised his glass. "Stronger than alcohol, vaster than your lyres, ferment the bitter reds of love!"

He took a drink. Then he took off his cap. He smirked. He let the smirk float around for a while. I tried it on, but it was too poetic for my taste, and more sarcastic than I wanted to be at the time. Then someone else tried it. It got passed around the bar. No one was any better for it in the end.

"**B**Y THE WAY, YOU NEVER ANSWERED MY question."

"What was the question?"

"What are you doing?"

"What do you mean? Where?"

"Here. Out here. Shouldn't you be going to college or something, smoking pot? Going to a rock concert? Ain't you a college boy?"

"I been looking for work. I don't go to concerts."

"You got wheels? You can pick, if you want work."

"I got wheels."

"We can go to the fields in the morning then. You can give me a ride."

"It's not a car. It's a bike."

"What kind?"

"Beezer."

He laughed outright. "Mechanic's training tool. Used to have a Triumph, myself. Pushed it more miles than I ever rode it."

I offered up a little bit of my story—of pushing bikes and riding—which led to how I got here, which naturally led to more drinking, and that of course led to talk of Tanya and Tanya led to Rolando and Rolando led to the dope story and the bust story and . . . I was about to go on.

"Wait a minute. This guy you're talking about, maybe I know him . . . Rolando Lopez?"

"No. Rolando Morales, Reggie actually"

"He had two names?"

"You might know him as Roland, or maybe Rodrigo. Apparently he used to hang up here in Portland."

"Yes. Yes I do know him. Least I think I do . . . but he was calling himself Billy at the time. Doing a lot of drugs. Had an old lady from what I remember—hard case. Heard he's a leech, though. Likes to live off the women. But he's dumb. Landed in county once because of he's so dumb. And that's all I know."

"That's a lot to know about someone you don't know."

"I know it is." He paused. "Your girl have money?"

"Maybe she did. She didn't seem to. Anyone ever really know a woman?"

"I don't know about that—maybe you're the lucky one that does.

Rolando Morales. Jesus. You are a lucky man to have them kind of friends. You got kids too, Pilgrim?" He leveled a hard eye at me.

"No. I mean, I hope not."

"I do. Two daughters. Two different women. One of them I never met. The other I never see. You should try it."

"I ain't got time for daughters."

"Yes you do. You don't look so young to me. I think you got time."

"I'm young at heart."

"Look here, I'm gonna get you a date with one of these bitches. Get you a line of offspring going." He yelled at someone at the bar. "Hey Connie. Get your whore ass over here." Connie looked at us for a second then turned away. Walker called her again. She got up and walked over to the table, irritated. Her hair was dyed bright yellow and her eyes were two different colors. She had a broad nose and a faint mustache and a mole the size of a Lincoln penny was visible on her back left shoulder.

"My friend wants to meet you."

"He does, does he?" She replied in a theatrical southern voice dripping with disinterest. "How you doing, you pretty young man? You wanna date?"

I didn't respond. Somewhere in the last hour we had switched to pitchers so I poured another glass from the pitcher and drank it slow. But not slow enough, cause I saw my face at the bottom of that glass and it was talking, telling me to get the hell out of there.

"C'mon Pilgrim, you said you wanted a taste."

Connie was drumming the table. "You got any business for me, Birdman, or is this a fucking joke?"

"Later, maybe." I said. "I'm not quite drunk yet."

"You gotta be drunk? Get drunk. Take all the time in the world."

"Sit down with us, Con," Birdsong motioned to the space beside him. "You talk to him a little bit, he'll learn to love you. Just like I did, remember?"

"I'll sit down . . . back at the bar." She turned and walked away.

"Well what do you think, Pilgrim? Everybody's got to get down. If you don't you'll go crazy. I know it. I been crazy. All that jazz backs up in your head."

"I'm a free man. I'm free to decline."

"Free my ass."

&

WALKER STARTED EGGING me. He took out a pen and wrote the words "Mary" and "Kali" on his fingers. Then he held up his two hands like they was gonna wrestle in some *Night of the Hunter* Robert Mitchum imitation. "See, you got your Virgin Mary on the one side. Everyone can get it up for the Mary, because you know her, you love her, and you know you can't have her. She's the girl next door, pure as your mother. And here you got your Mother Kali on the other; she lives down by the dark river. And you can have her anytime you want. But you don't want her because she is goddam *scary*. You never get it, what you want."

"I seen this movie."

"You believe in reincarnation, Mr. Lucky?"

"No. And where's all this crap philosophy coming from?"

"Some dude used to hang down here, Mr. Valentine Martinez. Called himself Bobby Valentine. Swami Bob, we called him. Strange dude. Half Mex, I guess. Said he was part Indian, a reincarnated Hindu priest. But he looked white. Always preaching to drunks. Here's a story you want to hear, see. One day this rich lady came down here, trying to get back at her husband probably, or just to prove she could. Anyway she picked him up and took him home and that was the end of him. He come back looking like the walking dead. Said he had a vision up there in that fancy apartment—a vision of how to do business. Now get this. He set himself up in a hotel across the road, other side of Burnside and 3rd I think. Started out as a joke. But shit, I never seen a man get so much chicken. And he was an ugly man. College girls mostly, and middle-age women. When he wasn't teaching he used to hold court right over there at the Seven Seas."

"What does all this have to do with anything?"

"This was the thing. Old Swami Bob used to say, 'You wanna be a true poet you got to de-range your senses, yep you got to *de-range your senses*. Find yourself the scariest woman in the room and you'll be halfway there, far from home, but closer than you ever been to God.'" Birdsong looked around the smoky yellow room. "Of course you kind of have to have a theory like that around here. I mean look what you got to work with. But then again you know what Mother Teresa says—the flesh of the lowly is the true body of Christ, and we should not be afraid to touch them."

Birdsong didn't look much like a guy with a guru, but then he pulled out a fat old leather wallet stuffed with papers and found a business card inside it. He handed it to me. Bobby Valentine, *Philosopher, Epicurean. Contractor. Past Life Chaneller.* And then in small letters it said "*Let Guru Sri Valentinus show you the path to redemption through the power of love.*"

I tossed the card back to him.

"Tell me something Pilgrim. Was your mother a pretty woman? "

"Might have been. I don't remember her when she was young."

"You ever kiss your mother on the mouth?"

"I probably did."

"You know your mother was naked the day you came out of her ass?"

"Don't talk about my mother like that."

"And you think you ain't been chasin' that since the day you knew you was a man. What you don't want will kill you and that's too bad. You look over there now." He pointed back to Connie, who now had an index finger stuck in her ear as if there was an alarm clock in there and she was trying to shut it off. "You got your whole Greek tragedy laid out for you. All you got to do is ask for some." Walker said.

"But I ain't looking for tragedy."

"I don't think that's true, Pilgrim. Look around you. Why you here? Why you talkin' to me? You got some self-hatred thing going on, don't you?"

"It goes against my personality."

"You watch too fucking much TV, Stranger. Personality my ass. You think you got one? What? Did you make it out of parts? Did someone sell it to you in the street? You think you get to choose who you are? Oh, I'm sorry. Maybe you are that lucky man after all. Hell, I say go with it. You might even get married and have some kids before the wife finds out you're a phony." He said it again, "phoooneeeeyy," stretching it out.

"You make it all sound so pretty."

"Don't know. I do know people been on the road so long, there ain't nothing much but a handful of mannerisms and a toothbrush left to 'em. Easier to travel that way."

&

THERE WAS A show about elephants on TV. Then some people skateboarding on Venice Beach in a commercial about diet cola. "I got a story for you," Walker said, then added, "But this is the last one. Don't ask me for another."

"I don't remember asking for the first one," I said. He laughed.

"Happened up in Yukon, 'bout ten years ago. I was working for the Union Pacific, layin' track in the sticks. A wolf been sighted in the area of our camp, which ain't necessarily odd. I was bunking with my brother."

"Your brother?"

"Yeah. Exactly," he laughed. "Like I'm looking in the mirror. That's how much alike we was. You got a brother?"

"No."

"Yeah. My brother, Holly. He was a kung-fu motherfucker, too. He studied in the service. Picked up on this theater shit, too, in Asia, brought it back with him. We hooked up with this street troupe in San Fran. See we were like beatniks, freaks, you know. It was like running away with the circus for me. It was cool. We were cool once, hell we all fucking were. Now he's a bum, a fruit tramp. Me, I'm not a fruit tramp. I'm just doing it for a while. Anyway, we left Frisco cause we heard we could make a bunch of money up north. We were up in the Yukon that summer, '65 or '66, I think. There was a drought. Everything was coming out of the woods, coming around the houses for scraps—bears, weasels, deer. Well we heard something hanging around the cabin getting into our shit. One night there was the devil's racket out there, with Benny howling all crazy, that's our dog. Then it stopped. That should have been a sign—that it stopped. 'Cause when we got out there Benny was dead. Now my brother, he loved that dog. I remember he was inside listening to some station out of Juneau that night. I was out back. I remember mostly the insects. It was locust time or something, sawing their legs and singing. Then we heard that howling. Well, Holly, he went out there on the porch with a flashlight, but couldn't see nothing. I figured there was nothin' to see, what the hell. Then suddenly there it was—the flashlight dead in its eyes. Usually they run or slink away. You never get 'em in the light. But them eyes was yellow. And it was standing still, I tell you."

"What was it?"

"The wolf, asshole, *canis lupus bellicosus*. Suddenly there was this silence round everything, I mean the radio was still playing and everything, but it seemed silent, like it was happening in another world. Seemed like all you could hear was the beating of your own heart. Then in a second it was gone again. Then it was there again. It kept slipping in and out of the dark—there one second, gone the next. Sometimes you knew it was closer cause you could feel it more. And then it just appeared 'bout ten feet away again, and you know if there's one, there's more. And we're both standing there with no one else around. It was Saturday and they's off gettin' drunk."

"Shit."

"Tell me about it. Then that wolf jumped like nothing I ever seen. Just charged, you know. Went for Holly, not me. I was on the side. Well there wasn't much he could do, so he took one of his kung-fu stances, what he called the Steel Claw of the White Swan or some such thing. I thought he was joking or crazy. He had his arm sticking out stiff. But he had his switch-knife in his hand, with the blade retracted, and when that thing went for him, Holly screamed like Bruce Lee and just happened to jam his arm straight down that wolf's throat so hard that it went all the way down to the pit of his belly."

"C'mon. This is getting a little hard to buy."

"Yeah, well, by that time, the others were barking. I come out with the pistol. But I didn't want to shoot it with his arm down there and everything, so I shot it in the air. Anyway, he's down on his knees then. I looked at him and thought he was gonna die. He was scared as shit waiting to get his arm tore off. Holly swore he could feel that wolf's heart beating against his fingers, and how that pulse went traveling right up his arm and into his head, until it seemed like he was surrounded with it, like he was inside of it. And now, when I look back, I think it was true. I think it was like that."

"Uh-huh."

"Now get this. That wolf was stunned and so Holly pops open that blade and starts to cut around inside, then he let out some kind of god-awful scream, and I swear just at the same time I shot the thing in the ass he ripped it right out, heart and stomach and all and I seen it."

"Bullshit."

"Bull, you say? Baby, I seen it. Bloody fuckin' mess too. Like it puked all over him."

"You're full of shit."

"Believe it or don't. Wolf's dead. Top of that, we ate it—ate the wolf.

"You're lying like a preacher man, man."

"Ain't kidding, in a skillet, with potatoes, onions. Ate the heart and liver and even the legs. Taste like dog, too. You ever eat dog? Ate the whole damn thing, me and him, tough as leather. They say a man eats the flesh of another man he steals that man's strength. Romans did it all the time. Same goes with animals. Eat the heart of an animal and you steal that's creature's strength. You know what that is?" Walker's eyes were moving over to Connie at the bar. He was getting worked up by his own story.

"An elaborate lie told by a drunk in a bar?"

"No, sir. It's a parable."

"A parable is a riddle. That ain't a riddle."

"Maybe it's a psychological quandary then. The teeth-marks left scars like a bracelet of jewelry on his arm. He got all proud of it. All cocky and arrogant. Pride got him. Said he was gonna eat the heart of everything he killed, so as to acquire the entire knowledge of man and beast in this way. What I'm sayin' is, he overstepped. Not in the killing, but in the way he lived his life. We had our problems, but our problems got worse. And we used to be friends. Now we're like Cain and Able, oil and water. One ought not to overstep."

"So you don't see him any more?"

"We steer clear." He looked back at Connie, who shot him a smile.

"Why?"

"Says I stole some money."

"Did you?"

"I might have done. But that's not the reason. I'll tell you one damn thing, you will be what you eat. You eat a heart for courage, but a heart is more than that. You can't know what it is—might be the devil or a tick. Sometimes I think it turned around and ate us instead. Cause it made him petty and it made me a fool."

"I'll keep that in mind."

&

I MADE LIKE I was getting ready to go.

But Walker couldn't let me go, not without some parting advice. "Follow my directions, Pilgrim. Say no, that's what I say. No way."

"No way to what?"

"No way home. No way to all them clichés they use to suck you back in—make you think you're special. Money. Pride. Walk away from it. You have to be ready to give up everything at any time—father, mother, brother, sister, wife and child and friends. You gotta pay your debts and make your will, and settle every affair—then you are ready to take your walk. And that's my motto. That's my name. I been ready. Indeed, I'm a walking son of a bitch. 'Cause the minute you start thinking you're better than, or the savior of, any other man, well you better know arrogance is the next stop on that train to infernal laughter, Pilgrim. Your life becomes a parody of your every ideal. You'll see what I mean."

"I hope I don't."

He turned his head, looking toward the door. "I know what you're doing out here, but you ain't ready for it, you ain't ready for that walk yet. A self-hating man like you might never be ready. You don't know yet that you ain't never coming back. Don't think I don't know you, Pilgrim."

A fight broke out at the other end of the bar as if to punctuate the theme of discord and disillusionment. It was getting too much like a comic book for me, so I got up to go. "I'll see you later, Walker. I need some air."

"Yeah, you'll see me. But watch out for that parody, Mr. Goodman Brown. It's coming after you just like a hungry wolf. Your accusers may not be holy. Your Fool's Paradise grants no grace against the taint of their funny tongues. Your Vanity Fair will turn to an Insanity Fair when all is done. Your Beware now, Pilgrim. Listen to what I say."

"My name's not Pilgrim," I said.

"I don't care," he said, gazing at the table.

(12)

NIGHTS IN THE BURNSIDE DISTRICT COULD *SEEM* prophetic; they seldom were. Enigmatic encounters with mercurial figures were the norm. Weirdos, geeks, dubious ferry men might attach themselves, offering amulets or advice or guidance across the asphalt, all for the price of a drink, a hot-dog or a quarter. It was as if we were all traveling toward a bland eternity in which nothing would be solid or lasting. There was energy in the air, but life was unreal. Whole nights might pass in neon hallucination. I would live through events I might remember only days later—in a sudden flash, at an incongruous, unrelated juncture—it would all come back in ambush. I was a pawn on the fluid gameboard of alcohol and restless desire, as if the species were mutating at a phenomenal rate and the game itself was no longer understood.

The streets and bars were full of guys like Birdsong, who got emphatic and preachy the more they drank. The fast and gravely bar-bred patois could lapse into near biblical cadence. One such bard claimed riots would break out in LA, New Orleans and Chicago. He spoke of volcanoes, earthquakes and devils living in the minds of men. Another guy said the CIA was unleashing a new disease to get rid of poor people and fags. He said there was some heavy shit coming down, and it would only get worse, and that we might even see the apocalypse in our time.

The moon was hanging there like a single-barrel, sawed-off shotgun turned flashlight, the night I stepped out of the Morrison and ran into Nick. I knew Nick Raven through Tanya. Some ex-old man of hers had been army bunk-mates with the guy. But Nick had gone AWOL. Hounded out of the service for his sometime habit of cross-dressing in Monterey bars, he drifted up and down the coast for a couple years. One day he left a note on Tanya's door: "Tan, Got your address from Rainwater in Yakima, Remember? I'm at the Hamilton, #22. Look me up, let's hang. Nick."

The note made her a little nervous. First because Eddie Rainwater was a dealer who'd gone up on battery, after beating the crap out of one of Tan's best girlfriends. If he was out he was trouble; his head was a pressure cooker of grudges. Second, to her recollection, Nick Raven was a wild-ass conflicted freak and part-time fairy who courted abuse by inviting the fists of drunks and homophobes to aim for his face. But Raven had got his self-hate under control and we'd become friends. We lost touch with him more than a year ago, before New Orleans. Now here he was again, just in town from Yakima.

"Frank! My man!" We did some kind of brother handshake. I don't remember the exact mechanics of it. I do remember Nick looked different. He'd morphed from Native American Hippie to a "hep cat." He wore a Gatsby cap and had a jazz-bo goatee and a large stained pin-striped vest with lapels. He was a big man, six foot three or four, two hundred something pounds, easy.

He and I took to doing the Burnside rounds, drifting from bar to bar with occasional breaks for free dining. Nick was a self-appointed tour guide to the spiritual free lunch. "Any creed will feed you a meal for ten minutes of your attention," he loved to say. And sexual predators, chefs, holy men and plain old lonely people—they all knew it was true, too: food was a form of propaganda—you could have your cake but you had to eat your symbols, too. I ate mine and remained pretty much unaffected. Other people, less sure of themselves, suffered the consequences of their appetites. And there were plenty of holy rollers willing to buy a mark a sandwich or cook a meal for a little taste of one's quality time. Everybody had something to offer. It may not have been exactly what you wanted, but you couldn't say the world was stingy if you knew the way. Nick knew.

The price of a beer at a stripper bar could get you a ham sandwich with American cheese on Beefsteak rye. There were a few such lunch buffet bars around—Bangers, Boomers, Billy's Private Eye. Nick explained the pleasure of such a meal in terms of Gnostic spiritualism, equating corpulence, sexual indulgence, consumption and beatitude. Lechery as a path to wisdom—it seemed so easy.

And so we sang songs of love and drank the cherry Kool-aid of many a numbed-out utopian brotherhood. We ate sloppy joes with the Moonies. We enjoyed cold hamburgers and stale cakes with the Salvation Army. Up the street the Hare Krishnas offered their seed pastes and sweet sauces. Mid-afternoon, it was coffee and cookies at Captain Andy's House of the All-Merciful Lord. Captain Andy was a retired merchant marine with a plastic leg and a glass eye, whom Jesus had guided through many a storm at sea. He now offered what little solace he could to the men of skid row, whose storms still existed in their minds. The Captain's motto was "Nothing is free. And so is pain." It didn't make sense but he could prove it was true—while you were eating he would pull out his fiddle and start in on some old sea chantey. If anyone complained about the god-awful music he would tell them to just shut up and eat their cookies, while he rocked back in his chair, sawing away like some displaced Ishmael, only madder, hopped up on caffeine and sugar and living in the wrong universe.

&

ONE NIGHT NICK and me hooked up with this French Canadian guy—Randy Holiday, I think his name was, and his girlfriend, Terri Fandancer. They had changed their names to show they had some control over who they were, as if identity were a type of ownership. They were drinking a bullet, sitting on the sidewalk around the corner from NW 3rd St.

"Sing to me, muse," Randy sang, handing me a bottle. In those days if somebody had a bottle everybody drank until it was gone. "Let us sing of the wanderer harried for years . . . ." He paused as if unsure, then began again. "My friends, join us in our ritual celebration of God's liquor." Nick laughed.

Randy Holiday was a literary drunk, apparently—a hang-jawed, bony-faced road dog from Quebec Province who'd been in the States long enough to confirm his Canadian suspicions that the place was a pit of shallowness, ambition and violence. He didn't need our war machines. He didn't need our ghetto scenes. Terry Fandancer was mostly Mexican, a quarter German. She wore a beret. She loved America for the opportunities it offered. She met Randy in a bus station. Neither one of them had a ticket. She thought he was a poet. He thought she was a fine piece of tail, just his kind of sweet little "girlsoul." They bonded over a pint of Irish Rose and decided to make a week of it.

The four of us made the rounds. This bar, that bar. Randy talked about shrouded travelers and bodhisattva badboys, the wretched, naked, grieving ghosts of the road. He'd seen Walt Whitman once in a supermarket in California. He had a mystical bent to him that was both corny and annoying. Terri talked about death and the meaninglessness of the universe. She never went to high school, but somewhere on the road she got turned on to Sartre and Camus. Looking for the fifties, they were stuck in the seventies, a Buddhist wanna-be and an Existential never-was. And they both liked to get high.

Randy said he could live on cheese and crackers for weeks. He said one time he got so high on Mexican tea, he was running naked in Pecos Canyon when the state cops picked him up. He did some time because there was a gun in the car and a kilo of weed. His eyes glazed and a tape machine of remorse clicked on in his head, as he recounted details of big-house life. Now Mr. Holiday kept a knife in his boot. He would swing it over his head like a bullwhip handle or a boomerang, claiming he would cut that motherfucker's dick off someday, when he caught up with

81

him. That "motherfucker" himself, whoever he was, might not have been around, but Randy's histrionics successfully caused a circle of space to open between us and the throngs of pedestrians that fine summer evening.

"Write a poem about it, *corazon*. Hell, write a fucking novel, *pero ocultar el fierro*," Terri said with practiced disinterest. She struck a match.

Nick said, "I'm splittin', I'll see you tomorrow. These guys are freaks."

"Thanks," I said. "Thanks for introducing me to your friends."

Then we heard someone in the crowd yell, "Go man, Go!" It was Randy's friend Damian Pomeroy, a drifter from Denver who knew Randy from the old days. He probably saw a crowd of disgusted people and figured Randy would be part of it.

Damian thought any kind of absurd behavior was totally cool and logical—even cosmic. "Do and Be," he said over and over again. "Go man, go. Let it all hang out. Keep on truckin'." I was wondering just how many counter-culture clichés he could string together in his show of support before he started egging Randy on to public confession, like a proto-talk show host of the streets. "And how does that make you feeeeel?" Damian asked, half laughing.

"Fuck you, Perc!" Randy answered. He called him Perc for the Percodans he was so fond of popping when his quest for the perfect bottle of Mad Dog got boring.

The sight of his friend took the pluck out of Randy. Perc put his arm on Randy's shoulder and carefully moved him down the block to a different location. Terri and I followed. She accidentally brushed her hip against my leg. I let her.

"Let it go, baby, let the pain go. You got to feel it all go through you. It's all nothing no way but electrons and slime, atoms and time."

Randy shook his head. Perc looked back at me and Terri. "By the way, who's the new chick?" His interest was more than friendly and Randy knew it. He didn't appreciate his revenge fantasy being deflated by theories of a mechanistic universe either, but there was some comfort in knowing he had no choice. What he did appreciate was that Perc was trying to goad him into some embarrassing or illegal act, partly to make it easier for him to steal Terri. Because Perc was a dog. Randy knew this because he was a dog, too. They both equated power with sexual territory. And Terri was willing to be marked. She was flashing cleavage, as some women will around hopped-up males. Her walk had changed, too, from a straight gait to a provocative swivel, putting it out there, trying to ratchet up the rivalry so she could lean back and feed her anima on the violence.

Meanwhile Perc kept working the confusion quotient. He spoke in disconnected sound bites and cheap shots, and would string these bits together in extended forced metaphors that imitated sense only because they were so long you couldn't trace them back to any original idea to disprove them. When Randy said something about the road being an albatross around his neck, and a heavy and dead one at that, Perc fired back, calling it the metaphoric K-Mart at the end of the path of all questions. "The thing is not to get hung up. We can go anywhere, get anything we want. Let it go. Dig the time. God exists without qualms."

Randy passed judgment. "You're full of shit, man." And he was. This combination of Zen and pop culture seemed to indicate a subservience to the very power structure he wished to tear down. It was just as Birdsong had said about parody—it sneaks up on you. But then I was no different. I was guilty of adding intellectual gloss to a conversation between drunks.

Randy reverted to the default state of his obsession. "I don't CARE," he shot back, obsessively, "I'm going to fuck up that dude, I going to cut him up with my KNIFE. Cut off his dick with my KNIFE!" He was sweating profusely by then, activating the dried wine stains on his clothes.

"He's one deep motherfucker, isn't he?" It was Terri. I couldn't tell if she was being sarcastic. I didn't know who she was referring to either, but I knew the repetition of themes that evening was driving me crazy.

They're easy to make fun of, I said to myself, but why bother.

Terri was leaning on a lamppost now and her hand was moving her dress slowly up her thigh, exposing more and more leg, as if she had no control of it, and could not be responsible for any libidinous thoughts it might provoke. I was about to show some interest when a scuffle broke out between some drunks further down the street. The disease was spreading. The fight was about a nickel, somebody's wife, the nature of the Cartesian universe—I didn't know. Whatever. It all boiled down to spittle and fists. I used the confusion to lose my new friends.

&

THE NEXT EVENING, Nick took me to a party down by the bridge. As we approached the festivities, I saw a guy playing guitar and another man standing on a log clapping while a dwarf danced around the campfire. I'd seen the style of dancing before: an early kind of hopped-up, hobo break-dancing invented by guys with bad arthritis, gout, acute alcoholism, nerve damage, too many poorly-mended bones and no sense of rhythm whatso-ever—men who learned their moves mocking the flames of campfires, the herky-jerky of Ozark dolls, spook house marionettes, or their epileptic cousins.

They stopped dancing when they saw us, as if embarrassed by their low-down medieval ways. With the candles and bottles and fire, the camp had the look of an old tavern. They were drinking Gallo Tawny Port, too, the wine I drank the night I met Tanya. Tawny Port is an acquired taste; it goes best with train tracks and road shoulders and cold meat sandwiches and memories. And only at night. You can only drink Tawny Port at night. But it was night, about 10:30. And I was reminded how much I missed her.

The conversation was all over the place, as the talk of drunks will be, everybody stepping on each other, nobody listening. One thing was for sure. They all used to have regular jobs. They were all once respectable guys, only now they just happened to be drinking Tawny Port under the bridge. The man holding court was Luther Bearclaw, a burly guy with shoulder-length black hair. He thought of the campsite as Luther's Tavern. Nobody ever tried to take that away. But Luther's real name was Larry Hermes. It was said his taste for Satan and pastry made him change it.

At one point the conversation moved to unrequited love and the ridiculous things men had put up with in their lives to get laid. Ed Shuman talked about this chick he took in who stole all his money. One day he woke up without his car or his wallet. "Now I don't do that saint thing no more. Pussy and money and all of it up front. No more promises. I ain't that kind of soldier no more."

This guy Hector or Herman or something chimed in, "I knew this chick. We was always over at her place. One night I'm so drunk I . . . well I ended up doing the mother, but it was by accident. I swear."

"Shit. I don't believe that. You're too ugly."

"Well, goddam it to hell, she looked just like her. And here's the weird thing. I thought the bitch would be pissed. But she just wanted in on it. We ends up doing a three-way—the girl, the mother and me. It was too weird, and I been weird in my life, my friend. I have been weird."

"That ain't so strange, look at Ed. He got "Mom" on his arm to commemorate the loss o' his virginity."

The conversation changed again, from love to tattoos. Max had a rose with a woman's name crossed out and underneath it was written "Queen of Misery." Legs Barker had a snake taking a bite out of his heart. Joey Lazaro had a skull and crossbones that read "Love Kills." I didn't have a tattoo. They said there was a parlor on the other side of the bridge. I said maybe I would go get some wine. Luther said I couldn't cross the bridge unless I guessed what his tattoo was. I said I wasn't going across the bridge anyway. I was going to the liquor store. Then I sat back down.

"Speakin' of which, guess who I seen the other day, over at Morrison's?"

"The right Reverend Walker?"

"The same."

"The holy savior of mankind himself lowered his royal being, bowed and spoke unto me. Me, a mere mortal. Can yee imagine?"

"And what did the holy prophet say?"

"Why I believe he was cadging for a drink."

By this time half the guys were laughing their asses off. I could see the faces softening through my alcoholic lens, becoming rubbery and loose like masks hung on hooks in a Halloween store. It was around then Charley Coyote held his fingers to his lips. "Hey man, check it out." We could hear a woman's voice, but we couldn't make out any words because of the traffic noise and boat whistles. It was coming from the river, though, a stereo on a ship moving slowly down the Willamette toward the sea. The barge workers had cranked it up. Years later I would recognize the song from *Turandot*. Some princess with skin the pallor of the moon and a heart like ice.

"It's beautiful," Legs said, pretending he was gonna cry.

"There's no brick wall out there, man. You don't know what could happen to a dumbass like you. The universe is bigger than that there bottle."

"What universe?"

"Which bottle?"

"The one he ain't bought yet." Luther was looking to me.

"It's all the same fuckin' universe anyway."

"And that's *all* it is. Same *fucking* universe. Day in, day out." Ed said, looking a little perturbed.

"My grandfather said there was a time when the skies were darker, but the road seemed clearer."

"You gonna get that goddam bottle or not?"

I got up to get the goddamned bottle.

I woke up in the morning in a playground, rolled up in my jacket in some mud under some monkey bars. My mouth felt like cotton and the local bowling team was going for the gold in my head. A woman was telling her daughter not to get near me.

"Don't go near that man, honey. He's sick."

&

THAT MORNING I wandered around, trying to reconstruct the night. There were images, of course. But there was no sequence of time to tie them to. The candles of the campground. A pool ball flying across the room. A green station wagon. There were accusations as well. And Tanya, dressed in that red cowgirl dress. I got a coffee, sat on a bench in Harrison Park and rolled a smoke. It was still early. Off in the middle of the park, I could see a man and woman, trying to do it quick before the cops came. The ground was cold. It was a cold world. I took a cold nap on the cold bench, then went over to the Morrison. Walker Birdsong wasn't there.

I continued to walk. I saw some brainwashed hippie speed freak playing flute in the lotus position down on Couch, a garland of flowers about her scrawny neck. She seemed like Tanya in a parallel universe or some Lolita of Burnside, on the road too long and too early, and a little bruised. You learn not to ask questions. You might get them home, but there's always some brutality behind the desire. If you touch them, you share in it.

Later, I came upon an old sailor stationed on a side street off the park. His fake leg was propped on a milk crate. His one glass eye gazed nowhere. I knew the direction well. The sea was changing—it wasn't adventure anymore, it was confusion, spite, overstimulation—a cold, salty, gasoline-thin memory of the first moment of sentience. His arms were covered with bird tattoos—it was a simulation of escape I guess. So I counted my money—one hundred-something dollars—enough for a good meal, a bluebird tattoo and the grey dog out of town if I had the nerve. I decided to cross the bridge and check out the flash sheets. When I looked down at the camp where I'd been the other night, there was nobody around. Some empty beer cans, lots of ashes. No opera. To hell with Tanya, I thought.

&

TIME IS A river, and we are but stones disturbing its flow, each whorl a story, the ripples our souls make in the current, spreading out in vague waves, soon to be dissipated. I looked into the eddies of the Willamette and dreamed of suicide kisses and Rhinemaidens, and of simple women who could love me for what I was.

"Jump! Jump!" was all they said.

Part III
sacrifice in the apple camps

(13)

I WOKE IN THE MORNING DIZZY AND DISORIENTED. I WAS EITHER moving too fast or too lopsided or not moving at all. Or it might mean some idea was giving birth to itself in my brain. Halfway down the hall to the elevator, the lights went out. I had the newspaper and a cup of coffee in my hands, hoping to nurse my hangover with news about how other people's lives were worse than mine. Today it wasn't going to work. I went to the diner.

Tanya had done her time. She was a free woman now. Coming to rescue me from my life of decadence. And I must have wanted to be rescued because I heard a sound not unlike the howling of an over-tight fan belt on a dark night on an abandoned stretch of highway, I saw a bead of light in the back of my mind, and then I turned to see her standing in the hotel entrance with a backpack and a copy of Fitzgerald's *The Crack-Up*. She was bathed in light as if the headlights of a great truck were barreling down from behind her. She said she had just missed me at the hotel and then at the diner, so she came back to the hotel. And there I was.

I barely got the door locked before I had my face between her legs, along with other limbs. When we were done, she examined my bluebird tattoo, the bluebird carrying a banner in its beak that said *l'amour fou*. She'd been in jail and tattoos didn't mean much to her, especially this one. "It's a symbol," I said.

"That's a pretty lousy tattoo, is what it is," she said.

And she was right. I remembered how the guy looked at his work with a touch of surprise, like he knew he was bad . . . but not quite *that bad*.

"Did prison change you? Are you a lesbian now?" I asked.

She kissed me. "Don't worry. C'mon. Let's party." We put on our clothes and went and got some beer. When we got back we took our clothes off again. We were in a hurry. In the next room an old man coughed and wheezed, reminding us of how little time we had to get it right. We started making plans.

The next day we hitched down to Corvallis to pick up the BSA. I cut a piece of shoe sole for the primary drive-chain tensor and glued it on with heat-resistant epoxy. The clutch plates could wait. We spent a couple hours making nice with Neil and Kimberly, then we rode down to the Sandman family compound in Eugene. In those days Eugene had a shopping mall for a downtown. I think they were even recycling back then. They voted with their credit cards and shopped for a better world. They were way ahead of the times. At least they thought they were.

Naomi used to teach there. Tanya spent time there in her childhood. Tanya's father, Harry, was packing the family stuff for storage. He was renting the house out and moving in with his teenage girlfriend. He was dressed in a sweater of indeterminate color with a cowl collar and his hair was tied back in the manner of hippies trying to fit in with the corporate world. He offered us a drink out of pint bottle when we walked in— always a bad sign.

"Kids, good to see you." And it probably was good to see us. He needed help moving stuff. But modern life is fast. Time passes quickly. A minute later it wasn't all that good to see us anymore. "So how long you staying?" he asked.

Tanya had filled me in on Harry's background. Once a radical thinker in a weird way, he'd written a book of essays about street theater, revolution and commercialism. A Jewish man in a West Coast Waspish world: half his personality relied on clinging to old contacts; the other half didn't give a damn. He wanted to deny the clichés that informed his actions. But he used them, and he got used because of them. Like a badly dressed extra in a small-town motel lobby—not yet a bum, but making all the wrong decisions that would get him there. He would never admit it, and that's part of what kept him afloat—stubbornness. A bad day at the track, a bad performance in the sack, a sudden lack of funds and the chick might split, his middle-aged ego would collapse, and it's an easy slide down after that. The girl had something to sell. He didn't.

Harry spoke in clipped aggressive phrases, a patter born of years of defending himself to women and academics. He could act like he didn't care, but his nervousness betrayed him. He smoked a lot and pretended he had deals to make. He was too mild-mannered to be a real hustler but he would do just fine as an avatar of failure for anyone who was inclined to see him as such.

His face had that half-dad, half-professor, half-salesman over-full hybrid quality. There was too much in it and yet, strangely, not enough. The sternness of his jaw was opposed by the loose folds of his mouth. In fact, his whole face was a little loose, almost as if he kept it that way on purpose to hide his inclinations.

Tanya's mother was somewhere else. She always was. Somewhere inaccessible, often nameless. Somewhere that couldn't possibly live up to Tanya's stories, so it had to remain nameless so as not to be embarrassed.

Naomi once wrote asking Tanya to come live with her in that special nameless place, but that was a little too abstract for Tan. Too much responsibility. She wasn't quite ready for it. "You just have to do what's right for you, man. But it's not the time. Maybe if it turns out I'm there someday, then that's where I'm supposed to be."

At the time, I knew how she felt. One thing me and Tanya had in common was that every major thing we were going to do, we were going to do "later." It was part of our bond. For now we were happy sitting around eating sandwiches and trying to get high off leftovers from Harry's medicine chest, listening to the old man bitching about this and that: Naomi and Sandy and Ralph and John Smith and then Naomi again. Goddamn Naomi—who more than ever seemed like an improbable wife for Harry Sandman. Almost as improbable as Tanya was for me.

Tanya moved to a far end of the ranch house, no doubt to indulge in some psychological self-abuse. I went out to the garage to stare at the motorcycle. Harry followed me. I heard the door open, and there he was, hellbent on justifying his existence. We went through our catalog of conversational styles, eventually settling on a testosterone-charged rapport which was a little difficult to pull off considering I was a wormy hippie kid with long hair and he was hovering somewhere between has-been academic and would-be traveling salesman. More Mamet than Hammett, but mostly made for TV, we did our best. We'd both watched plenty of TV, so at least we had a base. We grunted a little bit, made some hand motions, then got down to it.

"Standing guard over the old castle?" He sighed, then laughed, as if he had told himself a joke. I didn't get it. "Looks like you need a refill." But I didn't have a glass. He handed me the bottle. Then his tone changed to one of fatherly advice. "You know they say that everybody that rides a motorcycle has a death wish?" It sounded like an accusation to me, as he fingered a dead flower he'd pulled out of the vase on the worktable—some souvenir of Sandy, probably. "But maybe it's the threat of death that lets you know what things are made of. Am I right or wrong?"

"Maybe," I said, surprised by my agreeability. "By the way, it's ours. We bought it together."

He crushed the dead flower. I laughed.

"Teresa always did go for self-destructive types: rockers, bikers, druggies. We were made to understand you were different."

"I thought you'd be different too, I mean the way she described you."

"Well, I don't know about that. Anyway, all I'm asking is this: if you've got some self-destructive agenda you feel like you've got to live out, leave my daughter out of it. She's a survivor, despite what you might think.

Besides, whatever her relation to you, it's her anger towards us, her mother and I, that's what drives her behavior."

"You don't give me much credit, do you? I mean that her and I could make this work. That maybe I can help her get where she needs to be," I said.

He looked at me hard, as if trying to highlight the lie. "I don't know you. But if you're trying to be a saint, don't bother. You'd be doing it because it sounded good, or because you read about it somewhere. Men are capable of sacrifice, but not of faith." He made a vague gesture with his arm, as if he were trying to include an audience that wasn't there. Then he changed the subject.

"Naomi was many things but she could also be a real bitch. Teresa uses her against me. But I'm used to it. Can't really blame her either. I'm sure you'll meet her one of these days. You'll like Mrs. Sandman. Or should I say O'Connell. She's a little difficult. Me and her, well, we didn't always see eye to eye. But we had our time. Amazing woman, actually. Never seemed to get any older. Can you imagine? Probably why she was so successful." His lip curled a little.

Suddenly, weirdly, I thought maybe he was trying to set me up for some inevitable future encounter, hoping I would embarrass myself in front of Mother Naomi. That could be a bond between us. Or maybe Harry was simply covering for his own inadequacy—a middle-aged man, unable to get it up for his middle-aged wife. I'm sure it stung him every time she picked up with younger men. But then he himself was on that same track backwards—back to virility, and further. Back to childhood and birth and further. Both Ben and Birdsong had been on about that. As if the female sex were just a long dark tube to the beginning of time where you could lay around on a beach in the center of the earth while warm black waves lapped the black sand. Drinks and TV were free. And all the ships were wrecked so you had no responsibilities and no desires.

I pulled myself back from the reverie. "I don't know what to say. We are where we are."

Harry changed his tone slightly, to one of fatherly wisdom. "It's mostly about making a lie you can live in, that no one can call you on. No one ever gets anywhere in this world telling the truth. They actually want you to do it, you know. They won't come out and say it, but they want you to go right on lying, as long as its suits their purposes."

He was sounding a lot like me, I thought. Or maybe I always sounded like him, and maybe that's why Tanya liked me. Or didn't. The cynicism, the resignation.

I could see his thought processes: the sparks jumping, the synapses misfiring, the facial expressions changing a little too quickly under the influence. "I'm going inside," I said. I made a move toward the door.

He kept talking. "You know, she used to be a college professor before the trial. Then she lost her faith. Something you wouldn't know about, I suppose."

I skipped over the insult. "You're right, I don't. What trial?"

"Forget it. You'll find out. Teresa will tell you if you ask her. I don't want to talk about it now, too complicated. But I do think that was the time Naomi understood me the best. Having your own peers pull you down. But no, it's true though, she's done a lot of good in her time." He nodded to himself like he wasn't sure. "Done a lot of good. I'm not putting her down, Luc. No, it's other stuff."

I felt he was baiting me. "All right. Well . . ." I moved toward the door again.

"Look," he said.

"What?"

There was something about the way he was standing, supporting himself on the workbench. It was a telephone call from a desperate man from a remote phone booth on a highway in the wilderness of middle age.

"You know, it's not natural for a man to stay with a woman more than four or five years anyway. Naomi and I were together almost ten." He looked around. "Jeez, I have to get out of this house."

"Really?"

"You raise the kids until they can walk and talk, then you split. It's nature's way. Besides, it was mutual. Naomi, she's in Calcutta now. She went nuts for a while. Got all Catholic again. Some nun out East talked her into going to India."

"Tanya thinks she's in Tunisia."

"It's Calcutta. I suppose you can justify anything with a 'cause,' but I'm the one who got stuck raising Teresa and Steve, and I didn't . . .." He trailed off, then started up again. "I don't suppose you know that she left Teresa with me for years while she ran off with God knows whatever leftist with a credit card fighting this and that righteous fucking cause. While I held the fort and paid the bills." He took another drink.

"She didn't tell me."

"Maybe she doesn't remember. She was pretty young. I love my daughter but I don't know what she's doing with herself. She used to be so bright. Maybe you were, too—but now the leather jacket, the whole look. Who are you kidding? Anybody can go shopping. I been there, you think you're a part of something. Everybody loves you. They're all with you for a while, pushing you to the limit, egging you on until you take a stand. Then one day you turn around and you're alone."

He paused, shifted his focus, then got on with it. "You think you're a free spirit, some Bob Dylan, Ginsberg beatnik with your motorcycle and your cowboy boots. But you're not free. And you are weak. And there are three things make men weak, Luc. Remember that. Fear, sin and travel. You can't get rid of the first two, but you can sure as hell stay home." Harry looked at his watch, then started for the garage door. I followed him back into the house.

After an hour or so Harry drove off. His features had grown considerably darker, taking on some of the color of the bourbon he'd been drinking. Tanya said he probably wouldn't be back till morning. She went back to the bathroom to rummage through the medicine chest. I heard a couple of bottles break. Her parents had a lot of headaches, apparently. She came out with some pills of various shapes and colors.

&

WE WATCHED TV while Tanya looked through the family PDR until she identified the painkillers. I swallowed mine. She cooked hers, but she couldn't find a vein. But her arms weren't *that* bad—the search was an act. I was fiddling around with the radio but I couldn't get a proper channel. Maybe the two things were related. Then we heard a car door slam. It was Harry. Apparently the teenager had thrown him out. Impotence, lack of cash. Who knows? In any case he didn't have anything to say to us. He walked by and went to bed, ignorant of the spoon on the counter, the matches, the candles, the whole occult altar.

Soon enough the old man was snoring. Tanya was singing something softly, unaware she had a little blood on her face. She was a clown. I wanted her to be a messenger. I wanted faith to be an act of will, not a fairy tale. I needed to see her as some kind of spiritual creature. But all I could see was a female St. Sebastian peppered with red pinholes. The dreary universe itself was her inquisitor. Besides I knew the attempt to apply religious symbolism to one's life is an adolescent thing to do, and I was older than that. And then the drugs kicked in, and I didn't need to worry about it anymore.

I read a magazine. It was just like old times. The TV was going in the corner. I could see Tanya absently nodding to that voice, and I realized that if she had to have TV on, or a radio, then maybe it was just for the voice; it made her think there was some game she had won—the game of friendship. It made her think she had a friend. And if she had a friend, they shared a common memory. I understood her better then, though I was starting to realize I didn't understand her at all.

She was singing softly along with the radio. She sounded good. She always did when there was no pressure. I got that old chill—that chill I always got when her voice got inside me. "You sound good," I said. "What's that song?"

"An old blues number, Bessie Smith I think. When we get to Chicago, I'm going to get a band together." She was planning something in her mind.

"There's enough bands already," I replied carelessly. I meant it as a comment on the state of rampant plurality in mass culture, but she took it personally. For the first time she thought that maybe I didn't care a whole lot about her musical career or take it seriously. I was surprised, too. I just thought she should be a solo act—musicians always diminished her. But then we were used to each other's misstatements. The blood running down her forearm made her hand look like a fat pink star on top of a pink Christmas tree tinseled with scarlet strings. I remembered how she used to say, "I'll eat anything, but I won't shoot anything." I could see now how she was degenerating—going against her own ethics, and it made me sad.

THEY SAY ANGELS appear in our lives only to bait us with their beauty into crossing some threshold. They hold out their hands and guide us through the window into the light of the free life. But if you turn around to ask why, or where—they're gone, and you're standing in mid-air about to fall. Happens all the time.

"**M**AN, DON'T YOU THINK YOU OUGHT TO GET UP some day?" she said pushing me playfully around in bed. "Hey, I put the bike together while you were sleeping," she said, swallowing her grin.

We had, oddly enough, found a British bike shop in Eugene and bought plates, points, plug wires and such. So while I "overslept," Tanya had finished torqueing the clutch nuts. She'd also topped off the oil, gapped the points, rebolted the casings, etc.—had practically done a whole tune-up. And it wasn't even noon. Her will, her wherewithal, often amazed me. Such amazement was always short-lived, however, being perpetually counterbalanced by some other completely fucked-up behavior. But at least it existed. It was there to be tapped when she wanted.

We spent the rest of the week helping Harry around the house. I came to like him more, or at least partially to understand him. Then we headed for the mountains to look for orchard work. No one would hire us. Maybe 'cause we were Anglos. Most owners preferred Mexicans. They would hire Mexicans and then complain the Anglos were lazy. Mexicans were faster, they would say. This was something I never witnessed. True, there were fast pickers, but it was not due to some inherited "agricultural" gene. In fact, the amount of work done was wholly dependent on numerous variables, primarily: when you woke up, the intensity of your hangover, how long a lunch you took, how late you worked and, factored in there somewhere, how quickly you actually did work, or whether you preferred to sit on your ladder and gaze out at the spectacular scenery. Introspection, aesthetic appreciation—these were bad work habits.

Another difference was that the Mexicans often worked as a family. Whites had long ago lost that nuclear faith. They were, each of them, alone. Also it was true that, while everyone who was working desperately needed the jobs, some at least wanted to be working at General Motors or US Steel making union wages and buying the American dream. But General Motors and US Steel were all moving to Mexico, where they could pay the workers less money than they made picking apples in the States. Meanwhile, supposedly, the Mexicans were moving up here so they could make more money than they could in Mexico. It was a twisted competition for a living wage in a twisted world. Global economics are based on rumor and disinformation. You keep people separated and tell them lies. Divide and conquer. Plus it gives reformers something to do. I could even imagine Naomi on the fruit-tramp activist trail. Campaigning for child-care, insurance, unions. Hell, maybe we would run into her at a soup kitchen or a family planning tent at the Hood River County fair.

Finally we scored. It must have been the fifth or sixth place we applied. The guy was just prejudiced enough that he didn't care how slow white people worked, or how dodgy or dreamy they seemed. Of course even this prejudice would give out later when his profit was at stake. There is a hierarchy to this kind of loyalty: pocketbook, family, race, in that order. Sometimes the hierarchy serves you, sometimes it doesn't.

&

APPLE PICKING WAS the Cadillac of fruit tramp jobs. Nick had said so. So had others. We were prepared to make some cash. Tanya and I worked hard. But we were white and we were city kids and we had a stigma to uphold. It took us a week to go from three bins to five. Eventually we were doing eight. That was the both of us. It wasn't good, but no one was laughing. And there were slower people than us. But not where we worked. Where we worked was a small orchard owned by the Hazeltons.

There was only one other hired hand—Hollis. Hollis Brown. He looked to be 60. But sometimes he looked younger. He looked older and younger at the same time. He might have spent his youth staring into a dust storm. His cheeks and chin were pointed. His skin was like pieces of cracked leather stretched over an aquiline skull. It was a face that could pass as a Reader's Digest condensed version of the Grand Canyon. If you got close, there were crags where whole mule trains went astray. You could hear the cries of lost pioneers echoing around his smile. And when the wind rising up the Hood River Valley hit that face just right, those cries became a shrill scream that made you long for your mother's arms. Hollis knew it. He knew his effect, even on a quiet day. He also knew your mother was dead, metaphorically. That was part of his power over you. And he showed no emotion whatsoever when he used that power.

His hair went straight back—that look of men who go racing through life. Hollis's racing days were over but he kept the style. It suited him. Fashion-wise he had the dustbowl thing down, though he wasn't a dustbowl man. He wore a crumpled felt hat, medium brim, suspenders and long-sleeves; the sleeves he never rolled up, even on 90-degree days. His movements were stiff, as if his whole body was calcifying. His lungs were way ahead on that track; they couldn't have been more than caves of hard tobacco-flavored coal, because he smoked like an old railroad engine

98

day and night. He smoked even when he was asleep. I never actually saw him without a cigarette. I never saw him drink either. Rumor had it that he once did. But then Hollis was an enigma. It was hard to catch him "doing" anything he "did." For instance, he never actually seemed to move much—that is, you never saw him working. Every time you looked he was sitting on his ladder smoking and coughing. And he still ended up with five bins. He quit working at five bins no matter what time it was—one o'clock, two o'clock, five o'clock. Probably some mystical significance to the number. But you didn't ask.

He claimed to be some kind of mongrel: Welsh, Blackfoot or Cherokee, Gypsy. The fact that me and Tanya were slow didn't matter to him, at least we weren't Mexican. He claimed to hate the Mexicans even though he was married to one. Maria was her name. She was waiting for him in New Mexico. Hollis didn't like most people, but he got along with us. I had a deadpan Midwestern quality he appreciated. Tanya was gregarious and didn't mind swearing. We used to speculate about Hollis at night while we laid in bed listening to him hack and cough in his cabin down the path. Sound carried, especially the sounds of mortality. Some nights you couldn't hear your own voice, but you could hear a car crash ten miles away and the fading beat of the victims' hearts. And you could hear Hollis coughing up his lungs.

All the rest was emptiness and you had to fill it in. We filled it with stories—long complicated made-up adventures of familial progress, mule-train tales full of hardship and small glories. Then we acted toward him as if these stories were true. Hollis never complained; he didn't really care. Some things we knew. For instance he'd lived in Canada when he was young. Apparently his whole family was up in Alaska for a couple of years looking for pipeline work. His father was away most of the time. The rest of them stayed in a cabin about seventy miles outside Juneau. Pop ended up working in a cannery. Mom brought the kids back to the states. Tanya picked this up from something he said to Gerry Hazelton. Hazelton had known Hollis in Korea.

&

THERE WERE NEW orchards and old ones, good ones and bad ones, orchards run by drunken individualists and those run by faceless corporations. The Hazeltons were a proper Sunday go-to-meetin' kind of family. All individualists. They didn't like government and they didn't like paying taxes but they did like guns and defending the land. Twenty years ago they'd migrated from Arkansas to Oregon and got into the orchard life. John Steinbeck it wasn't. Their kids didn't want to have nothing to do with it either. Nobody's kids in this valley wanted much to do with apples. Real estate, rock music, banking, grocery store managing, usury, drugs— anything but apples. The Mrs. was a hell of a cook, too, and put on a couple of spreads in the course of the season. Huge piles of steaming potatoes, lots of tender roasted meat, cooked carrots. Used to bring us pies and such, too. At first I thought it was some kind of bribe. Then I realized they were just being friendly. Paranoia like this has ruined my life.

Now despite all the other things I said earlier, the single most important variable in picking speed was the quality of the trees, which had a lot to do with their age. A young low-pruned heavily fruited tree, like those grown by the Hazeltons, could yield a bin in a half hour, effectively doubling your pay. Competition could get ugly. Pickers scouted the rows. Manipulating your position, however, by slowing your pace, or accidentally skipping ahead, was a form of behavior rarely tolerated by the owners. Still, strategy happened. If you weren't fast, you sucked up. If your boss liked you, he would hook you up with more work on other farms further up the mountain. The fruit ripened later the higher you went, until you got to tree line. Then you went back to where you came from, or somewhere else you didn't belong, somewhere down the line. We were about to move from a new orchard to an old one. It wasn't any higher, it was just a little ways down the road. Tanya, Hollis and I were all going. The Shelleys were expecting us.

Red Shelley was a frog-voiced South Carolina farmer, patriarchal and a bit aloof, but possessed of a hands-on plain country honesty. Rachel, his sun-baked wife, worked hard and repressed her vulnerabilities. There was one daughter at home. Another had gone to San Francisco. The son was in Omaha. Theirs was a bigger place with more cabins, some of which were already occupied with other waiting workers. Will and Dorothy-Anne, or "Doty," as he called her. She called him Buck. And Taylor Gordon, who went by the nickname Mad Jack. A family of Mexicans and a family of Okies—the Hernandez clan and the Carters. They were both singing families.

The Hernandez clan played accordions and guitars and sang Mexican spirituals about God, tequila and good times. They were not related to the famous Mariachi Hernandez family but they were well known in their home region of Tecalitlán, supposedly, and often played in festivals of the dead and festivals of the sun. They seemed as if they stepped out of a Mexican sit-com. The Carters played guitars and banjos. They also sang about God, maybe even the same one. They weren't related to the famous Carter family, but they did seem to have stepped out of an old radio. The kids often seemed quite docile, but they could play their fiddles and Tanya often sang with them, and it was a gay old time.

So we had plenty of entertainment while we sat around waiting for the sugar man to come—the guy from the packing plant who tests the sugar in the fruit and says "Go." One day he came, but he didn't say, "Go." He said, "Any day now, any day now." Any day now stretched to three because of the drought. We killed time riding on the mountain roads. The speedometer on the Beezer was shot long ago from vibration. I never fixed it. It was more than just disregard for the law—it was the idea of knowing your machine. You might end up taking a 40 mph curve at 60 and you wouldn't know it. If it didn't throw you, then that was the way it should be. Riding at night in the mountains was dangerous—blind curves, deer, fog. You can go from total to zero visibility in a second. If you want, every day you can have a near-death experience. You learn to like it. One night Tanya was driving. She was going into a turn with the clutch disengaged—always a bad thing, unless you actually like that feeling of being adrift in oblivion. We couldn't see anything except the fact that we were going down—a second or two of free fall that felt like an hour. Fortunately it was just a shallow ditch and we were back up in a few minutes.

When we weren't teasing death or talking with Hollis, we hung out with our new friends Buck and Doty who lived in a cabin down the road. Doty only had one eye and she was pregnant. Her skin had a strange glow. Will said it was the plastic surgery. Doty was ready to settle down. Buck, not so much. We would sometimes stay up and drink Ole River Bottom and listen to weird radio shows and think about faraway places. The hills distorted the signals. You couldn't get a local station, but you'd get something a thousand miles away, an old sea chantey from Mars, or a drinking song from some dead zone.

Three days was a long time and a few restless pickers left, but new pickers arrived. Two of them were named Brigitte-Marie and Percy. She was from Toulouse, he was from Tennessee. They married for the green card, but they loved each other. They were dumpster divers, too, and always had a supply of out-of-date dairy goods and crushed boxes of soup mix or noodles which they didn't mind sharing, so it was always good eating with them.

&

FINALLY IT WAS time, nearly five days late. We strapped on our sacks and headed out into the end-of-September mist. Unlike the young trees of the Hazeltons, those owned by the Shelleys were old. They were the kind that grew to monstrous size before the advent of modern genetic engineering and scientific pruning. Such a tree might seem ripe and bursting on the outside, but when you got inside you could see and feel the ravages of time, the arboreal osteoporosis, the reluctance to bear. You could see how much was paint and how much was sap. Looking down those acres of gigantic ancient trees, it was easy to imagine how explorers might have died in there and never been found. There was danger and a certain seduction, too. After all, there's nothing like the feeling of balancing on one leg out on the far reaches of some ancient brittle branch with forty-five pounds of apples hanging around your neck while you search the endless expanse of foliage in vain for the top landing of that fourteen-foot ladder you left behind so long ago. Way up there little things begin to annoy you. A bird might fly by delicately and freely and you might curse it. A squirrel straight out of the Peaceable Kingdom might mock you with its acrobatic confidence while some many-legged insect that time forgot might crawl closer and closer to the white knuckles of your hand desperately clenched around the crutch of a tree limb. And then comes that sound the apple picker fears most. It begins slow, maybe sporadically, a soft sometimes sudden cracking sound that elongates in duration and volume until it demands entrance to the emergency processing centers of your brain. You begin to make plans, desperately searching for an escape route. Do you jettison the bag? Or hope the weight will act as ballast? Do you jump and pretend to control your fall? Can you trust your reactions? Should you try gingerly to get back to the ladder? Or do you simply you put your trust in grace?

In trees like this, it can take three hours to fill a bin. By the end of the day you're exhausted, bruised, broken and still poor. But that's the luck of the draw. The next day might be better. You had to hope it would be.

(15)

IT STRUCK ME HOW WELL TANYA AND I SEEMED TO BE GETTING along. I suppose it was hard not to be happy up there in the lovely mountains with nature and God's grandeur and all. But the work surely had something to do with it. Good old work. What felt like twenty pounds in the morning felt like a hundred by night. The straps wore blue bands in our flimsy shoulders, which we would rub painfully as we limped down the road back to our cabin, too tired sometimes even to eat, much less indulge our unspoken animosities. There was a kind of contentment, though, and this is a secret of salvation as old as civilization itself—that fatigue is the true cement of marriage, more than sex or money or children. For career people too, but especially for the laboring classes.

Now I'm no Marxist, but I do believe successful marriage goes hand-in-hand with physical labor. When such labor decreased in our society, the divorce rate increased. Seeing this unrest, the gods of oppression tried to replace the benefits of physical activity with stress, but it's not the same. Stress does not unleash endorphins. Stress never satisfies like labor does. So the powers tried pathos. That seemed to work. People grew sadder and sadder, and those who could not placate themselves on entertainment would do so by complaining. You heard it in the cities and you heard it in the hamlets too. At night in the apple camps up and down the mountain, people sat around their campfires and bitched. We bitched about society, and how we were afraid of the neurotic lives we would have to live when our work disappeared. Perhaps we were merely justifying our lack of ambition.

&

THE PET BEEF of all fruit workers was, of course, encroaching automation. Already, at the packing plants, different machines were being tried, and there was a consistent rumor of giant picking combines that would roll down the rows by themselves, reducing whatever human labor was needed to the scavenging of cider culls. Someone even claimed to have seen one of these machines and drew a verbal picture of the thing—like a great metal insect moving slowly, mauling the fruit in its godless mechanical arms, with headlights like a mutant overgrown automobile glaring in the misty dawn. The only human around was a man far off in a lighted control tower. Rachel Shelley put it her way: "God gave us hands in order that we should use them." She was a dignified and sad woman and her Christianity did not suffer condescension. She knew the way of life that had fed them was disappearing.

In the face of such negativity, these campfire gatherings could become intense events. Especially when the sane people went to bed. That's when the "back of the bus" came into its own—the punks and the hobos and the drunks. The talk turned to all the crazy people they knew or had heard of, people who blew into the area and did something wrong or scandalous or criminal, like So and So from Arizona who got Mr. Cowper's daughter pregnant, or that hippie couple from Alabama who threw a party, attracting every trooper for fifty miles. Brian Carter told how he saw a guy rooting through the dumpster behind the Safeway who had supposedly died three years earlier. Turned out he had faked his death and started a new life with a new wife; problem was he didn't do it in a new place. And there were the stories of super pickers—some guy over at the Johnson's orchard who could do fifteen bins, even in high trees.

A lot of hitchhiking stories got told about getting picked up by killers or pervs, of week-long odysseys in party vans with pot dealers and hippies with guns. The killer on the road. The runaway on the highway beyond redemption. The hobo who looked just like someone you knew once upon a time. And then there were the stories of all the fucked-up things everybody had done to bring them here, to this point in their lives. One guy had stolen a car. Another was on the lam from alimony payments. Some just didn't give a damn about any damn thing—they were victims of other people's decisions.

There's a difference, I suppose, between romanticism and desperation. I may be a romantic, but I was never much of a storyteller. I confused endings and beginnings. That's where maps were different—you could pick a spot here and pick a spot there and draw a line between them. The division of space and time was vital, if only to dispense with it. Or, some might say, to "own" it. A good story was also a form of power. Which means they become a form of competition. Many stories started out, "Yeah, well that ain't nothin' pal, listen to this." And once the besting started, there was no stopping it. And Tanya was among the best. If there seemed even the slightest amount of cachet to be gained from having lived on the wrong side of the law, Tanya would stake her claim. If anyone began to interrupt her, she was quick to turn and reinterrupt them, by way of their having reminded her of yet another story of being so fucked-up or getting busted or almost dying or having taken more different types of drugs than the human body could or should be able to tolerate.

But she only blended in by her extravagance because everybody else was doing it. There was the guy who did a whole bottle of reds because he thought they were vitamins and had to have his stomach pumped. And another guy who OD'd on heroin in Alaska and had to be taken to the hospital on a dog sled. The woman who drank a little bottle of pure LSD, thinking it was airline vodka. Apparently in her coma she lived five complete and different lives: a whore in 19th century Paris, a Welsh princess in the late middle ages, a cavewoman, a spaceman and a pink dolphin. When she came out of it she was in the hospital and it was 1967.

I suppose there was some reason people lived their lives like this, pushing the limits, hoping to break through to some other side. I myself never had much faith that the other side was there. Once on purple micro-dot I met an old hermit living in a coffee can in the rafters of my friend's garage. He turned me into a skeleton made of oak twigs and scraps of rancid meat. The wind whistling through my bones played Beethoven's 21st symphony. I flew straight to the edge of the universe and looked beyond it. I saw what was there. I never went back. It was a decision I made and I was glad I could. One more second and there wouldn't have been any "me" left to make it.

But transcendence wasn't the issue here. The object was to stand out, but you couldn't stand out because no one was listening. The audience might even display disinterest by getting up and stomping around or pissing by the fire or loudly getting another beer, while waiting for a break into which they could interject their own story of getting fucked up or busted or almost dying. Drinking and fighting and spewing. It was a glimmer of what the world was to become, a passing that would take place subtly, in which we didn't any longer live in a common tapestry of mixed fates, but an infinite number of individual productions in which the teller of the tale was also the star, and everyone's subjective opinion mattered more than any collective destiny. It was a disease of democracy: rampant confessionalism posing as wisdom, personal validation posing as community. But I never said these things. Nobody would have cared anyway.

&

COLD RIDGE WAS the closest town, and it was a small town, and there was little to do except play pool in the local game room. We'd buy beer at the grocery next door and hide it in the cooler of the pool room. The manager pretended not to see, knowing if we couldn't drink we wouldn't be there. Afterwards everybody would try to start their cars. Nobody had a good car and the street often looked like the parking lot of an auto parts store.

Saturday nights we might hitch into Hood River for a night of drinking in the bars, especially the Hi-De-Ho, down by the river. The Hi-De-Ho was one of those fake cowboy bars with imitation wood paneling. They served burgers and fat french fries and sometimes mountain oysters. The jukeboxes played Tammy, Johnny, Waylon, Patsy. And occasionally Janis or the Doors or ZZ Top. We'd leave the bike at camp so we could get ripped. Hollis never went. Sometimes Taylor, Brigitte and Percy joined us. They usually stayed at the bar taunting the locals. Me, Buck and Tanya stayed on the pool table. Sometimes we'd get a few free drinks out of it.

The clientele of the Hi-De-Ho was mixed: hustlers, construction workers, pruners, pickers, townies, the errant sales staff of the local department store, maybe a railroad worker or a fireman, and always one or two dressed-out middle-aged women without husbands, intent on getting drunk and screwing some good old boy. Their daughters were there too— chubby young ladies in blue jeans and sweatshirts. They probably married when they were seventeen, but weren't divorced yet, or they were still raising kids, so they couldn't fuck around like their moms could, but they could get drunk and resentful and start fights which was the next best thing. And there was always one or two Hood River businessmen and maybe a proto-yuppie couple from Portland who got lost looking for that great little restaurant in the eastern suburbs. And there were Indians and Mexicans and assorted packing plant workers, and sometimes a hobo or two who wandered up from their encampment by the Willamette, looking to fill up on cheese doodles and corn chips.

After a night of drinking we might catch a late breakfast at The Pancake Pantry or the Bun & Yolk, then head for home. The road at that hour would often be a loose, intermittent parade of over-confident jeeps, shy station wagons and woozy sedans—the closing-hour migration of drunks up the hill. If you couldn't get a ride, you walked and if there was no moon shivering in the cold sky, you might walk right off the edge of the road. If some friendly lumber mill wasn't churning like a satanic factory in some misty hollow you might have profound feelings of isolation. You might be tortured by old grudges. Usually, however, you got a ride, and usually with somebody you had been drinking with a few hours earlier. Or some ex-con on the prowl. Or the guy who worked right down the road from you. Or the guy who cashed your check at the mini-mart. Or the lumber mill foreman. The ones who passed—those fearful parents in their Chevy sedan, those wigged-out freaks in their lime green wagon—you wondered who they were. But you didn't wonder too hard. Like I said, those roads were dark, but not so dark as the imaginations of the people who walked them.

(16)

ANTHONY BLOCH AND JOHN SQUIRES SHOWED UP IN A '65 Chevy Biscayne wagon, lime green with a plastic weasel for a hood ornament and white-wall tires painted purple. They rolled into camp that foggy Sunday morning while we were still warming our hands on our metal coffee mugs. Apparently they had been sent from some other orchard.

"Hey, didn't we see that car on the road last night?" Tanya yelled at them.

"Yeah, yeah, we saw you guys, we were gonna give you a ride but you looked like escaped cons," Bloch offered by way of explanation, half joking.

"You never know these days," added John Squires.

Squires was pale, Anthony Bloch less so. Citybillies. Blockhead, as he came to be known, was the Jewish comedian of the two. Except he wasn't Jewish. Squires was his West Virginia straight man. When something was funny to Bloch, it was passé to Squires. And while John Squires was abrupt and paranoid, Bloch was polite. But he was paranoid too. Hollis said he probably didn't trust himself. We both figured they were on the run from something, telling jokes so you wouldn't ask.

The two were unforthcoming at first, but one night after joints and whisky, they opened up. They had been living in Cleveland when they had a streak of bad luck. Blockhead's mother died. He didn't like to say what it was, but she was only 44. And Squires was sick. He was living in a special house. Bloch was living in that neighborhood, too. But not that house. He was working part-time and not doing much else. He and this guy Sam used to drink in the bars and talk to the hillbillies. The hillbillies put some ideas in their heads. One of these ideas was to get the hell out of Cleveland. They met Squires in a bar. He was hustling a beer with match tricks. A fight broke out. Bloch remembered a balled fist and a declaration: "Better get out of here. 'Cause after I fuck your mother and your sister I'm gonna burn your motherfuckin' house down, cocksucker, then I'm gonna fuck you in the ass with my .44." So Bloch, Sam and Squires decided to split. When they got to Sam's street there was a crowd of people standing around his apartment building watching it burn. It was a good thing he had some money in his pocket. A street sign pointing west said "One Way."

Sammy said, "Let's do it."

Squires said, "I'm going too."

So they bought a hundred-dollar car and drove to the coast. S.F. first, then north. Sammy met some redhead out there and went off with her, I think they said to Eugene. But the redhead ran off with an older man with money that Sam didn't have. Bloch and Squires came up to work the orchards in Hood River. They were still young. They did a day's work but got fired. The guy had hired them at night and didn't know what they looked like. So he sent them to the Shelleys' because he knew the Shelleys would hire freaks.

There were only a few more days at most of work, but there were already two empty cabins. The Hernandez family had left for a corporate orchard. The Carters had said it was too dangerous—the trees were too old. Nobody mentioned anything about the sheriff coming around the previous day. Block and John took the Hernandez cabin. They liked the chili and lime decor. The other cabin, the Carters', was filled later that afternoon by Tommy Burke and James Goodwine. Tommy had been in prison for beating a guy to death with a pool cue. James didn't talk much. Hollis Brown didn't take to Tommy and James. He called them trash. They called him an old half-breed fuck.

Tommy Burke was a razor man, he carried a straight razor and was always talking about cutting anybody that fucked with him. You didn't have to do much, apparently, to earn that status. One night he snuck up on Bloch over by the shower house. He had the razor out, standing behind him in the mirror, sneering. He said it was all for fun and he laughed, and Bloch pretended to laugh with him. James said Tommy always was a crazy motherfucker. Squires heard about it and got a bat and almost got in a fight over it, but then he backed off. Tanya did get in a fight with both of them, but all they did was yell.

&

THINGS WERE A little off. A few days earlier Doty had a miscarriage in the bathroom of Johnny's Tap out by Dee Junction. We were shooting pool. Blitz beer cans littered the table. Johnny Cash was on the juke. I played "Ball and Chain." Doty said she felt ill. She went to the bathroom for a while. "Here's to times that never were and friends we never had," Buck said. It was his favorite toast. Doty came out crying. Things got a little tense. Doty blamed Janis, saying the godawful voice scared the baby away from living. Buck said to hell with that, too much alcohol probably and the baby wanted out. They fought about it. Whatever the reason, Doty flushed the result down the toilet and we drove home somber. When we got to Buck's house the doors were swinging open. Right away I thought—burglary. But it was Beulah, his goat. The goat had been a gift for helping build a porch the previous spring. It was ornery and had an evil clown face. Buck kept it tied outside so it wouldn't maim or kill anyone. They found Beulah in the bedroom trashing their personal possessions. Everyone decided to eat her.

There was a dying tradition that, after the harvest, the orchard owners put on a spread for their pickers. Some owners just bought a bunch of beer, then tried to stay as far away as possible. The Hazeltons took us to the all-you-can-eat Chuck Wagon, a choice reflecting their personal values. The Shelleys usually provided a large piece of meat, a roast or something, then went home and locked the doors. This year they were off the hook. Beulah would be the harvest feast.

First we had to find someone with a gun to kill her, which was no problem. Bill Black, from up the road, had guns. Bill thought the solution to everything was to shoot it. He wanted to shoot the neighbor's dog and he wanted to shoot the tires on the Mexicans' cars. His wife had her tubes tied so at least they wouldn't have babies. They raised bunnies instead, and ate them. The bunnies had names and you would be eating one at their house and they would say "Oh, you're eating Muffy," or "You're eating Pinky." Anyway Bill came out and shot Beulah twice in the head, so we had to invite him to the feast, even though nobody liked him. He said he would bring some cleaned bunnies for when the goat ran out.

Turned out the goat was too stubborn even to die. She was tethered to a stake and kept bucking up. Everyone stood around watching, figuring it to die any minute. But she didn't. It was decided someone had to cut her throat. Suddenly no one had a pocketknife. There were a bunch of guys who could have done it, and should have had knives, but everyone voted Bloch should do it, just because he never had. Suddenly somebody had a Buck knife and handed it to Bloch.

So Anthony Bloch walked over and cradled the goat's head in his arms. He felt he was comforting a terrified child, he said. Then—whack! At least it was supposed to be "whack!" Actually it was more work than that. The blade did not exactly slide through the flesh like butter. It was more like sawing through living shaking leather. And the goat's cries were not so much from the pain, but the mechanical responses of its nerves—the panic that comes when the forest and the darkness close in. Bloch stood there looking lost. Squires shouted some encouragement. "Just do it, don't think!" He had done this sort of thing before. He had killed things. Bloch ran the knife through the wound again. Beulah went down.

"Jesus fuck," said Taylor.

Squires said, "I can't stand it, I can't stand to look at the thing."

Later, everyone would convince themselves that it was all right. Anthony Bloch turned his shame into pride, said the killing made him feel more alive than he ever felt.

We strung Beulah upside down from a tree and put a pan under her neck to collect the blood. Then we smoked some cigarettes and drank some beer.

Squires directed this question to the rest of us: "What the hell do you think an animal sees when it's gonna die? Nothing. Nothing at all. So there's no sense worrying about it."

Still, Bloch looked at his hands and he had blood all over his fingers and wrists. And maybe that was the beginning of the end for him. Maybe his jokes stopped working. Maybe he went on cutting things. We would never know. We did know his personality seemed to change. He started swaggering around and guzzling his beers. Blood can make men arrogant; it gives them a leg up in a world of punks. It's something that goes back a million years when cavemen shoved sharpened sticks into each other because they didn't have any way to explain themselves.

&

AN HOUR LATER we skinned old Beulah with kitchen knives by the light of a fire. Bloch said "Oh shit," as he looked at the raw hanging red corpse. For a few long seconds nobody said anything. We stood around looking.

"Let it go," said Squires. "It's not worth it."

Hollis said, "If you're gonna eat meat . . . you gotta kill meat." Of course, Hollis thought nobody didn't know anything about death but him, and he would tell us what death was about. "The only way to beat death is to roll in it," Hollis said. "Have to have a share in it," he said, "look into it till it don't make you sick no more. Use it up it. Keep doing it till it don't seem like evil no more. And then, by God, it ain't. Death is the same."

These philosophical waters were a little deeper than anybody wanted to wade in, so Tanya suggested an alternative: "Let's just not talk about it. Let's sing songs."

Meanwhile Hollis started putting all the goat entrails in a bag, figuring maybe the sooner it was out of sight the sooner people would forget. He picked up the heart and said, "Nakedness of a woman is the work of God, my friend. Yes, and the wrath of the lion is God's wisdom. Lust of the goat is God's bounty. Heart of a mother is the strongest and most courageous of all flesh. Can't go wrong. You want to know about death, I'll tell you. You see this?" He had the goat's heart in his hand. "Best thing is to eat it." Hollis squeezed it and a trickle of blood ran down onto his face and into his mouth. "Shit, that's good," he said. Then he tried to wipe his mouth but ended up rubbing the blood around. He looked like a clown. He laughed. Then he spit. You could smell sweet apples in the air, wood smoke, and blood.

"It's not funny, man," Buck said.

I turned to Tanya. But she wasn't by my side. She was standing with Brigitte. They were tipsy drunk and started singing "Piece of My Heart," I guess as a kind of joke. Brigitte-Marie in her French hillbilly accent, and Tanya with her West Coast hillbilly accent. Tanya could put people around her at ease. But she could also divide them. So, while Hollis was trying to speechify, they were shaking their butts in unison, holding their beer cans up in the air as they sang the chorus.

"Shut the fuck up," Hollis shouted.

But everybody just laughed at him. Most people thought he was a madman, anyway. And he thought they were all stupid. So he started off to his cabin mumbling, "Fuck every one of you. I'll do for myself. I'll take your trip. You fuckin' hippies don't know shit. Yes sir, Mexican taco, eggs and onions, cilantro, garlic, potatoes. Rest of you can fuck the fuck off."

"Hollis, what a clown."

"Old hippies never die they just get morbid," Squires said.

"Who's he to call us hippies? He's an old hippie himself," Percy added, feigning indignation.

But I was thinking about the long sleeves, the potatoes and onions. Something about it struck a note.

(17)

I FINISHED MY BEER, HAD A SMOKE, GOT ANOTHER BEER, THEN slipped over to Hollis's cabin to see what was up with him. Potatoes were boiling on the stove. Chopped onions were piled on the cutting board. Garlic. The heart was sizzling in a puddle of brown foam in a skillet on the woodstove. Some scratchy radio broadcast of an opera or something was playing, but the channel kept fading in and out as they tend to in the mountains. Hollis was staring in a mirror above the table. It was an old cracked dirty mirror and he was mumbling to it, the way people do when they think they're alone. He seemed to be examining his stubble. "C'mon on, baby," he said. Funny thing was, I couldn't see his reflection, but probably it was just the angle—me being still in the doorway and afraid to knock. He couldn't see me either. It took him a few seconds to realize I was there.

He spoke without looking at me. "Ever hear the story about the man who shot his double?"

"No, never heard it."

"Turned out to be suicide. Had to spend the rest of his life imitating himself, playing the part of himself so no one would know. The moral being: better be careful who you talk to in mirrors."

He stopped to get some spices out of a box on his bed. "So you come here to criticize my ways?" Then he turned showing me those severe facial outlines of his. Sometimes I thought some beast was pulling his skin tight from behind his head. Sometimes I thought his face was going to crack, like old veined stone. For a moment he was a piece of landscape. Then his features softened, lost focus. He became Hollis again. The radio channel drifted to a banjo tune: something about going down the road feeling bad, or breakin' rocks on a chain gang, or life is all sorrow and love is sad. Then the station fuzzed out and I realized the radio was on a shelf next to the mirror and his hand, which seemed to have been inside the mirror, was really behind it, trying to adjust the channel. "Goddamn hillbilly music . . . . So I'm a old hippie eh?"

"C'mon, Hollis. We were just kidding, man."

"It's my prerogative to be insulted, just like any man."

"Well, what the hell were you talking about out there?"

He'd got the opera station back in and was now waving the kitchen knife in the air like a conductor's baton. Then he stuck it out and said seriously, "C'mon baby, come and get me. Come and get old Hollis. He's a-waiting for ya." Then he remembered I was there and chuckled. "Ain't no mirror gonna kill me. Speaking of which, better watch that girl of yours, she's a wild one, some kind of mirror herself. I see a little of me in her, and that can't be a good thing."

"I'm not worried," I said, not wanting to change the subject.

"No? People ought to be worried. People are mostly *afraid*. But they ought to be worried."

"What are they afraid of?" I asked.

He seemed to want to change the subject. "Now. What's your name again? Luc? What? I know you told me."

"Payne. Francis Lucretius Payne. That's my name."

"Frank Payne? Ha! Is that another fucking fake name or something, like all these other freaks? Nobody has a name like that."

"I do. And what difference does it make?"

"You got me there. No difference at all."

I decided to get to my point. "Say, you ever know a guy, name of Walker, in Portland?"

"Might be."

"I met him on Burnside. Walker Birdsong. Another funny name, huh?"

Hollis started looking hard at me then. "Yeah . . . so?"

"This guy Walker told me . . . he told me a story about another guy, a guy that could have been you. Funny huh?"

"People tell stories son. You wouldn't be here if they didn't. Doesn't have to mean any damn thing. Campfire's outside if you want to hear plenty more."

"How come I never seen you roll up your sleeves? You never wear short sleeves, T-shirts, nothing. And in this damn weather."

He was starting to get an angry look to him and I was starting to think that I'd gone too far, made a connection that wasn't there.

"You want to know a lot, don't you?"

"Is that bad?"

"Can't say it is. And we'll leave it like that. No harm done."

The heart was frying and spitting in the skillet now and it stunk. It stunk like kidneys, and it wasn't supposed to. Maybe he had mixed in the kidneys. He dumped in the onions and garlic, but that didn't help. The potatoes were at a boil now. It was getting warm in there.

"You know, there are people what say the heart is really an animal all unto itself. Worse than a tapeworm or a tic or a harpy at the liver of chained man. It's got wings and it's got teeth. Suck all the life out of a man if you let your guard down."

"I'm going to get a drink." I said and started out the door, figuring to let it rest for a while.

"I'll see you later, then."

&

THE GOAT WAS hanging from the tree all clean. We sat in a circle around the fire drinking Jim. I guess about an hour passed. Then Tanya came back from talking to Tommy. "What's up with Hollis?" she asked.

"Eatin' dinner."

Anthony Bloch threw his beer can in the fire in disgust. "Shit, I can't believe I did that." Then he opened another one. "I'm turning vegetarian," he said.

Tanya said her mother was a vegetarian for a while, but she couldn't stand it.

"Oh that's right, you got that famous mother?" Bloch snarled.

"Famous for what?" Percy had never heard of her.

Hollis had. "I heard of her. Naaaaaomi McCoy. Didn't much care for her. Communist, wasn't she?" He was approaching the fire, still chewing, and he had a cup in his hand. "Somebody wanna pour me a taste of that red?"

"She was just for people rights, that's all." Tanya said. "She was in the march on Birmingham, even though she had a broken leg from a motorcycle accident."

This was news to me—this accident. Kind of like the trial Harry spoke of—more unfinished or unheard episodes in the life of Naomi McCoy. Next I would probably be finding out she went to Vietnam with her neck in a brace. She was apparently a woman who overcame all odds. Still, we all agreed that physical problems shouldn't hamper your ambition. Then we had more drinks.

Hollis sat next to me on a log, and talked below the volume of the general conversation. Okay, he said, Walker was his brother, all right. I had guessed right. But they'd gone their separate ways years ago. Birdsong had tried to make some bread being a mule for some acid coming in from Geneva via Mexico. A dumb move to start with, but someone called it in and Walker did time. And of course his name wasn't really Walker either. It was Seth. He changed it because of the biblical connotations.

"What biblical connotations?" I asked.

"Never you mind. If you don't know, you don't need to," he said. "But my brother would not be seen as a sodomite."

I let it go. Hollis went on. Apparently he did not think much of his little brother. Hollis had been in Korea. Walker dodged Vietnam—that was part of the reason he changed his name. And Hollis had no patience for draft dodgers, drug dealers or drunks. Hollis had a shell in his hip, and anybody that hadn't at least taken the risk for God or country was a little low on the moral ladder to him. You could beat your wife or shoot your best friend in a poker game but you had better have served your flag. And on that note we got up and helped to throw the goat carcass in the back of the station wagon and Buck and Doty drove it to the town market for cold storage.

&

THURSDAY MORNING I met Hollis at the fire pit out front of the cabins— we were drinking coffee and I asked him more about Walker. He started with the Birdsong name: they took the name when they were aspiring hipsters in 60s Seattle and Portland. In those days they were pretty apolitical, just gettin' over, catchin' a ride on the changing times. The hippie crowd didn't much like rednecks, but they would condescend to Indians. 'Pretentious fucking liberals,' Hollis called them. Birdsong was their mother's name, the father was Moriarty. So they were Hollis and Seth Moriarty, legally. One drifted right, the other left. Both claimed hypocrisy as the catalyst. But the filial split had really come earlier than politics or women. They had once even been close, Hollis said, as young men. Their parents had actually split a few years earlier. The dad supposedly was gonna be made foreman up at Walton Fish. His wife hated Alaska. She ran off with another man and later filed for divorce in the lower forty-eight. Hollis would have been in his early twenties around then. Younger than me. Beyond that there wasn't much I needed to know, which meant Hollis didn't much want to tell. When and where he met and married his wife and how he ended up in Arizona would have to wait for another day.

"So what's with the Brown? Why are you Hollis Brown? Not Hollis Birdsong?" I asked.

"I am Hollis Birdsong. I'm just holding it for a while till some trouble clears up. I don't want to talk about it. And you better keep shut up about it, too."

Brigitte-Marie was approaching. I saw Tanya running to the outhouse. People were getting up. Hollis stubbed his cigarette out in the dirt with his broken-heeled lizard-skin boots. "Let's go to work," he said. That day he picked seven bins—out of character for him. I picked four. I was thinking too much.

The next day, Friday, was hot, and there really wasn't much to do but clean a few trees out in the hollow. Tommy and James, the Cain and Abel of the Cascades, finished in the morning and took it upon themselves to dig the pit for the roast. With his shirt off, I saw that Tommy had a snake tattoo on his chest that wasn't finished. He said he would finish it when he got paid. Lots of guys it seemed had these unfinished tattoos—a heart with no flame, a rose without thorns, an empty scroll draped around a dagger. Money was short.

&

THAT NIGHT WAS a quiet one. Hollis smoked cigarettes and played chess with Anthony Bloch. Percy and Brigitte went to town. Tommy and James stayed in their cabin. Saturday morning, we skewered the goat, filled the pit with wood and rocks and started roasting. Round about 3 o'clock, people started coming up. Seemed like half the people in the town showed up. But it was a small town. Still there were way more people than anybody invited. Friends of friends of neighbors who had heard. People came on motorcycles and people came in new cars. One guy had a BSA, a lot like ours, but a '70. Another guy had a Harley, an AMF. There must have been thirty people. Respectable merchants sat down alongside fruit tramps, student types and hippies. There was a middle-class prostitute from California and her pimp. They were both good-looking blondes and Bloch and Buck had seen them working the bars in Hood River. There was a guy with a guitar and a guy with a deck of cards. Tanya sang a song. The guy with the guitar told her she should get a band together. They were going to jam later.

We kept the beer cold down in the creek, but the feast disintegrated after awhile under the influence of alcohol and it was all we could do to convince people to go home. But they did, and when everybody was gone we drank some more.

&

PARTIES OFTEN GIVE people bad dreams, maybe as compensation. We were nursing our hangovers the next morning and some of us decided to tell these dreams. Mine was of little goat heads hanging like plums in the trees. If you bit into one of the little heads the goat juice stained your chin. I let the heads roll down my arms into the apple sack. Each one cried, "Help me, help me!" Later in the same dream I heard a telephone ringing in the cooler. I went inside and the door closed behind me, and then I saw the stripped goat carcass hanging on a hook, and I heard that voice, "Help me, help me!" Then I got out of the cooler, but the goat was still in front of me. "Why have you forsaken me?" it said. The telephone kept ringing. But it was in a booth by the road. I woke up and went out to take a piss

117

in the moonlight. I remember the insane noise the insects made. The trees were full of them and they all had the heads of the Virgin Mary. Tanya came out and brought me back in. She'd been calling my name. She said I'd been out there almost an hour, mumbling to no one.

Anthony Bloch apparently also had a dream of the Virgin Mary. He said she was glowing like a lamp in the woods. And all around her, little bloody heads in the trees made sounds like tiny bells or murmuring water. There was a goat there, too, that romped and frisked like a kitten and sometimes laid its head in the Virgin's lap.

Everyone was astonished by the consistency of the dreamscape. Not Hollis. Hollis said, "Dreams ain't nothing but pool games in your head, only no one's playin', just a bunch of balls rolling around. Don't put much stock in it." And so we all agreed not to put much stock in dreams.

Then Bloch said, "I'll show you something."

And he did. He had Tommy's razor. He showed me. He found it lying next to him when Tommy passed out at the party. Bloch was going to keep it too. We passed it around. It was old and notched by hard use and it looked like some kind of key.

Tommy spent most of that whole day looking for that razor. He said he was gonna hurt somebody if he didn't find it. Brigitte and Percy were gone within an hour. So was Mad Jack Taylor. Bloch and Squires got in their car and split that evening. Buck and Doty had their own problems.

That evening Hollis showed me the scars on his right arm—they looked like Arabic writing or something, white and grizzly on his grizzled skin. "The thing I remember most about that night," he said, rolling the sleeve back down, "was the way everything seemed so soft, so natural. There weren't no borders to anything. Whether I died or stayed alive. I felt like finally—I have no choice in this, no choice at all. And when I felt that wolf heart beating I knew what I had to do. The whole night was beating like that. We were all inside it. I never felt nothing like that in my life. You got to kill something to know what that's like."

I didn't know how to answer that, so I didn't. Hollis got up and walked off.

There were a couple of orchards still picking higher up, so I decided to chase the harvest to Parkdale, and get in a few more days. It was getting colder. There was frost on the bike tank in the morning, and flecks of ice in the air and on the apple leaves.

At the absolute end, me and Tanya cashed in our bin tickets and went to Portland. We bought a beat-up canary yellow Corvair van, loaded the bike, all our clothes, a case of transmission fluid, a case of oil, and drove to Chicago. We arrived Halloween night, picked up a couple six -packs and a pint, bought some rubber monster masks at a dime store and drove around the near Westside neighborhoods with our rubber masks on, honking at kids. People thought it was cute. I'm not so sure. It felt more like an alibi.

Part IV
the elasticity of time

(18)

MAYBE IT HAD BEEN GOING ON ALL ALONG, BUT I didn't notice it until we moved to Chicago—a phone booth on the street, or someone's apartment window, or a room down the hall. Tanya must have noticed it too. Or she noticed me noticing it. "Maybe it's for you," she'd say. "Aren't you going to answer it?" I laughed. But sometimes I did dream about it—a phone sitting all by itself in an empty basement, or out on some gray street in a crowded city, ringing for me like a flashing neon light. You pick it up, it changes your life—not always in a good way. It was happening all the time. In fact, it seemed like the streets of Chicago were alive with ringing phones that nobody answered. Why should they? Apparently most of these people were done with fantasy. But, of course, I was wrong.

We took an apartment in one of those gray areas between neighborhoods, where Wicker Park meets Humboldt Park, and the American dream meets sad economic reality. It hadn't picked up a marketing tag from the real estate people yet, so it was still cheap—eighty bucks a month—and still sad. But you always knew you could move to some other gray neighborhood. I say "neighborhoods" but these were not the neighborhoods the politicians talked about with the cute "neighborhood" names, the ones they put on banners on telephone poles on the main business streets. Most natives didn't use those names. They used the closest major intersection, say Western and Fullerton, or Ashland and Chicago, or Racine and 51st, or Armitage and California. That's where we lived and, like I said, it was off the map, even though it was on it.

Where the politicians and the real estate agents failed to exercise any control there were local "sets" or gangs that kept the neighborhoods in line. Some were large enough to run vast indeterminate areas of the city like corporations. Others were confined to a few streets or even one block. The names were confusing to strangers. Conservative Vice Lords, Simon City Royals, Latin Kings, Apache Stones, East Side Disciples, Blackstone Rangers, Mickey Cobras, El Rukns, 2-Sixers, Insane Popes, P-Stone Nation and on and on. Their graffiti read like an arcane book of sigils and signs across the alleys and storefront steel doors of the city. The territories were all mixed together and you never knew where you were. Every street had a storefront church, a thrift shop, a taqueria, a hot dog shop, a liquor store and bars on two of the four corners. There were no Starbucks or Benettons in those days to run into if you felt afraid. And it was easy to feel afraid.

Down the street from where we lived there was a club called the Armitage Iron Men. They were local, and they strolled around their locality in beaded colors toting sawed-off golf clubs decorated like dandy's canes. Two blocks away was St. Helen's Alley, which belonged to the Gents. The Insane Unknowns were around, as were the Almighty Gaylords.

&

TANYA COULD SEE the interest in anything—it was part of her mechanism. We'd see some fat lady laughing in a dark doorway and we'd laugh along with her. Our soundtrack was the wind making its low-toned organ drone over the manhole covers and gutter vents on empty mornings. Our dramatic backdrops were vacant lots with abandoned cars, the lamp-lit alleys, and the ancient theatrical arches of the el tracks where sparks fluttered down from the iron rails beneath the passing trains. There was a natural splendor as well: the geological cold of the winter, the spring with its tree blossoms dripping perfumes, while the cilantro and chili scents mixed with motor oil fumes. In summer the fire hydrants spewed cool fans of fetid river water into the air and the regular thunderstorms choked the sewer grates with banana skins, cornhusks, papaya peels, cigar wrappings and condoms.

Being off the road, the city became our road, and we drank in the Nelson Algren bars of West-town, and listened to country music in the hillbilly bars of Uptown. We'd find old theaters in remote corners of forgotten time-warp dime-store neighborhoods with 60-cent double features, places where you could take in a cooler if you wanted. Time was space. You could cross some street and walk into the 1940s, the '50s, the '60s or even the '80s, even though it was still only the '70s.

For all the local color, I often felt we were living in a black and white movie. The Victorian industrial past melded with contemporary migratory neglect, making for a kind of organic decay. And we came, like the citizens there, to see the architecture as a spiritual thing, both by intention and result. Bleak as it might have seemed, the jagged arpeggios of the grey streets served as a conduit for the eye, from the gray and brown stone façades to the erratic roof-lines of the utilitarian blocks of wood-frame row-houses, painted or wrapped in asphalt siding, built to last no more than a generation, yet they were still there, taunting the present with tenacious decay. At night I'd strap a six-pack to my bicycle and go riding down alleys, under the wires draped with tennis shoes, past the anonymous ancient satanic industries, the foundries, tanneries, smelting yards and scrap yards by the river. I'd ride and drink while looking for that rough angel or some fantastic animal forgotten by time.

&

IT WAS A city of junk—junk lives, junk neighborhoods. On Sunday mornings we'd go down to Maxwell Street, a whole neighborhood given over to the recycling of junk, as people from all over the area parked their trucks there and just dumped their junk on the street. People sat around garbage can fires eating pork-chop sandwiches while old black men in stingy brims or straw cowboy hats played guitars on their stoops. God-fearing women in proper Sunday dress sat on milk crates singing spirituals in vacant lots. Somebody would plug an amplifier into a telephone pole using ten or twenty extension cords and you had a night-club at 10 a.m.

There were a couple of Jewish delis that opened around daylight and sold six-packs and sandwiches. Mexican women sold enchiladas and tamales from five-gallon paint buckets. Tanya and I would spend the whole afternoon down there going through record bins, eating, drinking, talking to freaks and eventually riding the Milwaukee back north, busted, baked, and drunk, with some ridiculous plaster statue in our laps, or a box of tools or useless motorcycle parts or cooking utensils we would never use, or ten pounds of bananas, lemons and twenty-five cent hardback books on the occult we'd never read. Once we bought a broken accordion that would eventually end up as a window decoration.

Used bookstores were everywhere, as were warehouse-sized thrift stores and small mom-and-pop junk shops. We used these thrift stores as private clubs or personal attics. We loved the smell of stagnation, of ghosts and lives in abeyance—it was the odor of the parallel universe of the desperate and the disappeared. You could sit on a couch for hours with an old encyclopedia or some yellowing National Geographic, while watching the latest installment of your favorite talk show or soap opera playing on the color TV next to the cash register.

It may not have been the Grandma's house of Tanya's old heroin daydreams, but it was a collective Grandma's house nonetheless, where Grandma was an insane poverty-stricken leftist with a boyfriend who used to be in the SDS and an uncle who traveled the country as a hobo bone player. If anyone was looking for you, you could be lost and lost was good. And you always felt that somewhere in a backroom there was a secret rite being enacted, some ancient Illuminati or Satanic ritual that

125

needed to be regularly reenacted in order to keep the world in this state of sacrificial splendor.

This great material turnover also symbolized some kind of change we were dimly aware of in the world, as if the world we knew or wanted to know in all its detritus and funk was being sold off before our eyes. This city was still a haven from the malling of America that was occurring elsewhere, but it wasn't going to last. They were already tearing down the YMCA at Milwaukee and Division, to build a Pizza Hut. The old bank would soon be a McDonalds. Maxwell Street would become another Higher Education Shopping Mall.

&

UNSKILLED LABOR WAS still a going thing in the US of A. Monday morning, if you wanted to, you could go and get a job. I was a bicycle messenger for an architectural drawing reproduction service, a stockman for a department store, a machine shop metal bender and an ambulance man. I did demolition and I did rehab. And this was all in one year. You could look in the paper one day and have a job the next—if you wanted. If you wanted, you could live in a hotel next to your job, or you could rent your own place a block away. Vacancy was an everyday word. It shouted from the windows of the lonely neighborhoods like a homecoming cry.

Tanya took a job in a kitchen. And since you're supposed to drink when you work in a kitchen, she was trying to live up to the stereotype. Eventually I was working in a kitchen, too, in a big downtown department store. We were both drinking and working in sad kitchens. If you've ever worked in a kitchen, you know how that is. What started as an appreciation of "real" life turned to spite as the city made demands on us that had never before been made in our constantly mobile life. Maybe it was not the place, but the relationship that established this new tone— not the soul-crushing, mundane, back-breaking, dollar-a-day, reality, but something else that was happening, a kind of subtle slide into a domesticity that we had never experienced. In that sense the city tricked us—it kept us busy and made us forget we weren't going anywhere and that we were, ultimately, together.

To come from the pastel optimism of the West to a monotoned working-class metropolis was hard for her. There were no pretty people, no blue oceans, no soft breezes. There were, however, plenty of ugly people, a polluted lake, and that old "hawk" like a knife that whittled away at the sunny sanity of the newly arrived. Tanya was fighting against this reality, chafing against its grain, and the fight would exaggerate certain aspects of her behavior, aspects that might be counter-productive. Maybe she was trying to challenge herself. But she wasn't being real. She was baiting reality at whatever the cost. But unless you're strong enough or insane enough, reality usually wins.

&

ANYWAY, YOU NEVER saw two people more miserable than Tanya and I. We weren't moving and we were miserable. As a cheap fix to the situation we decided to buy things. Hell, we were working people. We could make some money and buy shit and drink and smash the shit we bought and buy some more shit. We even put $20 a week in the bank to pay for our future, whatever that was.

There was a logic to this kind of magical thinking. You see, I used to believe that maybe the number of things I owned multiplied the surfaces and thus the potential for adventure. Now I realize it was just clutter—all of it, the cars, the vans, the motorcycles. It was as if by multiplying my means of escape I was buying myself insurance against some impending cosmic frieze. But owning something doesn't mean you're engaged, just as going somewhere doesn't mean you're taking a trip. The heat death of the universe is writ equally large and stagnant on the surface of the world whether you own shit or not.

The van kept running, but it seemed to be shedding parts like a tree sheds its autumn leaves. We tried to sell it. A one-armed guy tested it. Then a guy without a leg. Finally some punks solved our problem with crowbars, smashing all the windows and tearing out the dashboard. We filed off the VIN, took the plates and let the city have it.

&

SOMETIMES WE STRAYED away from our neighborhood and went east toward the lake. Lincoln Park was over there. It was a semi-bohemian neighborhood in those days, in a state of transition. Anchored by the Biograph, the Three Penny, the Body Politic, and at the south end by the Old Town School of Folk Music and Second City. There were a number of bars—Kingston Mines, Wise Fools, Katzenjammer, etc.—that made up a near north "blues scene." Up to now Tanya had been mostly a country-western woman, a latter-day Patsy Cline wannabe. However, a shift was beginning to occur in her tastes, a concession, perhaps, to the environs. I couldn't tell if she was giving up or merely mutating.

Once I had the big idea to find Mother Blues, the club where Big Brother supposedly originally played. I figured Tanya would get off on that. But that bar no longer existed and instead we ended up at Mothers, a sleazy singles pick-up joint down on Rush. They wouldn't even let us in.

The bouncer said we looked like junkies. Tanya said she was in a band, a hopeful statement.

Of course, she never did get a band together. But she kept singing. More and more she was singing blues with a guitar player named Larry King who we'd met at the Drunken Clown Lounge on Armitage. She tried to get gigs in some of the Lincoln Avenue bars. She actually got a gig singing for a couple of weeks at the Katzenjammer Bar. It wasn't really a gig, but they used to ask her back. They had a kind of open mic with a house band. You could sing there every week and, if you were good, they sometimes gave you a gig. The first couple times, Tanya did country numbers. They told her they wanted blues. Then she tried "Ball and Chain."

"You sound too much like Janis Joplin—we want Bessie Smith types here," the guy said.

"Fuck you, the place is empty," Tanya shot back.

&

I COULD ONLY speculate on the cause. Tanya had the lifestyle but not the luck, the voice but not the drive. And it was ironic that the more she approached the Joplin style the more she denied it. She saw it as an insult that people would compare her to Janis even though the comparison was increasingly obvious. Oddly, in Tanya's mind, if they were going to do it, then she would play the game, maybe even turn it on them with a vengeance.

But the problem was that she was never quite mad enough, egocentric or arrogant enough to look into the souls of others and believe she understood them. Nor was she very ambitious. She was actually rather modest and self-effacing for all her bravado. She as much as admitted to her lack of ambition and understanding, often in the same breath, as if the two were related.

"A pessimist is never disappointed and an optimist is constantly let down." I think I said that, not her. But she lived it. Another thing I noticed was that, when she sang, she started to do this leg-shaking thing that Janis did, as if by mimicking the mannerism you could somehow come to know the neurosis that drove it. She picked this up shortly after having watched the Monterey Pop Festival film.

(19)

WE BECAME REGULARS IN SOME LOCAL BARS. TANYA could shoot pool, and I gave her the nickname Fast Edna. She was best between two and five beers—that was her window. I was slower and not as clean. In reflective moods we might wax mystic about tangents, geometry, the unpredictability of the table bed, and how the universe was like a billiard game except nobody was shooting. We sometimes stole dialogue from *The Hustler*, our favorite movie. Tanya would light up a cigarette and cock her hip. "What are we gonna do, Luc, when the liquor and the money run out?" I would say something about our "contract with depravity" and we'd spill through the room laughing like drunks in lust, which we were. It was fun even if it was somewhat foreboding.

But our life wasn't really like pool; it was more like pinball. Pool requires some skill. Life is a bunch of dumbass rolling around, like the Hollis dream theory—something happens here, causing something else to happen over there. The reason you lived in this apartment and not another one was the product of three cushions and a kiss-off in your social relationships, knowing someone who knew someone who had a grudge against someone else—the cue or clue being nothing more than a tone of voice five years earlier that drove you across the street into another woman's arms, or made you lose your job.

There's logic there if you want to find it, if you break it down fine enough, but we also knew there was no reason for anything, except the need to see it that way. Otherwise the world would simply stop, people would be standing around scratching their heads. Eventually the sympathetic nervous system would give out and that would be the end of the production of goods and services—period. The god Entropy would return to the throne.

The pool table was also a way of meeting people like us. There were, after all, things we had in common with certain demographic groups. One night we were shooting and drinking at the same Lincoln Avenue bar where Tanya had been thrown out for being another Janis Joplin. She always liked to go back to the scene of her humiliations, to experience them more fully. It was like the idea of expunging evil by indulging it, as Hollis had said. Or maybe she was just a masochist. I was starting to believe she was. Or at least I was starting to pay attention to, or maybe just reinterpret certain tendencies in her.

That night, as a means of getting back at the manager, Tanya kept playing the same Joplin song over and over on the jukebox. But the manager wasn't there, so it drew the ire of the bartender instead. It also got the attention of Jack and Ruby—Jack Algiers, and Ruby "Tuesday" Beauvoir. He was Back-o-the-Yards, son of a union organizer. She was a community activist from Bronzeville. They met in Hyde Park a thousand years ago at some Yippie rally and moved uptown. They came to this joint most weeks because of Joffre Stewart's anarchist open mic.

"You play that song as much as you want! He's only going to throw you out again, anyway."

"Huh?"

"You're the girl who was singing here the other night, right?"

"Yeah, so what?"

"You in a band or something?" Ruby asked.

"No band. I just opened my mouth one day and that's what I sounded like."

"Well you sounded good, lady."

"Thanks anyway," Tanya said, not really buying the compliment.

&

WE SAT DOWN at their table, finished our beers, then went into the alley and smoked some pot. There was a partial eclipse of the moon that night, although no one seemed to be paying any attention. Celestial events couldn't compete with real entertainment, and no one had time for paganism.

I usually didn't talk much with strangers and even less so when I was stoned. Jack kept looking at me. "Frank is one of them guys who doesn't say much, isn't he, he's always there, though, watching you. He's a watcher not a talker."

Tanya came to my rescue. "He's just quiet until he knows you. Then you better watch out, 'cause he won't shut up."

Jack laughed. "Hey, check that out." He was pointing at the graffiti on the building that seemed to glow in the aura of the streetlamp, UNKNS. All is All. '76. There's your Proverbs of Hell, Jack said as we walked around the corner stoned.

We went back in the bar and caught up on the Jack Algiers and Ruby Tuesday story. They were part of a surrealist/anarchist group who put out a magazine called Pensee Sauvage. They had once been radicals—still were, in a redefined way. After Joffre's gig, most of the anarchists went home. But Jack and Ruby often stayed around to drink, like true believers. Jack had been an anarchist filmmaker. Ruby Tuesday did anarchist crafts—wine bottles wrapped in beads and string that symbolized anarchy. Her name was her brand. They also published a radical poetry broadsheet called *Jack Ruby*. As a couple, people often called them by that single name, as in: "Jack Ruby are coming by with some weed," or "I saw Jack Ruby in the council meeting the other day."

Lincoln Park had once been the kind of place where anarchists lived. But Jack Ruby didn't live in Lincoln Park anymore. They used to have a used bookshop on Southport. Now rents there were too high and, despite my experience, jobs were tough to get. Jack couldn't get a job because all the acid had irritated some dormant nerve disease. He wore dark glasses all the time to hide his eyes. Ruby refused to work for "the man." They were living on SSI and street fairs. So they moved downtown to the Croydon Hotel, a small pocket of sadness in the North Loop. We had a car so we gave them a ride.

&

THE AREA AROUND Ohio and Wells had a number of once-swank joints with piano bars that had grown either seedy or closed. The old and insane lived there now, a lot of them on SSI. The piano at the Croydon was presided over by one Frank DiAngelo, or Frankie Angel, as he called himself. He wore a sponged brown sharkskin suit straight out of an Algren novel, and a matching dishwater rug held on by visible bobby pins. 55 going on 65, he did his best to keep the memories alive on a minute income. Stray torch singers gave him a hand at this—men and women who'd spent their lives belting out the standards with that show of passion their audience craved.

There were only a few places where these people could play. They might find work in a lounge here or there, the Marriott, or the Drake, or maybe the Hilton. Most did not. It wasn't that the swank hotels lacked piano bars, they just didn't want people like this hanging around. So they walked the streets like ghosts and dropped by the Croydon every once in a while to do a guest set. They always pretended they were on their way to other gigs so they wouldn't have to stay around embarrassing themselves when the repertoire outlasted the illusion.

The male singers usually had Italian or Spanish names: Dario de Silva, or Hector Velasquez or Fernando Feliciano or Bobby Palermo. The female singers often had French names. Some were once opera singers. And there were a fair number of Lees—Charlotte Lee, Patricia Lee, Anne-Marie Lee. And they weren't related to Peggy or Brenda or Sarah either, but they didn't mind it if you thought they were.

Ruby Tuesday thought these old-style torch singers might show Tanya another path besides the country-western, rock-and-roll road of self-destruction she was on. It was an odd assumption, not only because it was simply trading one dead end for another, but it was like telling her she was washed up before she'd even started. Still we ended up going to the Croyden numerous times over the next several months. The wood was dark and the place stunk with nostalgia.

One night we dropped by. Frankie DiAngelo wasn't playing for another hour or so, so the four of us went up to Jack Ruby's pad, room #61. They had a two-room kitchenette with a walk-in closet. We got stoned and started to take an interest in minutiae: a poster here, a bandanna there, a pot pipe Hendrix had supposedly used—a picture, a parable, a past joy.

"I always thought the '70s were the '60s," I said.

"That's because you weren't there," Tanya said. "Besides, it still is the '70s."

"I mean, it was all something I watched on TV," I added.

"That's why it's over," Jack said. "The revolution *was* televised."

"I mean, it was just the news," I continued. "It had nothing to do with my life."

"Yes it did, more than you think," Jack shot back.

&

NOTHING IS WHAT it ever was, they concurred. But they had no regrets. Regrets were for cowards, even though the world had become a trick. They'd gone to California, but the "dese" and "dose" of their accents didn't sell in La-La Land. And they didn't have the right clothes. So they headed up to "liberal" Frisco, which Jack described as a masked fascist state whose entire population had been duped by the storybook color scheme into a misguided belief in their own evolutionary ascendancy. According to Jack, California was the first culture to create itself entirely from a self-generated media image. "It's all a kind of Disneyland imitating a Disneyland imitating a Disneyland, until no one knows which Disneyland they are living in anymore—the real imitation or the xerox of the imitation."

Ruby Tuesday said something about a *mis en abyme* of mediated reality. We didn't know what she was talking about, but that didn't stop her. "It's like standing in line to visit the Bohemian Village Exhibit. But if you don't buy into it, you shatter the illusion. It's this weird kind of fear. That's why we came back. No one's trying to be famous." Besides, they liked the working-class traditions: the Social Realist School, and what they called the "Night-Shift Surrealismo."

"I don't know, I like it out there better. This place is kind of dreary," Tanya said. "Sure, there's a lot of assholes out West, but that's true everywhere. Assholes are a fact of life." I never heard her say she wanted to go back, but now I wondered.

As for Jack Ruby—for years now they hadn't been west of California Avenue. Violence was changing things. Even Humboldt Park gave them the willies, what with the recent gang escalation. They liked the scene around Armitage and Halsted but they saw it being trashed by the banks. "Everything is a product," Ruby said, "even the notion of community, even individuality. Everyone's selling themselves like a new brand of candy bar to the sweet-toothed masses."

"The media is a virus. Information isn't knowledge," Jack added, "and fashion isn't thought."

"The 'left' is the worst," Ruby added, "and the best are doomed."

I heard a phone ringing. Everyone stopped talking. No one was answering. "Never pick up the phone," Jack said. "It might be the feds."

&

I DIDN'T WANT to hear a tirade, but I didn't want to be a passive ear, either, so I said, "Maybe technology *is* the Brave New World. You have to open up to it." I didn't really believe it.

And Jack wasn't buying it. "Exactly," he said. He never believed in that global village crap for a minute, except as a means of speeding up people's perceptions so they had less time to think before shopping. "Things keep going faster, man . . . . But there's nowhere to go."

"But the beat goes on," chimed Ruby.

Despite this annoying tendency to offer poetry in lieu of real conversation, it was becoming apparent these people had something going on. It didn't jibe with their graying hair, rounded shoulders and archaic mode of dress, still it was good for us—it elevated our own level of discourse, made us remember things we had read, things we used to know, or thought we knew.

Jack believed that the boomers were a sacrificial generation—that a whole generation had to be sacrificed like a chicken or a goat so that Capitalism could really get going. And, of course, they regretted the hell-bent-for-leather attitude of self-destruction that they had taken on years ago—all that hard subscription. Of course, they didn't think of it as self-destruction at the time. It was just life. Apparently a lot of their friends were dead—liver disease, syphilis, meth, motorcycle accidents. And of course Janis and Jimi and Jim died from dope.

I rolled my eyes. But Tanya bit. "You knew those people?" she exclaimed, reaching. Her tone was that of a non-believer who wanted desperately to at least pretend to believe. "You're shitting us."

No. They weren't.

"Let me show you something, honey," Ruby said. And before anyone could stop her, she'd placed several boxes of hippie memorabilia out on the table. Articles from old papers: the *Seed*, the *Barb*, the *Free Press*. Ruby, however, couldn't seem to find any picture that proved she knew anybody, but while she was looking, she happened upon an article in which Ruby Beauvoir and Miranda Conner were arrested in Madison at an anti-war sit-in—August of '66. Then everything changed.

"That's my mother!" Tanya shouted, grabbing the article, surprised and oddly perplexed, as she examined the picture.

"What? Wait! You're kidding. Right?" That was all I could get out, though I knew I should be more engaged.

"No shit. Check it out."

"Wow, Naomi's your mother? Wow. We were in jail together," Ruby said.

"Cool," Tanya said.

"So Tanya, you're Teresa?" Jack interjected.

"Yeah, changed my name, couple years ago."

Ruby Tuesday laughed. "So did your mom, she changed her name all the time. We were afraid of the FBI."

Tanya sat there quietly. I took the picture out of her hand and looked at it.

"Christ we must have met you when you were like five years old, man," Jack added. "Harry and Naomi drove out in that old Rambler wagon. Remember, babe? And Steven? What's with him? Is your dad still writing? I think we even have a copy of his book around here somewhere. What's the name of that book, Rube?"

"*Consumption and Revolution*, no *Consuming Revolution*, yeah that was it."

"I can't believe this shit." Tanya was excited and exasperated at the same time.

"So did she ever come back from Calcutta, man?" asked Jack. "We haven't heard anything in years."

"She's in North Africa . . . Tunisia."

"Oh, we heard she went to India, you know, to get her head together."

"Yeah, like she was starting to lose it, you know, paranoia, depression, all that shit. That was the rumor anyway. Who knows? She always took

134

things too seriously."

"I never heard that," Tanya said, surprised.

"You know, Tan," I said, "your dad said something to me about it. That she was having psychological problems."

"Thanks for telling me, asshole." She seemed genuinely pissed.

"Sorry, I thought he was making it up."

"Makes sense, though. Dad always thought she was nuts. Who the fuck knows? Everybody lies."

"Yes they do," Ruby added, then she went on: Naomi had stayed at that apartment on Page in Frisco for a while. She apparently knew Kristofferson, the Angels, Neuwirth. She was at Pepperland. She knew Peggy Caserta and Donovan, too.

During a lot of that time Tanya was growing up with Harry—so of course she hated Naomi for that, for missing out on all that, even though, at the same time, she loved her for being who she was.

"Shit, I could have even met Janis Joplin when I was a kid. Wow, what do you think?"

"Maybe, man. Hey, I think you actually did. Why not?" For his part, Jack hated Janis. "She's a bitch if you ask me. You didn't miss nothing."

"Nobody is asking you," said Ruby.

Ruby claimed Jack was an asshole back then because he took way too much speed. Naomi's friend Walter was getting it from a guy named Manzoni who used to manufacture acid and then switched to crystal meth when the scene turned south. A lot of their crowd got strung out.

"Is that Anzo's dad, the guy I met out in LA?" I asked.

"Yeah, must be." Tanya said.

"That kid's still alive?" Jack asked. Tanya and I nodded.

Ruby changed the subject. "It's funny but when I heard you sing the other night, you reminded me a little of her."

"People always say I remind them of Janis. I'm sick of it."

Ruby did a double take. "No, I didn't mean her, I meant your mother."

If it was backpedaling, it worked. Tanya would rather remind people of her mother. Jack and Ruby were practiced at quick conciliation, and part of the technique was to backpedal easily or change topics seamlessly.

"So, what's up with Steven now?"

"He's married, I bet," Ruby said. Then she got up out of her chair to empty an ashtray.

"Yeah, he is. I saw him at the wedding a few years ago. Other than that I don't know. I mean, now I think he has a job, or he's teaching college or something. We're not that close." Tanya was distracted—she was studying the article, lighting one cigarette with another.

"Speaking of North Africa . . . ." Jack brought out the map to tell us about their trip to Tangier, six or seven years earlier. On the way, they passed through Algeria. It was only a few years after independence. The mood was high. Jack was totally into it, he even changed his name because of it.

"Bliss it was in that hour to be alive, but to be young was very heaven," Jack recited.

"Get over it," Ruby said, and went back to the map. They had traced their path in red ink from Marrakech to Tunis, which Jack pointed out had once been Carthage, where St. Augustine lived.

"Tunis—*that's* where my mother is," said Tanya. "It's Tunis."

"Cool, man." Jack went on—they had been tracking down this Sufi mystic who played music that caused perpetual insomnia. Once you heard it you would never sleep again. It just kept playing in your head, lifting and driving you toward some kind of spiritual exhaustion—kind of like an advertising jingle but with a more noble purpose.

"I don't get it. It's hard enough to sleep as it is," I said. "Why would you look for it?"

"Precisely, you can't sleep. So there might as well be some point to not sleeping. I spent a lot of sleepless nights trying to figure it out man." Jack broke out laughing. Ruby Tuesday was laughing, too.

Tanya just kept saying, "I can't fucking believe it. I can't fucking believe it."

&

I WAS BEGINNING to like these people. They left me feeling a little unsettled. But then most people left me feeling unsettled—that was no reason not to like them. Jack went on to explain how he'd started out a Socialist, went on to Communism, and then somewhere along the line he met a Social Darwinist who turned him into Anarchist. But before he was an Anarchist he had always been an Artist—first a poet, then a filmmaker. But he gave up filmmaking and turned to photography. Then he abandoned that and took up philosophy and neuroses. These days he was retracing the maze, trying to pin down his personality, which he thought he had lost. And the medication was helping.

Then Ruby showed us some of her anarchist wine bottles. They were based on Haitian voodoo bottles but were meant to be used as Molotov cocktails when the revolution came down. But it didn't come down so she called them art instead and began vending at street fairs. She used to write articles for the underground press, too, mostly music reviews. She started looking through the box to find some.

Meanwhile Jack had reels of film documenting their wild hippie adventures. Fortunately their projector was broken. But there *were* photos—some in a big portfolio—pictures of men standing on street corners, road-shoulders: hitchhikers, hobos, flower sellers. It was a study, Jack said, for a book he was gonna do called *St. Francis Descending the Staircase*. Carl Solomon was supposed to write the text. Jack had dropped the project though, but now he was interested again, probably because he didn't have anything else to do.

"Cool, man, what's it about?" Tanya was into it.

Ruby answered for him. "It's based on an old traditional story of a man who can't die because he's fated to wander the world forever, haunted by sin and unlived dreams." There was just the tiniest hint of sarcasm to her tone.

Jack said he had gotten the idea from Duchamp and just run with it. The thing was that the soul descends the staircase into planes of lesser and lesser resolution. We begin in some primal unresolved grainy plane, like a bad photograph in which everything was true and possible. But in this, our loaded and focused state, we bear the burden of uncertainty. "It's about giving up possessions," he said. "It's like, when you become aware of your ego, it's like that wrenching of the nerves, you feel yourself waking from the fluidity of a dream."

"Cool."

I didn't know if Tanya was really following him. She saw something in it, though, and that was enough. I myself felt some contradiction, but I couldn't quite figure out what it was. But I was confused to begin with, partly because we were pretty wacked. But according to Jack, one day we would return to that mist, and it would be like all the ghosts of wandering souls going backwards and blending together again into some kind of utopian mind, the original collectivity or singularity.

"It's about reclaiming potential," said Ruby. "Changeability as power."

"It's all very Blakeanesque, man," Jack added. "The fragmented soul searching to bring itself together in the war within the self."

&

I WONDERED IF it wasn't rather an elaborate excuse for doing nothing, for never becoming a complete person. You could say that to over-define yourself was somehow to defy God or the spirit of creativity. I didn't say it quite like that. But I said something. I know I did, because Jack answered. But first he scratched his chin, "If that were true, it might explain the kind of eternal adolescence of the culture, as if the capitalist perpetuation of "want" was actually something holy. Or at least we were supposed to think so."

"That's exactly what I mean," I said.

"Oh yeah, right," said Tanya, "like you have any idea what we're talking about."

"Hey I hope *he* does, 'cause I know I don't," Jack added, laughing.

"No really, it was!" I stuck to my guns. I had nothing to lose after all.

"Maybe the real reality is actually more solid than we are. Maybe we're more like the xeroxes, man, hundredth-generation photocopies, and the originals are lost."

Ruby Tuesday put it her way. "Yeah. All these people you meet—you need them. It's like collecting baseball cards. You look at them to remember what you forgot."

I agreed, at least at the time. Because as the waves of cannabis rolled through my veins I was actually beginning to feel a little like a bastardized photocopy myself. I had no idea what the original picture had been. In a way, it was a relief. I had nothing to live up to.

"For every St. Francis, there's a Manson, for every Kerouac, a Speck," Ruby added. "Convictions turn to paranoia. That's the curse of the liberal imagination. Without God, the beatniks became hippies and the hippies became entrepreneurs." Ruby didn't go on to say who her God was, but she obviously had less faith in the human soul than her husband did.

"That may well be true," Jack answered, "After all, the tigers of wrath are wiser than the horses of instruction."

"I don't follow," I said.

"The road of excess leads to wisdom," Jack continued.

Ruby stood up, "Here we go," she said.

"Heavy cat, heavy cat," Jack mumbled as he nodded to himself, well pleased with his literary allusions.

&

IT HAD GOT to the point we had no idea what we were saying. But we just kept saying things anyway. "I can't fucking believe you guys knew my mother," Tanya said again and again.

Then the phone rang.

"Watch this," Jack said as he picked it up. "See, there's no one on the line."

"That's been happening a lot these days," I said.

"That's because there's nobody out there. No one alive, anyway." Ruby Tuesday started whistling the theme from the Twilight Zone.

Silence followed, accompanied by a gigantic heartbeat that seemed to enclose the room. The discomfort grew until Jack had to get out of his chair. He tripped on the lamp cord pulling the plug out of the wall and accidentally knocking his glass off the table at the same time. The glass broke. A Doors' song was playing in another room down the hotel hall, something about a killer on the highway, and the danger of the strange.

Jack went, "Wow, man," and winked. He loved serendipity.

In the light from the window, he looked like a completely different person—a rapist, a child pornographer. It was as if this world were one side of a coin. On the other side everybody was different. On the other side Jack was a pervert, a serial killer, a sick fuck, and Ruby was a conjurer, a whore. I was a snake-oil salesman and Tanya was the Harvard scholar writing her dissertation on chaos theory and the fact that the four of us were together, at this exact moment in this exact hotel room. It was scary for a second.

Jack wrestled the plug back in the socket and everything was all right. Electricity saved us. By now we realized we'd been upstairs in their room for over two hours. "Hey, let's go back down to the bar."

"Yeah, I'm ready for a scotch and soda," Ruby enthused. It was a good idea, too. Jack and Ruby gazed at each other. You could see the love like a rope of barbed time binding them. They tugged on it playfully. Me and Tanya didn't have a rope. So we went down to the piano bar to listen to Frankie Angel.

Ruby told me that Frankie's name, DiAngelo, was made-up. He wasn't Italian. He was really Polish. Then she switched the subject to herself. She was African–American, but part French—an atheist. But Jack was a pagan. His real name was Starkweather. Jack Starkweather. He had changed the last name for obvious reasons.

Tanya brought up the fact that I was named after St. Francis, like Jack's art project.

"You Protestant or Catholic?" Jack Starkweather asked.

"Neither," I said. "Hindu, maybe. Or gnostic." They were unfazed. "I'm joking. But I do believe in multiple personalities." We laughed.

I was staring at a picture of Lazarus on the wall. At some point I realized most of my dialogue was really a monologue taking place in my head. We were listening to another Frank, one Frankie Angel, singing that old standard, "Once Upon a Time." It was a weird world. We thought we liked it. But it was also late, so we got up to go.

"Safe home," said Ruby Tuesday, going for hugs all around.

Jack shouted, "Stay crooked baby, keep to the crooked roads!"

"I know, I know. But we gotta go, anyway," I said.

"But you know what I'm talking about? Right Babe?"

"Right. See you later." We started out the door.

"Later, Jack." I said.

"Take it easy, Frank. You too, Honey. Call us," Ruby called out.

Frankie Angel shouted, "See ya kids," as he adjusted his wig. We were all laughing now. Laughing at the Croydon way back in 1977.

(20)

I FOUND THE MAPS AT AMVETS ON MILWAUKEE AVE. IT WAS JUST A couple days after the Croydon affair. They were stacked in a broken blue shoebox held together with rubber bands and twine, sitting on a shelf next to some old shoes, a bundle of *Life* magazines, and a line of once-futuristic chrome coffee percolators straight out of the Jetsons. I bought the whole box for a dollar—nearly 50 *National Geographics*, most with maps, mostly of the US, but also South America, Europe, Africa, Asia, and something called the Theater of War. Someone's old uncle had no doubt collected these for years, along with boxes of receipts, great gaudy wide ties, and garbage bags of sports coats. You could smell the old dead uncle odor of moldering dreams.

We were mostly interested in the US maps. The oldest of these went back to the '40s, before super highways—a time of small towns and actual regional differences, before everyone watched the same TV shows surrounded by the same furniture they bought at the same stores. It was interesting how the color and style of the maps changed with printing technology, history, and the country's sense of itself. A 1940s map, for instance, had a certain innocence, all the states were the same color, the names of cities were printed smaller because they weren't as important, and you could almost sense the danger and strangeness of the land. The later ones were more colorful, aggressive and cluttered with a sort of strained emphasis on boundaries, as if in ironic reaction to the increasing sameness.

We picked 1947. I covered Tanya's eyes while she circled the tip of a pocketknife over it like the diviner on a Ouija board, finally letting the tip rest on a supposedly arbitrary spot that ended up being Kansas, as if the knifepoint were drawn by the magnetic aura of the cliché that existed in our minds. We let the process work itself out, concocting in our imaginations a scene derived from album-cover art, Norman Rockwell, Edward Hopper, Thomas Hart Benton, *The Wizard of Oz* and *The Grapes of Wrath*.

It would be a gas station or a Howard Johnson's somewhere out there on the terra incognito of pre-TV, post-war America. Kerouac, that king of road clichés, is gassing up the Oldsmobile at a Sinclair station outside Lawrence. Meanwhile, Humbert Humbert is off buying ice cream while Neal Cassady puts the make on the kidnapped nymph, Dolores Haze. Simone de Beauvoir is having a cheeseburger in the diner next door, as she watches from the window and jots down notes about brutish American mannerisms. John Steinbeck is walking Charlie in the parking lot. According to what we read or believed, all these people could have been crossing this spot in 1947. Andy Warhol might have liked such a moment, but he would have been just a teenager then, and besides it's really his absence that gives the scene its power. Such things may very well happen, but once the trick of second-hand consciousness is introduced, it acts like a virus.

Now according to the laws of equilibrium and the heat death of the universe, it is the nature of things that they should become, over time, all alike. I knew there had been a time when there was difference. We hear it in stories. We see it in old world cartographic representations of pitching ships held thrall to wind roses and the fins of sea monsters. Unexplored coastlines, interior regions populated by Troglodytes, Turks, Mongols and Tartars. Tanya and I substituted our own cheesy post-card exoticism: the Hillbillies of the Blue Ridge. The mysterious Hassidim of New York. Amish and Quakers of Indiana and Pennsylvania. The terrifying Satan Worshippers of the Midwest. Cajuns who lived in over-wrought swamps. Forest dwellers called Rainbow People.

Despite our jokes, the maps exerted their fascination. We spent hours enthusing over place names: Paris, Fez, Prague and Calcutta, Madrid and Marrakech. We could go! We could go mostly because we were young and we were drunks and drinking produces dreams. All we needed was ambition. And money. Those unholy friends. Once Tanya saw an ad in a Sierra Club magazine for a pontoon boat trip on the Rio Negro. On a whim we got passports, a major act of faith for people like us.

But there was more to these maps than celebration or county-fair adventurism. It was a quality of absence, and the idea that distance and vagary could lend a certain transporting quality to a landscape, a process of abstraction which, taken to its extreme, leads to the map—flat, pragmatic, empty, but capable, in a perverse twist, of providing a screen upon which one could project any number of geographical fantasies— suggesting but never really presenting, surrendering itself in fragments to the interested party. Indeed the map could seem to undress haltingly before the would-be traveler, with that slow anticipatory thrill that might be felt by shy teenagers alone in an attic, with a bare mattress, a pint of Southern Comfort, and a single condom—an eroticism based on possibility which could seem more intense at times than TV or rock-and-roll, because it was still undefined by images.

It seemed like something was happening to me and Tanya, something that was both splendid and disturbing, and somehow related to these seemingly arbitrary events. It is said that early humans projected the form of the body upon the landscape in order to define it—the fingers of lakes, the foothills of mountains, etc. But what if it's really the other way? What if those rivers, ravines, peaks and forests have been slowly twisting, wrenching, and pressing out over the course of millennia, this human body with its veins, intestines, cleavage, gardens and lagoons? Of course, both are true—the anthropo- and the terrapo-morphic. The path of causality morphs both ways—forms interpenetrate. Ancient seashells can be found in the stone of skyscrapers, and the bones of the hand can be seen in the mountain's flank.

Now I know I'm pushing this metaphor beyond its actual capacity. But I'm trying to get at some idea. See, I won't say that these maps became a perversion. I won't say that we spread them around the bed like porn magazines, or used them as aphrodisiacs. But for some reason their presence did reawaken our sexual life. In part, I suppose, because they made it seem bigger than us: part of the world. And that made us more interested in exploring it, finding in the act that same kind of sublime transport found in the sight of a forested gorge, a waterfall, or a thunderstorm by the sea.

I sometimes thought of it, or remembered it, in terms of light—the moon breaking around the rim of a cloud, flooding the land with a soft pallor, providing that same kind of exquisite wash across the body that affection can produce, as I might remember Tanya's body on any number of outdoor occasions. Tracing my finger across her hip or shoulder brought to mind a cool night in a mountain glen or a desert way station. The smell of wheat or swamp water on her breath recalled the highway's flanks. The rumblings of her stomach remembered impending rain. The smallest details took on a certain grandeur, as our bodies became huge with shared history, which of course included the ravages of war, old needle marks and minefields, indistinguishable at times from the scars of childhood accidents. But that shared history was both a bond and a detonating device.

&

ONE NIGHT, DRIVING over the Chicago Skyway, the moonlight on the jagged red landscape of the Eastside seemed to press a question, which she picked up on. Tanya turned suddenly and uncharacteristically asked if I really loved her, and I said I did. She replied only that she hoped I would "remember." It was a somewhat foreboding response. Perhaps I had been over-anxious to admit to it. But then I couldn't deny it either. I didn't know if I meant it, but I wanted to. If I didn't mean it, it wouldn't be the first time, but it might have been the easiest. If I did mean it, I didn't necessarily know it. I knew about fantasy. But I didn't understand how dangerous words were. And since I didn't know what I wanted out of life I might have said anything. But just by having these thoughts, I was confusing myself.

Later that night we decided to go to a movie. Kubrick's *Lolita* was playing at the Parkway. We liked it, even though we had seen it before. Afterwards we got a six-pack. Since it was becoming our habit to imitate classic movie scenes, we settled down on the bed and unfolded one of the more recent highway maps. We decided to trace our journey up to now, just as Jack Ruby had done on their map of Africa. And just as Sue Lyons had done in the film, we traced a path in lipstick. Starting from Portland, we followed the roads we could remember, passing through towns that had faces and events attached. The ancient grocery in the pine forest with its bottles of pickled ears. The laughing man with the metal foot. It was funny how much you could remember with a graph to hang it on. I hadn't realized how haphazard our travels had been until I looked at the result—something like the sketch of a mad child or a drunk trying to write the word "desire" with a shaking hand that finally skids off the page. But that's all right.

I've read that one aspect of love is the way it allows for the compression of time, and by projection, a concentration of experience—so that the accumulation of years can be refined into a few hours of ritual. I won't go on to describe the acts that followed that evening except to say the red line of the lipstick moved off the paper and into our imagination, its continuity breaking up periodically into brief arcs like bird wings in the mist. You can't see anything. There's no direction. And no sound either except for inarticulate cries and questions that always seem to be moving away. And there's nothing to do for it but to follow them.

&

IT WAS A week later, I think, that Tanya's brother, Steven, came to town for a visit, actually sort of a reconnaissance mission for the Sandman family. In contrast to his sister, Steven was supposed to have made something of his life, but no one could quite figure out what it was. Certainly he was an achiever—an odd combination of perpetual student, proto-corporate go-getter and apostate liberal. He'd been going to school for probably eight or nine years with no end in sight. And now he seemed to be involved in some kind of marketing job. He was in Chicago for a trade show or a convention in one of those big halls where people who looked like him could walk around freely. Him and his wife, Ely, were staying with friends on the north side. We met up with him twice. Once in a bar. Another time he stopped by our place in Humboldt Park. We never met his wife.

I quickly learned he was Steven, never Steve. Tanya called him Stevie. He was well-put together with the button-down pressed threads of a Young Republican—mustache and sideburns never less than immaculate, groomed like the suburban yard of a Doris Day movie; you could have set up wicker furniture, umbrellas and a swimming pool alongside his facial hair and no one would have given it a second thought. No one ever saw Steven naked or get-down funky. He was either your ideal college roommate or your worst nightmare. There was a feeling of strained containment about him—displeasure and unease.

Steven had a greater affinity to Harry than to Naomi, but he was far less liberal than Harry, with rationalism being his dark side. He liked to sum the world up in terms of Darwin and Hobbes. It's natural and evolutionarily beneficial to want to make money. Weak people, those who got fucked over, deserved it. Life was nasty, brutish and short, etc., etc. Still in homage to the family's liberal tradition, he balanced his can-do American greed with acts of grace as he ladled soup to the Milwaukee homeless on Saturday afternoons. But you can't mix Ayn Rand with Weekend Liberalism, and his tightly controlled personality tics eventually became visible for the mask they were. He tried to shore up the fragile facade with some proto-new-age-psychobabble, but this only exposed his familiarity with AA, perhaps as another victim of Naomi's drinking gene.

But that was over now. He had wedding pictures to prove it. The wedding took place before I met Tan. There was a picture of her in a bridesmaid outfit singing with the wedding band, probably doing "Proud Mary." Harry was there. Naomi was not. If Steven was less enthusiastic about Naomi, it was for that reason. She was in Calcutta at the time. Not Tunis. Steven hadn't wanted to postpone the marriage till some indeterminate date of her return. He needed to shore up his "respectable" life as soon as possible. His wife's family would be there, along with plenty of representatives from the Naomi world. We looked at his pictures. Tanya showed him our passports.

"Going on a trip?" he asked.

"We're going to the Amazon," Tanya said, laughing. It was a laugh that showed she didn't really believe it was going to happen.

Steven looked around at the cans and bottles littering the floor. "I hope they sell beer down there in the jungle." Maybe he thought a case a day between two people was too much.

"It looks worse than it is," I said.

"Hmmm. You know Dad wouldn't mind if you called. Mom will be back from India soon and he wants to have some kind of get-together out there. I think he's trying to heal the rifts before the divorce gets ugly."

"Oh, it's not ugly now?"

"Well, we don't have to make it worse. Sometimes you have to be part of the family."

"Uh-huh. Uh-huh. You know, as far as that goes, there's a rumor around that you're only my half-brother anyway, which means I should listen to you only half the time."

"C'mon Teresa, don't start that shit. Besides you know they both want this, so we should stay out of it."

"I'm not starting any shit or anything else, Stevie. You know as well as me what I'm talking about. You know they're hiding something. I think Dad would just blurt it out, like, what does he care anyway. He could get back at her that way, but somehow Mom has power over him."

"I don't know how, she's never around."

"It's always, you know, 'One of these days we're gonna sit down and talk.' But that day never comes. And another thing, man, maybe you know—did mom go nuts, Stevie? Is that why she went to India? We met some people who said she did."

"Teresa, you know her as well as me."

"That's just it, I don't."

"I think she got depressed or fed up or something. Crazy, I doubt it."

"Maybe you should let this be, talk to your mother, Tan," I said.

"You know something Luc? Why don't you just stay the fuck out of it? You don't know anything about it anyway."

"What the hell, what are you turning on me for?"

"What about it, Luc? Do you think I don't know about your fucking around? I could smell it on you, and you stunk like hell in Portland. Shit. Men are all alike."

Steven didn't want any of this, but I needed to keep him in it. I nodded to him with a secret "men-are-all-alike" bonding nod. And we *were* all alike, at least in our disinclination to deal with hysterical women. Still, I was freaked out and quickly tried to change the subject. Tanya seemed equally willing. Somehow we managed to short-circuit the rest of the argument and headed over to the White Castle on Milwaukee for some local color. Two days later, Steven was gone.

I felt sorry for Tanya. She had really wanted to impress him, not threaten him. She just didn't know how. Plus the combination of various pressures—what was beginning to seem like an unwanted long-term commitment to me, Steven's delivery of the suitcase full of buried family issues—it was all starting to increase her sense of self-doubt.

"I guess that's it. I'm a middle-aged chick with a drinking problem, and a fucked-up family." I didn't know how she could feel middle aged at twenty-four, but a lot of people do. But then just her saying so made the tiny flecks of grey in her hair more prominent. "All I wanted was something besides bowling alleys and drive-ins."

"I know. I know."

"But maybe I'm fooling myself. I guess at bottom it's all a big joke, ain't it? Well, whatever it is, just let it happen, that's all I got to say. Let's have a toast. To anarchy, autonomy, automatism, whatever."

&

AND THAT'S WHAT we did, we opened the door and invited anarchy in for a party. The plans that connected her and me and made us crave the future began to degenerate. Increasingly, they gave way to the drinking that inspired them. And, finally, the plans disappeared altogether and only the drinking remained. She had her bars and I had mine. Soon we had different groups of friends. I started staying away in the evenings. Some nights I'd stumble onto the el train and pass out, not waking up till morning. It was hard to explain. We hung out with Jack Ruby a couple times but that didn't take the edge off. Besides I think we started to make them nervous. There's nothing worse than hanging out with a couple that doesn't get along.

One night I gave Tan a call from the Old Town Tap. She was going to a party. She wasn't asking me along. The next day she cut the tip of her thumb off with a butcher knife because she was drunk, taking shots in the walk-in with the pastry chef, a vet named Eddie. I met her at the emergency room. Eddie was there. Tanya got fired. I told her maybe she should use the opportunity to go back to California—it might be good for her. We could reconnoiter later. I told her she was never meant to live the tied-down life. I made it sound like a compliment.

"This isn't for me, Luc. It's for you. You know that. Me, I gotta go on doing it the way I see it. I ain't got no choice but to take it as it comes. You start worrying about cholesterol and cirrhosis . . . I'm not like that. I'm not planning anything. I gotta get it now, not later."

She was right. The truth was I'd had enough, and I was calling on the highway to save me. After all, this was America, nobody stayed anywhere, nobody knew their neighbors, and people didn't miss you when you were gone. You could make it work for you.

&

AS LUCK WOULD have it, some old friends of ours from New Orleans were passing through, Kyle and Jamie. They weren't stopping long so we made some arrangements that Tanya should go back to California with them—supposedly to hash things out with her father. The four of us ran around for a couple days. Then they all hitched out to the coast. I got a postcard from somewhere outside Salinas. It had a giant artichoke on it and an address in Santa Cruz. I never wrote. Maybe I was shallow. Maybe I was cold. I know I *was* surprised at how quick the break-up had been— zip-less, ghostlike.

"Nothing makes the great spirit laugh harder than a man with plans." I read that. One should, however, be careful about shopping at the K-Mart of convenient epiphanies. Besides there's a difference between owning and using, and unused epiphanies are like unread books: you can browse the spines but you don't know why you bought them. And wasn't it Uncle Remus who wrote that telling parable of the man who collects antique straight razors—it's a riddle, see, he either goes to trade shows and shakes the hands of fellow collectors, or he stays home and slashes his wrists. That may be true. But it was Ross McDonald who said, "Human beings are just too damn adaptable for their own good." That's definitely true.

(21)

IWAS DOING MY OLD "WAKING UP IN A ROOM AND NOT KNOWING how I got there" bit. Some time had passed that I wasn't able to account for. The decade had changed for one thing. Tanya wasn't around anymore. I took stock of the room—stove, refrigerator, a copy of *Down and Out in Paris and London,* a duffle bag, partially packed, with some folded clothes next to it. A cigarette was smoldering in an ashtray, I could hear it. The phone was still ringing, I could smell it. The prostitutes down on Lawrence Avenue seemed to be aware of it as well. They were looking up at my window, waiting for me to answer that smell. The moon was in an evil phase. There was a bruise on my leg.

There was a large folding table covered with paper in the left-hand corner of the room. On it sat an old Underwood typewriter and some maps. The chair was positioned so you could see the graveyard if you were sitting down. There was a hole in the paper right in the middle of a sentence. "As I came down the impassable rivers . . . ." The page looked old—not faded, just old. There was no way to make out where the sentence was headed. Apparently the carriage had frozen and whatever followed got typed into the void.

I pulled the paper out, folded it and put it in my wallet. Then I looked in the mirror. I might have looked older, but I couldn't be sure. My fingers found a thin cut under my left ear. A nerve was twitching in my cheek, and I seemed to be winking at myself—a tic I must have picked up somewhere along the line. A truck started up in the street outside to remind me that the world had been, and would go on without me.

&

I BRUSHED MY teeth for the first time in two days and felt reasonably virtuous. Then I got a beer out of the refrigerator. The phone was ringing again, so I answered it.

It was Jack Starkweather Algiers. The Doors song, "Roadhouse Blues," was playing in the background. Other than this unlikely clairvoyance, he had not changed.

"What's your road, man? Holyboy road, madman road, serial killer road? Frank! How's it going?"

"All right, already. What's up?"

Him and Ruby wanted to meet the next night.

"What night would that be?" I tried to phrase it as a joke, like I had a hangover or something, but I really needed to know.

"You know, Thursday. We want to hear about your trip. We have some news for you too, from Tanya."

"Good news or bad news?" I asked sarcastically.

"No. Really, we heard from her."

"Tanya?" I didn't know if I wanted any kind of news.

"Yeah. We'll tell you when we see you. Glad to be back?"

"Yeah, sure. By the way, how'd you know I *was* back . . . and where to find me?"

"You left a message at our old place, remember? Jimmy gave us a call."

I didn't remember. "Seems like ages," I said, then I faked a yawn like my memory was clouded by sleep. "You moved? Where to?"

"Yeah, we got out of that old hotel, man. The depression has passed."

"How long has it been, anyway?"

"Year and a half. No. More than that. You been gone awhile."

"I guess so."

"The last postcard was back in July I think."

"And where was that from?" I asked. "I don't even remember."

Jack repeated the question to someone in the room with him.

"Paris." Ruby Tuesday said from the background.

I felt a sense of relief.

"'Epiphany in Paris,' remember? That's what you wrote. It was funny. I thought it was a joke. Man you *are* out of it. Go back to sleep."

I had one of those flashes that usually only occur in movies. Quick cuts of scenes from another life. The *rue de Maison Dieu*, a woman in a scarlet dress with a briefcase, a distant explosion. This was followed by a vague feeling that something had happened around me that I didn't understand.

"It'll be good to see you," I said. "Let's get together tomorrow night at the Katzenjammer. Around nine?"

"That place is closed man. Went out of business. Let's meet at . . . uh, Body Politic. You remember, right?"

We hung up. A year and a half. I had some catching up to do. Problem is you need to know where you are in order to go back to where you've been. You can then extrapolate an identity from there. I went back to the window. I was on Lawrence and Dover, that was certain. The same old place. I was looking out at the same old St. Boniface tombstones. Same odd ragged overcoat stranger leaning against the graveyard wall. I didn't know how it could be possible but I decided to celebrate the continuity. There just happened to be a half a bottle of bourbon on the window ledge.

I took a drink and decided not to do anything for the next 24 hours. Then the phone rang. Apparently my decisions didn't count for much.

&

I HOOKED UP with Jack Ruby at the Body Politic. I don't think they had changed clothes during the whole time I was gone. But they had both lost weight. Jack stood up and gave me a hug, then went off to the bar. They didn't have a lot of time either—some film screening to attend. Everybody was busy in this new world.

"So babe, what's up?" Jack set three cold brown bottles of Old Style on the table. The bottles looked nervous, sweating.

"You know as well as me, man."

"Good to see ya," he said as we all clinked bottles.

"So what's the news?" asked Ruby.

"Nothing. How about you?"

"Plenty man.

I broke it off. "So, you heard from Tan?"

"Oh yeah. We heard from Tanya. She's still out west, Oxnard. She's getting a band together. She's doing all right, I guess."

"How'd you hear?"

"She wrote to us. It was a while ago, actually almost a year, while you were gone."

"That's all? What else she say?" They looked at each other, deciding who was going to tell me.

"She wanted us to tell you . . . your friend John died. Said you'd want to know."

"Who?"

"John . . . what was his name . . . Squares, Squires, somebody from Oregon. She said you knew him."

I went along with it. "Oh yeah. The apple-picking guy." Tanya always considered people good friends whom I thought of as mere acquaintances. It was a different scale of friendship—the barroom scale.

"I guess he died out in Portland. It would have been about seven months ago now."

"From what?

"Pneumonia, something like that."

I looked confused.

"We thought you were keeping in touch with her."

Ruby's hair was a little longer, a little greyer. Otherwise she looked the same. Jack had grown a beard. It suited him, made him seem less middle-aged, more professorial in carriage, more the international radical that he always saw himself as being. He was still wearing dark glasses. And the bar was dark so I don't know how he could see.

"I haven't spoken to her in awhile, actually."

"You are out of it man. All that Amsterdam hash, huh?" They laughed.

At first I thought it was odd that they would bring up Tanya, since they knew we had broke up. But then to them we were always a couple, always would be, never individuals.

"How *was* Amsterdam, man?"

"Amsterdam was good," I said.

"You got any pictures?"

I thought that was an odd thing to ask. "No. I never use cameras," I replied. "Depletes the soul."

Ruby opened a tin of aspirin and took a couple. Apparently she had what seemed to be a perpetual headache and her mind wandered constantly.

"You look bad," she said. "You okay?"

I didn't know, maybe it was the cold wind running around in my head. Maybe she'd caught a whiff of that. Maybe it reminded her of some kind of cosmic malaise.

"It's nothing," I said, even though I was about to pass out.

"You didn't pick up a habit over there, did you?"

"No. I'm fine, but I need to go home, I'm exhausted. Sorry. I didn't realize I was so tired."

"But you've been back for two weeks. Maybe you got a bug in Morocco or something."

"I know. I don't get it either. Maybe."

"Hey man, no pressure. We were just anxious. There's been a lot of trouble around here."

"What? What kind?"

They looked at each other again. "Nothing man. We're just tying up some loose ends, in case we have to leave town. We'll tell you later. Get some rest. We gotta be somewhere anyway."

"Oh yeah, there's going to be an opening over at Randolph Street. They're gonna show some films. Some of my stuff, too. Charles Tucker will be there. He was an old friend of Naomi's, and rumor is she's coming to town to see him. You should come with us. You might meet her."

"When?"

"Next week. Thursday. From five on. Can you remember?"

"Okay. Yeah. I'll definitely be there."

"Call us in a few. Oh, listen, you know we moved. Here's our new number." Jack handed me a business card that read, "Free Jack Algiers." I started to ask, but stopped myself.

I got back to my apartment and stared at the wall, the blank wall at the end of the journey that had begun at a blank wall. I felt like a clown in a parenthetical set of blank walls, jumping up and down with a glass in my hand. The glass wasn't doing it, so I took some pills. I don't even know how I got those. They were waiting for me on the kitchen table when I got back, like little clowns.

"C'mon Luc, eat us," they said.

So I did. I ate them.

&

I DON'T REMEMBER exactly where it was, I think at the corner of Division and Milwaukee; I stopped suddenly as a car went by in slow motion. The radio was playing—"Piece of My Heart." It would be tempting to call it coincidence, but it was more like an aura. It only goes to show, you can go do whatever you want or you can stand in one place. It's the same.

I was having a lot of thoughts and I wanted to think they were revelations. There was a good chance that I knew these thoughts all along but had chosen to ignore them. The world had grown away from me and I didn't like it. So I put my alienation down to the second-hand nature of life in our time—that we only experienced things through windows. See, we like to think reality is changed by our being there, changed from a free autonomous event into an obligatory one, begrudgingly living up to our expectations. But reality doesn't play that game, or rather it doesn't do that except in the minds of sociopaths. And I wasn't ready to go there yet.

(22)

SOMETIMES THE SPEED WORKS FOR YOU. SOMETIMES YOU'RE left behind. The latter is my usual state. It was the early 1980s. Reagan was president. Subtle changes had taken place in certain Chicago neighborhoods. Where sausage-eaters once gossiped on stoops, you now saw well-dressed kids sneaking into condos with bags of arugula from Treasure Island. Early in the morning you could see people running in the street—and they weren't running away from anything. Cheap nihilism could be made to turn a profit. Once again it seemed there was a future that the working world could strive for.

I decided to change my entire life for the nine hundred and ninety-ninth time. I started hanging out in the West Lakeview scene—punks, poets, painters and drunks. I also took a job working for some lackey in a company full of lackeys. It was new for me—a real job. And I sold the '69 BSA Lightning too. I could have paraded it around or worn it like an expensive watch, but I had no place to keep it except the sidewalk where parts seemed to disappear daily. Fights started in its vicinity for no apparent reason. Perhaps it reminded people of their own stalled dreams. I ripped off the buyer too. Jed was his name, my new friend Maddy's friend. I told Jed it ran. It didn't. Actually it did. But it wouldn't for long, and I knew it. Bad crank. But Jed got back at me. He introduced me to Isabella who introduced me to Eddie, and that's how I met Sarah Townshend. It's a long story.

See, this guy Jed gave me a ride home in his pickup, and we stopped by this woman's apartment in Wicker Park for drinks. Her name was Isabella Yoon Yi, an Art Institute girl with all the requisite fashion baggage. She was Italian, Chinese and Korean with jet-black hair, skin like cream and a body that justified nearly any transgression. Something in her blood could buckle a man's knees from across the room while his brain fizzled and misfired. And she liked that—she liked to watch men decay. Tough-minded American romantics were quivering in jail for her, for some crime they could barely remember. I was sure I wasn't gonna be one of them.

"I've always wanted to know someone named Isabella," I said. It was a bad line. I laughed.

"Well now you do." Her tone indicated I might get to know more.

But that was just her tone—nothing ever came to pass, which was all right. With women like that, even if you're the man of the hour, you're still only an excuse in time.

There was a phone ringing somewhere as we spoke. It just kept ringing. "You gonna answer that?" I asked.

"I would if I heard it," she said.

Isabella walked over to Jed and stroked his neck. Jed was sort of going out with her at the time, but you wouldn't have known it the way they verbally abused each other and openly flirted with both friends and strangers. They called it their "dynamic," and claimed to be ahead of their time. It was true, too, and sadly prophetic. Jed was about to fall and was resigned to that fact. He was already dreaming of riding his BSA off into the sunset, a free man and I encouraged his fantasy. It could leave a void I might be able to fill by parlaying my "stranger-in-town" status into a cheap sexual conquest. This was not to be. One night I showed Isabella my soul, or some facsimile thereof. She got the joke. Maybe that's why she introduced me to Ed. Ed was a romantic, too, supposedly.

&

ED WAS ONE of the new "conflicted" people. He'd been trying to live in two worlds for some time and he thought he could resolve the situation by flooding the intersection of those worlds with alcohol. Me and Eddie hit it off right away. One night he had a get-together. A few hard-core drunks were coming over and it would be a big night of drunks drinking. Me and Maddy were there. Isabella with someone, but not Jed. There was another guy, Roberto Costello—a singer. I'd met him before through Maddy. But he knew Eddie through Devon, back when they used to live over on Hermitage.

Everyone knew Roberto was some kind of fabrication, but no one cared. There was a lot of doubt about his name, for instance. His name was really Bob, or rather Robert Cohen. He wasn't Italian at all. But he could pass. And with a couple of drinks in him, and little provocation, Roberto would burst into some Italian aria. It was always the same one, too, from Turandot, *Nessum Dorma*. No one sleeps tonight, he said, and on nights like this no one did. It was Bob Cohen's good trick—people wanted to feel exotic because they knew an opera singer, and he exploited that need in them as a kind of symbiotic social contract with the hipster lifestyle.

And there was another girl, a French girl, Claire Colette. Claire had a thing for Roberto Costello. She put on some Wagner record hoping to impress him. But Roberto hated Wagner and gave Claire the shoulder. Feeling undesirable, she proceeded to get wasted. Devon claimed

Claire was too drunk to drive, so she left the party in Claire's car. Claire's boyfriend went with her. Claire stayed on. The boyfriend was some loud literary phony from Poland, named Stash—at least that was his pen name. Isabella had already gone. Then Jimmy came over with some pot.

By the end of the night Ed was sodomizing the tenor on the back steps. Claire was half passed-out at the table in a funk, having been dumped by both Stash and Roberto. In the middle of all this, another guy named Oscar fell off the roof and broke his wrist. Nobody even knew he was there. He was talking lawsuit. Ed was talking cops. Oscar claimed passion drove him to it, though, and being romantics we all let him off the hook. Apparently he had climbed on the roof to spy on Claire, because he had a thing for her. But he hadn't planned on witnessing any homoerotic porn scene. He lost his grip on the gutter just as Ed was letting fly. After the ambulance left, me and Sarah ended up staring at each other over a trashed chessboard. It had been a long night and she looked like death warmed over, but I recognized her as a character from some ancient tragedy and realized I had been in love with her my whole life. Maybe it was her accent. Maybe it was the alcohol, pot and valium.

We spoke of Isabella and her disregard for people's feelings.

"Isabella's cool," Sarah said.

"Yeah, really cool," I replied.

This Sarah character seemed smart and a little aloof, which was nice. I began to imagine the whole future life we could live together: I would be with a smart woman who actually had a job and could take care of me. She had no relatives or friends in jail. And it would be good to know someone with a real purpose in life, other than looking over your shoulder for the next kick. I could tell I had her interest too, so I balanced my normally effective stylish cynicism with some sympathetic humanism. "Sometimes, it's just so sad," I said. "I mean look around—violence, divorce, abandoned babies, where does it end? The world is sick."

She agreed, putting it all down to Inhuman Capitalism and Social Darwinism. I added Emotional Marxism to the mix, figuring the *isms* would win the day. She was a leftist after all, and a sarcastic one on top of it. And I was just her type—at least for the time being. We hit the sack. But we were too drunk to appreciate it. That's how it was in those days. And if it wasn't intoxication, nostalgia and regret were always around to weigh down the pleasure of the present tense.

&

ANYWAY, LIKE I said, things moved fast. I quickly discovered that Sarah really didn't have a job, she was an "occasional" worker, a "freelancer." She had no intention of taking care of me either, and her intelligence was extremely circumspect, being too closely dependent on what she expected to gain from it. She talked about things that she was going to do as if she were actually doing them. I think she even believed she loved me for a second or two because it would help her feel better about her goal, which was, oddly, simplicity. But people can *seem* simple when they are really mixmasters of contradictions: the reason they love you is because they hate you; they hang out with you because they can't stand you; they order this when they want that; they wear clothes that make them fall down. They see the contradictions as some kind of test.

Sarah's real name was Sandra, Sandra Gombrowski. She was part Polish, part Scottish. She pretended to be British. She *was* born there, but she'd lived in the States since she was a kid. I didn't mind. I hated the name Sandra anyway—it was too blonde. And it's not that blondes lie more than brunettes, they just do it differently—almost without any sense they're lying. In any case you can't call them on it—you're playing their game, they're not playing yours. So you swallow hard and feign tolerance. But tolerance was a trap in and of itself, a sort of uppity kind of cowardice. I had a theory about it. Apparently I had a lot of theories in those days.

The theory went like this: the liberalism of the '60s had bred a kind of perverse tolerance which, in the '80s, could be used both as license and as entertainment. People could laugh along with the contradictions in others as a way of excusing their own. They could even revel in the fickleness of their friends while indulging identical behavior, assuming all lapses would be accepted. In fact, it mattered little, as the whole social façade was fragile and doomed to bottom out eventually in bad manners and egotism. We supposedly lived in a "classless" society, but class always got in the way. So did spirituality, which in this crowd was merely another type of class.

Sarah was playing a game in which I was supposed to save her. I was never sure from what. Cynicism? Duplicity? However, she wanted it to look as if I was the one being saved. Or maybe she didn't want or need to be saved so she picked me, a man who wasn't going to save anybody anyway. Perhaps the idea was to humiliate me, and make me so angry about it that I would play the game out of spite. But I couldn't see the game. Not then, and barely now. And if I had, I wouldn't have known how to play it. And even if I did, she wouldn't let me, because it was a one-person game; my playing would defeat the purpose.

It was what drew her to me that made her reject me in the end. She saw me as some unkempt, un-presupposing foil to the viciousness and falsity of her friends. If I said she was St. Catherine to my St. Francis, or even Judy to my Punch, I'd be playing into her trap. Hell, I wasn't even the road bum she wanted to tame, I was just a way for her to beat herself up about the fact that she really loved somebody else but thought he was boring. When she found out that I was more boring than him, she realized she'd lose face if she admitted it. The only way out was to drive me away by suffocating me. In her mind that meant casting me in the role of somebody who could be suffocated. But I already was, so that was misspent energy. It went on and on like that—at least in my mind. She had her own take on it.

Indeed, both our ideals were based on false projections. She wanted one thing and I wanted another. She was functional in a dysfunctional way and I was trying to be the opposite. I needed to suffer, according to her, and she, of course, did not. More likely I had refused to acknowledge her need to suffer, and she was pissed. I didn't know how to spend money either and that embarrassed her, as did my wardrobe. Experience was not valid currency to this crowd. Image was however, and I had none. I did have a tattoo on my chest: the aforementioned bluebird of *l'amour fou*. Sarah had liked that. And I had a leather jacket that was increasingly too tight, probably because I was eating too much out of frustration. I was existing on momentum.

&

ONE DAY JOHNNY showed up on the scene. I called him Johnny Denouement because I could never remember his last name. Apparently this John Denouement used to be a nice guy, but now he was a little off, and he liked people to know it. He acted crazy, not because he really wanted to—but because he was living up to the code of some book he'd never read, a book written by drunks and desperate men. I got the run-down. A while ago he'd quit his job as a clerk and ran off to LA. He got stuck there for two years. The dream became a nightmare, but a dull and dumb one. Now he was back in Chicago, fabricating an attitude and making life hard for other people. Especially me. Because he was trying to get in Sarah's pants. He wormed his way into her confidence like some bozo Iago and turned her against me. He called me a phony.

He said, "You know Frank, you're a phony. I bet you're really just some suburban shmuck. I bet your mother teaches high school."

I should have been hurt—my mom did teach high school—but I wasn't.

One day I caught myself looking backwards with a tear in my eye. The past began to seem better, easier at least, than this complicated social terrorism I found myself involved in. But where and how was I involved?

159

Did I even fit in? Was I becoming one of them? Maybe I wanted to serve Sarah right by becoming what she thought I was, even though I wasn't. The next day I didn't go to work. Two days after that I got fired from my job at the lackey house. I had an intense hangover and a bad attitude apparently, and the lackeys didn't like it. When I tried to tell them that life was tragic—we were all just trying to get by, and that they should have some compassion for my embattered soul, because we were all, every one of us, really shining aspects of the one great "world soul"—they didn't buy that either. While I was riding the elevator down I noticed a Hollyridge Strings version of Janis Joplin's "Piece of My Heart" playing on the Muzac system. It was a perfect example of that socio-economic Darwinism Sarah was always on about, by which everything you believe or like eventually turns against you.

Speaking of Darwin, I'd read that evolution doesn't make things better, it only makes them different. It has no goal, no purpose—it's just a series of accidents. Thus this song, "Piece of My Heart," which had begun as a kind of primal scream, could now be pasteurized and fed through an anonymous PA system to distract office workers from any meaningful thoughts. The song's strange path may indeed have been an "accident," but it also served the needs of the corporate junkies—the way they live off the desires of "the people." And so they stuck a hypodermic into the heart of those same people, and drained them. Then they forced the people to buy back their own life-blood as a means of pacification. Simplicity indeed.

&

I DIDN'T EVEN like the song anymore. I don't know if I ever really did, but now I hated it. But I'm sure it hated me more—if only for not living up to it. And now I was on the street, mid-afternoon, unemployed. I went down to Madison Street for something to do. They were tearing down the old Starr Hotel. It had been a landmark in its time. In fact, it had been two things at once—an example of old Art Deco architecture and a skid-row cage hotel. The city of Chicago thought they could solve their "hobo" problem by bulldozing blocks and blocks of hobo-land, apparently figuring the people who lived there would just disappear if there was no place to live. Then they were going to build some new subsidized luxury housing for middle-class office workers on the site, something less contradictory.

The hobos stood on one side of the street, the yuppies stood on the other. It was a split in constituencies and I was being forced to choose sides. I wasn't actually, but I thought I was. So I did. I bought a pint of Night Train and sat down with the road dogs. At least I could talk to them.

"Fuckin' city," I said, "times change faster than the human heart." I was shooting for poignancy.

A hobo called my bluff. "You're not one of us are you? Go over to the other side. Leave us alone."

"Hey man, I ain't one of them, either," I said, "At least I've been there," indicating with a sweep of my arm some distant mythical land beyond the city limits, where Woody Guthrie, Leadbelly and Cisco Huston still sat on top of boxcars singing about America.

"Oh yeah. You've been 'there,' huh?" He stubbed out his smoke. "You don't know shit." He was wearing a worn suede jacket with a Gatsby-type hat pulled low over his brow, shading severe hawk-like features. "You're playing games," he said. "I don't play games."

"I don't play games either," I said, feeling confident.

"Tell me then, how's life . . . out there?" He made the same sweeping gesture I had just made, but mockingly.

"What do you mean by 'life'?" I asked, feeling clever.

"Look," he said, "Don't fuck with me. You got some money, give me some. You got a girl, let me do her. Otherwise, go the hell away. You think you're free? I can't afford your freedom. I haven't got anywhere to go, but I'll get by just the same. You have everywhere to go, but you'll never get by."

"Fuck you," I snarled. "You know, there used to be a sense of camaraderie. Brothers weren't always trying to put you down." At the moment I was unaware how pleading and pretentious I must have seemed to this guy.

"Used to be a man took you as you are, that's true. If you needed a smoke he gave you one, and showed you the way."

"That's what I mean. What happened?" I asked.

"You happened, dude. And I'll tell you one more thing. Don't go to that town called 'Used-to-Be,' because it ain't there no more. It is a Town Without Pity now." He fixed his eye upon the crane and the hovering wrecking ball, and refused to speak with me again.

&

THAT NIGHT I was supposed to meet Sarah and some of her freelance friends for dinner. In her world everybody went out to dinner all the time. They were at a restaurant I knew. But it had changed owners and now catered to a more moneyed crowd. I walked in. I told Sarah I lost my job. I don't know what I looked like, but her companions began to cringe at my appearance, like cave creatures when the lights are turned on. It wasn't a good report. My boyish innocence had failed to elicit any mothering instincts from the freelancers apparently.

"Face it, you just want to be a bum," Sarah said, pretending such comments were part of our rapport.

"You don't know anything about me," I shot back, not pretending to any rapport. I believed what I said. But I wanted to believe that she didn't believe what she said. But maybe she did. Or maybe she just said what she said because it fit the narrative in her mind. But I wasn't a bum. At least not in the way she thought. So I sat down anyway. I didn't eat. I just drank. I was on a roll. I was hurt, but I was also glad the end was imminent. Johnny Denouement had served his function; the great unravel was upon us. It might take three times as long to break up as we were together in the first place, but when it does finally happen, it's based on something that could have been said the very first day we met.

At some point my face started twitching uncontrollably in the restaurant light and I had to excuse myself. I threw some money on the table and left. I walked north. By now I was hungry so I bought myself one of those hammered-to-death over-salted, thawed pieces of meat they call a steak at the Best Steak House on Broadway. I had a couple of beers and tried to make sense of things. I couldn't. Others would. Life would go on without my running commentary. The phone was ringing in the booth by the cashier. No one answered it. A man in an overcoat stared at me through the window. I ignored him. Then he put his tongue on the window glass and licked it repeatedly. The Uptown zombies passed behind him like a ghost parade of the broke and the broken. Archetypes of failure were out there all right, and they seemed to be breeding. I wondered if I could head off that gravitational pull before it became my future. After all, according to the fantasies of the middle-aged and all the victims of advertising, it was actually possible to do just that.

Part V
going back where we come from

(23)

PEOPLE LIKE TO BLAME THINGS—THEY LIKE TO PRETEND life is an accident, that it's not their fault. But accidents can be intentional. We make ourselves magnets by our aggressive apathy. On top of that we are fascinated by the idea of contingency—it suggests a value to individual existence. But there is none really. And so I was working on the Papa Sri Frank Payne path to nirvana—drink like a fish, speak to no one, indulge regret—alcohol, asceticism, hindsight. There was no way to explain it. Stability was good, I told myself.

I was on the far end of a six-pack of Drewry's with kindly Mr. Beam waiting in the wings. I was randomly severing emotional ties to inanimate objects—a favorite pastime of mine. As they say, a rolling stone gathers no moss. *The Honeymooners* was on TV. Ralph and Alice were going at it. I was half-asleep, using my old brown leather jacket for a pillow and a beer-can for an ashtray. Question marks of smoke peeled off the cigarette tip. The scene was classic down-market noir, so at least some goal in my life had been achieved.

Suddenly, like one of those slow gunshots that sneak up on you—I heard the telephone ring. Apparently it had been ringing for a while, possibly for months. This sort of thing is bound to happen—you get a phone, it's going to ring. Too often self-revelation begins in this way. I crawled around for a minute looking for the phone. I found it under an old copy of *Psychology Today* magazine.

As soon as I lifted the receiver, I wished I hadn't.

&

"LUC? IS THAT YOU?"

It was Tanya. I could tell by the upward lilt of her voice, the anticipation hanging there, that she was waiting for my happy-to-hear-her-voice reply.

My astral body left me for a second and I heard heels clicking on iron steps, down, down deep into the catacombs of the House of Used-to-Be, searching for that special old cask of Amontillado—the one tainted with the blood and grudges of long-gone friends. And there she was—Tanya, back in the corner, covered with cobwebs behind the furnace, where I hadn't really noticed her before, probably because I hadn't been paying attention.

"Luc?"

I had forgotten to speak. "Yeah, it's me."

Tanya had taken the phone company's advice; she had reached out and touched someone. There's no abuse hot line for it. Not yet. You're supposed to like it. That's the curse of telecommunication—you can't lose your past anymore. No matter where you go you're still in the same place.

Her slightly slurred and incomplete utterances clued me to the drink. I looked at the clock. 2:30 am. 12:30 to her. I must have asked how she was doing—because she told me. I made out that she was working, getting along. So okay, that's good news.

"What else?" I asked.

She mumbled something about getting married and having a great stereo.

"Married?" I was surprised. She wasn't the type.

"Surprised?" She asked.

"You're not the type," I replied.

"Are we types?" she asked.

"Yes, I believe so," I said. "Eventually, everyone is."

She laughed. "Is that what I was to you?"

I balked.

She claimed I had not been paying attention—or I would have an answer.

I wasn't sure of the question, though.

So she answered for me. "No. No, you don't know."

She was right on both counts. I hadn't been paying attention. And I didn't know. It bothered me that she would assume I wanted to.

I tried to picture her husband. I could picture them in a bungalow on the beach in Oxnard or where-ever-town California, preparing barbeque for guests. I was happy for her. I told her so.

"I'm happy for you," I said. "What's his name?"

"You don't know him."

I was glad of that, but there was more. There always is.

The husband was already gone—back to where he'd come from. Apparently there had been some trouble. She said something about a car crash, about having an operation and losing all her hair. The scene was going downhill. I noticed there was opera music playing in the background. It was vaguely familiar.

"Jesus, you lost your hair?" I said.

"I lost *all* my hair," she said. Laughing again. "But it'll grow back."

Suddenly I saw a huge, hairless baby, a crazy female Buddha-child sitting in the lotus position, holding a liquor bottle and slurring through the story of her life while a painted wall listened furtively, a wall poorly illustrated with an opera-hall audience composed of everyone she ever knew or wanted to, everyone who had wronged her or needed to be impressed. She explained she might be going back to jail soon, if the lawyer didn't come up with a deal. She'd been set up—so she said.

There was a pause. "Are you listening?"

I mumbled something sincere like, "No, I am, really. I'm sorry."

I doubt that I was really sorry, though, because being sorry would require some interest on my part. I was perfectly happy not knowing these things. I found a cup of cold coffee near the bed. I figured I better start waking up if I was going to participate. She asked if I was different, after all these years. Was I a teacher, a writer, a guitar player? Or was I still a bum? It was okay from her, the "bum" thing. She didn't mean it in a derogatory way. We were, both of us, proudly bums.

"Actually, I guess I am a bum," I said. "I've done nothing with my life." It was dismissive and it rolled right off my tongue, no burden at all. I was slightly surprised. But it was no burden for her either. She was only ever mildly interested in any ambition I might have had. But maybe my thinking that thought was a kind of resentment. Or maybe that was a trait we shared—a mutual lack of interest in each other's ambitions. Indeed, ours was an operatic ambivalence.

Whatever song the singer was singing in the background finished and then there was applause. Then there was the sound of a bottle breaking on her end of the line. Someone in another room perhaps, wherever she was living at the time. I didn't want to ask, but I did.

"Where are you?"

"Olympia." She thought I would be surprised.

"Olympia, what?

"Washington."

"What are you doing up there?"

"I told you, I was in an accident."

I didn't see the connection.

She said something offline, to the bottle-breaker, apparently. The man's reply, the voice, the breaking bottle—it didn't sound pleasant. I let it bother me.

"Are you all right?"

"Yes, fine." She was lying. The radio applause was fading, unsatisfied. Maybe she was looking to me for comfort or something. Perhaps I should have been sympathetic. I briefly scolded myself. Then, having forgotten what we had just talked about, she started over. She asked what I'd been up to.

I told her I didn't know.

Was I having any affairs, any chicks?

I said no chicks, no old lady.

Then I heard the man in the background again. "Tan, are you finished? I need the phone."

The music came back on, heightening the sense of tragedy. There was something very incongruous going on. "Since when did you start listening to opera?"

"I don't. Paulie likes it."

"Paulie?"

"Yeah, Manzoni. You remember? Paulie Manzoni. Anzo's dad."

I did remember. I wished I didn't. The son was bad news. I could imagine the dad. Still, I couldn't let it go. I was being drawn in.

"What are you doing with him?"

"He gave me a job."

"Doing what?"

There was a pause. "A little of this, a little of that." She chuckled. You know, I can't get around very well and we needed money."

"We?"

"Yeah, my husband, remember."

"But I thought he was gone."

"He is, now."

"Jesus, Tanya. What's going on?"

"Nothing. Look, don't get all judgmental. What did you do today, Mr. Righteous?"

"Same. Nothing," I said. "I got up. I made breakfast. I wasted the day." I paused. "I waste every day, it's a hobby."

I could tell she wanted to laugh but she didn't. "You're full of shit, man."

"Always was and will be. Nothing weird there."

"You know what *is* weird, though—thinking about the kind of person you end up being, like god how did I become this middle-aged chick with a back problem. I look at myself and I look run-down, you know. But I'm better now, though. Not drinking. I really think I'm getting it together."

"I hope you're better," I said. But she didn't sound better. And she *was* drunk. But then again I'd never heard her express any recognition of a problem before. So maybe she was better.

"Remember when you said that things sometimes seemed like you watched them on TV. Well everything seems that way to me." She paused, thinking about her own statement, maybe even a little surprised by it.

"You're like that to me now. Not to offend you but . . . I don't know what I was doing, you know. I still don't, but I guess I'm trying."

"What do you mean?" I was starting to feel I should be offended.

"I mean, I like to think those days, you know, that they were an important part of my life. But now, it seems like trying to remember a dream or something, you know.

"Yeah, so?"

"Soooo. You can't trust it. And I know I'm adding and subtracting, stuff that maybe didn't even happen."

"Fuck off Tanya, what are you trying to say? You don't want to remember the past, don't remember it. Why pull me into it?" I didn't know where the lines were coming from, or why I was saying them. I wasn't that upset. It's just that I felt I should be. And it came so easily. Self-doubt usually does, I guess. But this wasn't really self-doubt. It was something more sinister. It was theatrical self-doubt. It was an act. I decided to push for a conclusion. "Really, I mean why are you even calling me after three years. You're life has gone on, and so has mine. Let it go."

"I'm just thinking about stuff. I get down about it, thinking about it, you know. Like maybe I ain't capable of loving anything, or anyone for that matter, or even myself. What do you think Luc?"

"About what?"

"I mean do you really think we were in love?"

I needed to deflect this fast. "Tragedy maybe."

"You would think that. I think you can only fall for tragic women. It's something in you. And you saw that in me, or at least you wanted to."

I tried to take the slight lightly. "Tragedy is the easy part, Tanya. Tragedy has an end." Unlike this phone conversation apparently, I was thinking. She sidestepped my profundity.

"Here I go again, being the morbid reflective chick, stuck in a box, trying to analyze something that never was. I'm not saying this to make you mad. I just wonder."

"Uh-huh." I *was* mad, just not enough to make it matter much.

"I mean half the time I was only trying to get along with you. But it wasn't fair. You saw it as a weakness. I couldn't win."

"But that wasn't my intention," I said, defending myself.

"But you know, I was thinking, I wouldn't be in this position if it weren't for you."

"What? You're blaming me . . . for what? Anyway, you're mixing up different things." I said. "Your life's your own, Tanya, the results of your own actions."

"My *re*-actions you mean."

169

"They're the same."

She said, "You're missing the whole point, it's not your decision to make, man."

"What do you mean?"

"I mean . . . your intention is not what's important. You're not the one defining it. It's your . . . I don't know . . . we all have a certain effect on people, you know. That's what you have to think about."

"I don't know what you're saying, but it sounds fucked up to me. I'm sorry if you're in a bad place, but . . ."

"I'm saying it made a difference to me, that's all, it made a difference how I lived.

"It didn't seem to then."

"Don't you see? You have to be responsible a little. That's kind of what I'm realizing now. I'm not trying to say I was any better, I'm just saying, all right?"

"Look, Tanya, to tell the truth, I have no idea what you're talking about, and I don't know if I want to. I don't like it. So let's just forget it."

"Forget it? Yeah, you're right. Maybe I should go." I could hear her tiredness building up over the phone, her voice coming through the lines slow as syrup, thick and viscous. I didn't want to get stuck.

I said it was good to catch up or some such slick sign-off.

"Did you hear about John Squires?"

I said I'd heard, but that I didn't remember him that well.

She changed the subject. "Hey you still got the bike?"

I said I did, but that the bike didn't run. I lied.

"Mechanics training tool." She tried to laugh. She failed. "Forget it. Look, there's something I want to ask you."

"What?"

"Naomi. I need to get in touch with her. She's back from India, but I think she's out east. Can you to do me a favor? Find out where she is."

"Me? How? You don't know where she is?"

"Did I ever?" Again, she laughed. "Listen. Can you find those old friends of ours? I'm forgetting their names. Maybe they would have an address."

"Yeah. Actually I saw them the other week. But I thought you were in touch with them. They said you were."

"I was, but . . . like I said I lost all my addresses." She paused. "But you saw them?" She seemed oddly shocked, which didn't make sense, since she had given them a message for me.

"Well, a few weeks ago. Maybe a couple months actually. They said your mom was supposed to be here. I didn't follow up on it."

"She's in Chicago?" She asked this like she didn't believe it was possible.

"I don't think so. It was a while ago, Tanya. Besides, they would have called. Jack and Ruby. That's their names."

"Right. Will you call them again and find out?"

"Sure."

"There's another thing. Are you at the same address?"

"Yeah?"

"Cool. Listen, if things work out, I'm going to move back to Portland. I'm going down to LA first, then back to Portland. You wanna visit? We could hang at Alice's, the Seven Seas, all the old stops. It'd be fun."

"Ha ha, Tanya. I hate it out there."

"Seriously. It's gonna be my birthday. Man, I'm going to be 27, you know. 27 fucking years old. I never thought I'd be 25."

"You did say that. I remember." I'd forgot her birthday was coming up, but why would I remember. Still, I tried to cover with humor. "Another couple of years you'll be 50." She was already claiming to be middle-aged. We all were, so the comment seemed apropos.

&

THERE WAS A long pause, as if we were sharing breath, sharing thoughts. Maybe she *was* thinking the same things as me. Or maybe she was on the nod. I don't know. She started to wind down like a doll whose mechanism was exhausted, repeating the words, "Forget it then. Forget it then. Forget it then." At least that's what I thought she said. It *was* what I wanted to do—to forget. And I had, until the phone rang. I was still holding that phone in my hand until I realized she had already hung up. That was fine too. The conversation was getting deeper than I wanted to go. And though depth is often mistaken for truth, death is the only certainty. One day you wake up and you're old. The next day maybe you don't wake up at all.

I did wake up, though. It was later that same night, but not yet dawn. I looked around the room. It seemed a little duller than before, as if the color had sort of bled out of it. The clock ticked slow and loud and sinister like something from an old black and white movie. I could hear the blood pumping through my veins in time. My unshaven cheeks scratched the air and the air made a sour noise. A pile of salt on the table blew slowly away in a draft from the window. Moonlight clung to the floorboards of that old Uptown apartment like a stain.

(24)

APPARENTLY WE HAD TALKED ABOUT FORTY-FIVE minutes. it seemed like days. But time didn't seem to be the problem. I don't know why I thought there was a problem. The mechanistic aspects of the final moments of the call had been picked up by various inanimate objects. The radio came on. I turned it off and poured myself a drink. Something to warm me against the cold. A little hard-boiled role-playing wouldn't hurt. As they say, good form is a weapon against chaos.

For the first time in a while I thought back on my life with her—the movie version, the camera pulling back to show us crossing some great bridge into the future while the music swells and the audience tries to dry their tears before the lights come up. I did remember the cold night air on our cheeks and shoulders as we crossed the San Bernardino Mountains, the vibrating lights of the valley in the heat as we descended. We had the staccato hymn of the BSA pipes for a soundtrack and the smell of the empty road and rubber, and the gas stations and the snapshots in front of the hidden destinations and the warm afternoons and long stretches of indecision. It was all stored up there and ready for editing and I was the man to do it all. It was my movie.

Somehow me and her, we had a resilience, an optimism as two that neither of us had as one, even if it was only a belief in pure momentum, even if it was only primitive catalytic effect. I have read that sometimes the beauty of the world is so great that we have to turn away. I think, at such moments, we don't want to acknowledge beauty, because we would then have to take responsibility for it, and consequently for our own sadness in its presence.

And then I thought about how that all seemed so impossibly long ago and abstract now. Sentiment was a trap, and I wasn't going to fall into it. Nostalgia would not lure me. Nostalgia is sort of a sweat of the material world, a sickness of matter manifesting itself as memory, as propaganda. It makes objects shimmer with a subtle softening of their color and form. But memory is a slipshod thing. Hindsight is flavored by present desire. The details come to seem invented. Half the facts turn out not to be facts. And the images, well, we can't be sure where they come from either. Finally, one cannot tell the difference between the cumulatively constructed tableau and what really happened. We look in the mirror and wonder how we could be born so old and so naïve.

&

I DIDN'T WANT to think about what might be going on with this Paulie Manzoni character. Was she working for him? Renting a room at his house? Maybe it was some weird father fixation. Manzoni would be about twice her age. And he would be the type to take advantage of that. Or was it an alcoholic thing? Hard drinkers searching for comfort with hard drinkers. Had she merely jumped from one script to another and neglected to inform me? Of course she had informed me. She had just called, after all. Still, I felt guilty about it.

The mood had changed. I now needed a soundtrack for my misery. Sorting through some cassette tapes. I came upon *Kosmic Blues*, probably one of the few albums ever made where a woman is allowed to scream for forty minutes to the accompaniment of an off-key horn section. At first I thought to avoid it. Stick with the good stuff. Nina Simone and Billie Holiday. But I liked the half-assed garage-band ambiance of the album, so I played it through, listening with earphones. I fixated on one song: "Work Me Lord." That was the name of it. I played it four times or more because within it there is a moment, I can't describe it exactly, except as a kind of primitive vocal event, something free from any significance. I'm not sure of the time frame either, perhaps it comes three minutes into the song. The brass section is going, the voice is rising synchronically, and then she does this rolling dip, and then ascends again, and it is at that moment her mouth appears in my mind like some kind of grotesque cornucopian horn, whose corkscrewing tip could be traced back to a punctured heart, like a pin punched into an invisible balloon, letting the pressure out. And that's what was happening. And I wanted it to happen. That's what's weird about it. As if my soul craved it, and her job was to provide it.

There are many who put down her talents, call her a screaming bitch, the progenitor of numerous screaming bitches to come, a fat pock-marked junky whom you wouldn't even want to know if you met her in person, a woman who barely disguised her self-hatred with cheap flamboyance. She was almost tenaciously tragic—a product of a world so overpopulated with "individuals" that you had to learn to scream at a young age. And of course there's the whole Freudian Biker Mama thing, playing to the Oedipal unconscious of her fans. On top of that she made herself a target, a victim. But all that had nothing to do with anything. What was important was how I reacted, where and when certain things occurred and how they tied themselves into my psyche. The foundations were laid long ago.

The buildings went up. The train tracks went down. The town got built, even though the highway went somewhere else.

&

THEY SAY THE ultimate vocal act is the name of God. But God may well be a masochist, or a parasite. This goads the question: Does God feed on human emotion? They also say rock-and-roll is the last refuge, a grave-yard for the clichés of Romanticism. Tragedy is one of these. Tanya had accused me of tragedy. But she, too, subscribed. Blaming it on me was a joke. The creation of archetypes is a dangerous profession. They give people something to measure up to. Usually the creators cannot measure up themselves. That's why they do it, why they create. At first it seems like a victimless crime. What starts out as a joke or an exercise in passion, in "feeling," becomes way too serious at some point. But that's part of it too, to go out and trash your life in pursuit of the impossible, the ridiculous. After all how many people become junkies because of Burroughs, bums because of London or Kerouac? How many ended up on skid row having chased a literary illusion so far they couldn't go back?

Tanya wasn't dumb but she had a tragic willingness to believe people who were, and her information was often second-hand. And if it was a dead icon that baited her, or me, does it matter? People like to see others act out the impulses they cannot. But that was my excuse, not hers. Still, I should have hated Janis for inspiring that symbiotic dependence. I should have hated Janis because of what numerous women, Tanya included, had become because of her. I wonder what it is that makes people think they can manipulate emotions without responsibility?

But there's another angle to it. Icons bleed the living through compar-ison. The fear is that there can be nothing new. The psychic damage cannot be gauged. In a world of degraded forms, Tanya may have indeed felt like a lesser reflection of some Platonic ideal. Or at least she might have thought that's what I thought. And that might have been part of her reason for continuing to denigrate herself. After all, if you're already falling why not continue—it's better than hitting the ground. And maybe someday you'll actually fall right through the bottom of everything and into a better world.

I may have tried to dismiss Tanya, claiming she spent her life nursing a grudge. But life is only a symptom, not the cause. The arrow of time points to increasing disorder. She was going to be 27. She never thought she'd live to be 25. I was already 25 when I met her. Maybe we did live fast. But we had failed to die young. Because you have to have a belief first and I wasn't sure I did. I mean, I thought so then. I don't now. And in any case I had already failed, if the cliché was the test.

It's possible we saw ourselves as characters in a Harlequin romance. And had we been more beautiful or born to a different social class that might have been the case. But then again Romanticism is a middle-class notion and we are only showing our middle-class conceits by subscribing to it. We would not talk about it. We did not even think that we thought about it. This phone call was the first time I had heard her acknowledge that she had. The world was speeding up, she said. As if we had no choice.

And as far as the motorcycle inquiry—she probably just wanted half the dough if I sold it. Maybe she had no sentimental attachment to it at all. Maybe I gave her too much credit. I don't know what she wanted. It's true, though, I was always attributing emotions and motives to her that were really mine. I wasn't going to send her any money, and I resented her connecting memory and money that way. But then she was only following my lead. And of course she hadn't really asked me for money. That was me, manipulating her, in memory.

This whole John Squires thing was funny too. He wasn't really an important figure. Maybe she was trying to bond with me over his death, when any death would do—anything to stimulate or simulate common experience. Or possibly she brought him up for the selfish idea that it might stir some empathy in me that could then be transferred to her. She was wrong.

I could have tried harder, though. I could have told Tanya about the dream I had in which I was driving down a dirt road. I ride up to a cabin and John comes out to greet me. The dream ends as we are shaking hands. I could have told her about my dream of Naomi, in which she appeared as an insect sitting next to me in a bar asking questions about the decay of nuclear family structures and the plodding nature of geological time. But dreams are boring to other people.

I could have told Tanya a lot of things, but I didn't. Because I had realized now that it wasn't Tanya who called. Tanya would have never talked like that in this world. She never took life that seriously and she never looked back. It must have been a ruse, something I made up. And then I was relieved.

Dreams play funny tricks on me. Sometimes I wake up only to wake up again later. Which makes me wonder what I'm making up about waking life. But I didn't make her up. I was sure. Because three days later I received a letter from Tanya. There was a photo enclosed. It was the treasured picture of Tanya and Naomi, the one that was supposedly taken in New Orleans. The black and white one. This must be why she asked about my address. And there was a note. "Luc, hold on to this, bring it when we meet next time. I'll ask for it back, you better know that. I hope things are going well for you. Peace, Tan." I had the funny feeling that this picture had something to do with her wanting me to contact Naomi. I couldn't figure it, though. Not yet.

I got out my other photos for comparison, especially the one of me and Tanya, also taken in New Orleans. We took the picture in the same location as Naomi's. It's a dark photograph, the one of me and Tan. Blue and green were the primary colors, as if the photo had been taken in some timeless grotto of the sea. Both pictures were taken under a street sign. Dauphine and Bienville with the bus called Desire behind and to the left. Another cliché. But like I said once you start you can't stop. Clichés attract you with a gravitational force. They need you as much as you need them.

Tanya is wearing what she always wore, jeans and a sweatshirt, looking utterly happy to be in the moment—transient, unbound. By moving constantly, we managed to live in this state of perpetual desire. Thus the sign. Certainly we did covet that spirit. But we could not deny that we were chasing a world that was dying even as we were trying to experience it. As if the world had a disease. Or maybe we had the disease, and were carrying the infection into the world. Maybe we *were* the disease, and the world was dying because of our presence.

In somber hours I might express thoughts like this to Tanya, about how hard it was; the way it started out like a blessing but ended up a curse; the way it left us sleepless, the highway leaping like a whip. She jumped on it, of course. She was always too enthusiastic, even about bad ideas. But everybody's ideas were great to her, really great, man—she understood them, and she wanted them to exist, as long as she didn't have too big a part, or any responsibility. That was part of her problem. Too much enthusiasm. Too little engagement. It used to break my heart to see that enthusiasm constantly battered.

I looked at the photo of us— 24, 25, whatever our ages were then, we seemed older at the time, but that's because the culture was older. It had not yet settled into a state of permanent adolescence. And that's the irony of Desire, that the marketers would pull it out of the collective unconscious and use it to oppress us, to create a society of children. It was the very act of parody that Walker Birdsong had warned me against. But I hadn't known what Walker meant at the time.

&

WHAT FOLLOWED WAS a long night, actually more than a night. In fact, it was several days later than I thought it should be, when, some time before

177

daylight, I heard a knocking on the door. I didn't respond. Eventually the knocking stopped. I lit a cigarette and stared out the window, watching shadows darken the cemetery wall—it was just starting to snow. I saw my old friend down there in his ragged overcoat. He was leaning against the graveyard wall smoking his cigarette. He seemed to be mocking my mortality. The white tombstones behind him were like the rows of teeth in the mouth of a shark, shining in the intermittent moon—a shark called Fate, waiting for my next bad decision. I didn't make it wait long.

IHAD NOTHING TO LOSE. NO JOB, NO WOMAN. MAYBE THE USED-to-be *is* pitiless, but I was its pawn. So I called Jack Ruby to tell them my plans. Phone disconnected. I went down to the Old Town Tap where they hung out. The bartender claimed he didn't know who they were. Wells Street itself was barely there. I mean the old Wells Street—with the ghosts of head shops and folk clubs. I did notice a brand new photocopy shop where the wax museum used to be. The forms of reproduction were changing. Maybe there was some trend in society I wasn't aware of. It was late. I heard footsteps but I didn't see anyone. I went to the Greyhound station and bought one of those 30-day, See-America bus passes. Then I had a beaten-to-death steak at a State Street Diner, while I waited for the 2:45 a.m. express to Memphis. I sat in the Ratso Rizzo seat, as usual, way in the back, on the right side.

Maybe I *was* going in circles. You can spend the second half of your life going back to check on the first half if you want. It's like standing in line at a carnival ride you've been on a hundred times. You like being sick and that's the reason you do it. You ask the woman who hates you for a date. You tell your boss the job's a joke. Maybe the road was only a rope holding some kind of albatross around my neck. Maybe there was a noose at the end of it by which I would end up swinging at the anti-climactic finish of yet another bad movie.

As the bus rolled down the Dan Ryan, I watched the weak lights of Southside life struggling to be seen through the blue-green dark of swamp and squalor. The Robert Taylor homes were looming in the haze like prison hulks with their hateful eyes. Some had tiny television sets inside flashing perpetual images of violence and unattainable joy. Then the bus bore right onto 57 South, and my mind went with it, leaving the present for the past, domestic anxiety for the dream of the road.

I went to sleep. Somewhere in Southern Illinois they woke us up for the breakfast stop. I thought I'd give it a try. I had a donut and a can of root beer. I went to the bathroom, then bought a package of aspirin. I got back on the bus. It was getting light so you could see the scenery. It was beautiful—a picturesque parade of discount cowboy boot outlets and food franchises. Next time I woke it was late morning, Memphis. King Tut and Elvis. I walked around. I ended up at a restaurant called the Hillbilly Cafe. They had pictures on the wall of every hillbilly musician that had ever existed. I had a beer. I'd never been in Memphis before, so I asked the cashier where Beale Street was. He seemed ticked off but he told me anyway.

"It's that way," he said, counting some change needlessly.

Beale Street was in a state, half-abandoned, decayed. A lot of it was undergoing renovation—or rather evocation. I think they were even calling it "Old Beale Street." It looked like "Old Wells Steet" in Chicago, or "Ye Old Seaport" in New York. Everyone was trying to make it look like it used to be while ignoring the fact that nobody liked what it used to be and that's why it looked like it did. Additional irony was provided by the fact that whatever they did, they couldn't make it look like the postcards. The postcards made everything seem bright and funky and crowded with people seeming to enjoy themselves when all they were really doing was buying things. Still, there were stars on the sidewalks along Beale Street with famous blues musicians' names inscribed in them. You could walk along and remember how much you loved whatever it was.

I joined in the fun. "Here's to times that never were and friends we never had." I repeated those old lines in this new context, as I held my bottle up to the light of a Memphis streetlamp, a piece of "Art Americana" newly manufactured to look antique. Then a woman with a bloody nose came running out of an alley next to the photocopy shop. I heard sirens.

I missed my bus and had to take a local through Mississippi. I saw a sign for Clarksdale, with highway numbers and vector arrows instilling a vague sense of having been there before. The state passed like a sinister forest full of liquor stores, incest victims, crumpled fedoras, and oddly contorted men with grizzled cheeks and guns. Then I realized I was just remembering the movie *Deliverance*. Or maybe it was remembering me. I do believe that thoughts can think themselves, spreading out like an electric oil slick, and sometimes we are in those thoughts. Then the highway turned liquid on me and the memories that populated its darkened flanks began to merge into a single beating, breathing thing that oddly lulled me to sleep like a mother's lullaby.

We arrived in New Orleans around 10 a.m. the next day. I went straight to the Hummingbird Bar and Grill for grits and coffee. The Hummingbird has a special menu of items "Under a Buck." Grits and coffee was one of them. The place used to be full of working girls, traveling salesmen, tourists and local losers. If you hung out there long enough you got the feeling that everybody who worked there also lived there and ate there and that, occasionally, an outsider dropped in. I was the outsider today.

There is also a Hummingbird Hotel so I took a room. Room #33. I asked for it. It was available. Tanya and I had this room back in '76. Number 33 had a bed but there wasn't any table. There were 15 electric sockets, but there was nothing to plug into them. I pulled the picture of Tanya out of my bag. I looked at her. She looked back with a certain grainy, back-of-the-milk-carton sense of urgency, as if to say, "Hurry, Baby, I won't last, I won't last much longer."

It was hot. The air in the room wouldn't move, despite the ceiling fan pushing it around. The light was too dim to read the *Times Picayune* and the St. Charles street car would pass every five minutes sounding like some great metal beast caged beneath the street trying to swallow the last drop of water in the metropolitan sewer system. I got thirsty. Then I got nervous. I looked around. I moved the bed. I looked behind the mirror. Inside the closet someone had written, "Say No to Sainthood" on the wall. Years ago, apparently. The letters were faded and barely legible. It had even once been covered by wallpaper that had peeled away. There was some other writing: "Freedom is slavery, ignorance is strength." And something about the doors of perception needing to be cleansed so eternity could fall in love with time, blah, blah, blah. I didn't try to read all of it.

&

DOWNTOWN NEW ORLEANS is divided—the old town and the new town, the past and the present. I was in the new town, which was actually pretty old. It used to be the hard part of town where roustabouts and river workers put up—an archaic race of unenlightened men who wore broken hearts on their arms, who smoked and spit and drank hard and no one jogged. Now there were red bricks paving St. Charles. There were a couple of art galleries, a boutique and a photocopy shop. Oil men and river workers never need to copy anything and they don't care about art either. But the bars were still open 24 hours, and you still saw people carrying suitcases and bedrolls around just in case the world might wink back to the way it was.

I took a walk. Most of the old hotels were gone, including the Charlotte—there was an empty lot there now—where Tanya and I had lived eight years ago, before we lived at the Hummingbird. I looked up into the air and could see the space in which we lived. There wasn't anything there, though—a bird, a cloud. The Del Ray Hotel, The Orleans, and the YMCA *were* still around, and so was Tony's Port & Starboard Lounge. I decided to have a drink at Tony's—to celebrate. But a fight broke out. One guy said he was going to come back and kill Tony, so I headed over to the Circle View.

The bartender at the Circle View was wearing a pink tuxedo to match his red mustache. His name was Red. He didn't remember me. The guy on the next stool was talking about boats. He knew everything there was about boats. He wasn't a warmonger, he said, but he was impressed by the firepower of big ships. He remembered a lot of facts and stories and he was going to tell them. Nobody wanted to listen however—they were all preoccupied. Another guy challenged him to tie some nautical knots in a shoelace and the guy couldn't do it. He called the guy an asshole. Another guy said he would beat his ass. Then the first guy left. I decided to head over to the Quarter.

I walked to the corner where the picture of Tanya and I had been taken, at Dauphine and Bienville. The corner looked the same. It hadn't changed at all in a hundred years. Only the clothes the people wore and the brand-name signs. The Bureau of Tourism had done their job. They knew there were dozens of people like me sitting around with pictures of themselves in New Orleans in front of a bus called Desire, and that someday they would go back to visit, to reclaim the memory, thus doubling the tourist trade.

Some of the old characters *were* still around, I think—The Chicken Man, The Bean Lady, Lucky Charlie. There were no old buddies coming out of clubs and doorways to shake my hand. No one was standing me to drinks. I went up to Lucky Charlie, who was selling Lucky Dogs from a cart at St. Peter. He was older but he looked the same. Maybe he didn't. At least I thought he did.

"Hey Charlie, is Mary Stone around?" It was an absurd question. He had no idea who I was. "You know, Jessica, didn't you used to hang out with her years ago."

"What are you, a cop?" He looked past me, his cigarette rolled across his lower lip in sync with his eyes, both rolling away from my question. It was a practiced eccentricity, but I wasn't going to call him on it.

I told him my name. "Lucky. Frank. Luc. Don't you remember me?"

"*My* name's Lucky, asshole. Lucky Charlie, the Lucky Dog man." He paused, giving me the once-over. "What do you want her for? She owe you money?"

I attributed his hostility to the idea that he was (or at least I wanted him to be) ashamed that he'd had this same job for eight years, even though I knew he probably wasn't ashamed really. He probably wasn't even Lucky Charlie, just a photocopy of the original.

I wasn't more than a block away when I heard some guy singing "*The day I was born they told me I was dead. Everything blue turned out to be red.*" The song was familiar. There are lots of street musicians in New Orleans.

Some have talent. Others are playing at "paying their dues."

I went back to my room. Glass was breaking as a couple fought on the other side of the wall. Then they stopped fighting and started fucking. Fists first. Then bed springs. The ceiling was swirling faster than the ceiling fan. I guess this also reminded me a lot of the old days. I knew it before and now I knew it again. I figured I better eat something. I went downstairs. The special of the day was Grandma's Cajun Snapping Turtle Soup. There was a badly drawn picture of a snapping turtle done in chalk on a blackboard.

The counterman had roses tattooed on his hands. He said they were tearing the Hummingbird down to build a Banana Ranch Adventure Clothing franchise. The headline in the paper was about a mass murder in Chicago—a woman shooting kids in grade school because she didn't want them to grow old and disappointed. Page three had a guy jumping out a window in a building set on fire by arsonists because the owner wanted to collect insurance before he got too old to enjoy his lucre.

Analysts were scrambling to explain this trend of despair and violence. Apparently there had been a conference. Tulane said Nature. Loyola said Nurture. U. of C. claimed heat and hedonism. One guy said men beat their wives to get back at their mothers. Someone else put forth the idea that all of us were simply ciphers, drifting through Zones of Loss. No one mentioned anything about Hell.

The rosy-handed man was frying my eggs. Outside an elderly woman in a black veil walked by. She had a little girl with her. "As Good As You Been to This World," was on the jukebox. I checked my wallet. Two hours later I was on the hound jerking north through the traffic past the endless empty motels of Metairie—the vast parking lots and vacant spaces waiting for the festivals to come, waiting for the memories to set up shop.

&

IN ST. LOUIS, I took a westbound bus out 70 toward Denver, then up 25 to 80 and Portland, where, I pretended, there was some absurd chance I'd run into Tanya. But then if you want something to happen it probably won't. One trick is to wish for the opposite of what you desire. But it's hard to fake without getting pathological about it. Still, when I talked to Tanya she had mentioned something about heading down to Portland. That is if Manzoni didn't have some kind of hold on her.

As I looked out the window I saw several hitchhikers on the on-ramps. Maybe it was the season of the hitchhiker again. Maybe it was evidence of our overcrowded hospitals and prisons, or possibly a rebirth, a new "greening of America." A lot of these people looked just like me and Tanya in the old days, waiting for the ride that would change their lives. But they were wearing Jack Kerouac brand-name leather jackets and East Village trademark underwear and Ernest Hemingway copyright backpacks.

&

IT WAS GOOD to get back to Portland. I liked the way the city smelled— the roses, the bridges, the mountains in the distance, the clean dirt. The Estate Hotel had been rehabbed. The Freeway Hotel wasn't there anymore. Morrison's Hotel was there but the restaurant had turned into a fern bar. I ended up at the Old Town Hotel, which used to be The Providence. The sign said "New Management." The desk clerk's name was Jones. Something in his manner told me I was wrong to be there. I think it was when I asked, "Is this the place that used to be The Providence?"

And he said, "You're wrong buddy. You're in the wrong place." I took a room anyway.

I lit up a smoke and did the tour: Couch Street, Third Street, Burnside. It looked so quaint. But then I wanted it to look small. I wanted to feel on top of the town. This was the Burnside district all right, but they were calling it Old Town now. There was a sign that said, "Welcome to Old Town. Please respect our neighbors." It had all the signs of an Old Town too—the bean-sprout sandwich stand, the Old Town Tap, the ubiquitous photocopy shop which seemed to be replacing liquor stores and store-front churches as the most common feature of the American city street.

Still this was the fourth Old Town I'd been to in a week, and I needed a theory to explain it. So I came up with what I called "Old Town Syndrome." It would predate Chronic Fatigue or Attention Deficit, all those more personal versions. The OTS instead would manifest itself in the public sphere of city politics as a hankering after a "used-to-be" that maybe was once, but doesn't matter anymore, because what matters is how do you get home from your fun dinner without getting mugged. The parking lots had nicer cars but the men still carried knives. Most often in their eyes.

All these Old Towns were trying to be what they thought people "wanted." But people didn't know what they wanted. And so whole constellations of humanity had come to see themselves as focus groups, demographics, sets of extras in TV shows or movies about "themselves." Any other people around were forced to become characters in those mini-movies, despite themselves. It was all a mass effort to keep each other

184

entertained in a life where in fact no one else really existed except you.

Burnside was no longer that carnival neighborhood of sailors, farm workers, hobos, hard-timers and pool-hustlers that I remembered. Odd pockets of debauchery and spiritual weakness could still be found, but they were not pervasive. Once an area of schizophrenics, it had become schizophrenic itself. Personalities passed on the street and their various perfumes of body odor, booze, vomit, Chanel, Brute, Hi Karate seemed never to communicate.

This isolation was nothing new. Cars crash, the victims don't know each other. Men and women stay married for years, then discover they are strangers. Everyone's locked in a box. On the cusp of the age of communication there seemed to be none. There were only statements. Autonomous statements that thought they were true. The men of skid row had no place else—but they didn't even belong here anymore.

Apparently the decline of the industrial age along with the increasing lack of traditional career choices had bred an increase of designers and artists. I read this in the fashion section of *The Oregonian*. There was an article about Skid Row Chic: thousands of kids had recently gone to school to become artists, and apparently these kids were dressing by choice like skid row people used to dress by necessity. It was a new interpretation of the "classless" society. The downside was that you couldn't tell who anybody was.

I certainly couldn't. I couldn't recognize anybody. I couldn't spot the runaways, prostitutes, and cons the way I used to believe I could. So I told myself they were gone. That *it* had changed, not *me*. Impostors were playing the traditional roles, and they didn't care, didn't have a proper relish for it. Not like we did, back in the old days.

The phrase "the old days" started to bother me. Had I become one of those "yearning" people, perpetually interpreting my desires on the level of economic needs and projecting them onto the world as an emotional marketing device? Was I little more than a walking Old Town Syndrome myself? Maybe I too could make some money off of it. I could take on the moniker, "Old Frank."

I began to anticipate the tourists milling around the cobblestone streets in my head, visiting the Old Frank Memento Shop, the Old Frank Black & White Cinema, the Old Frank Wax Museum where characters from Old Frank's past held life-like poses in dusty dioramas. All this extra life was giving me a headache.

185

THERE'S WAS A bar down on Burnside called Alice's Restaurant. It was a renovation of the old Alice's All-Nite Café. They changed the name so people would think about the movie. Probably it was owned by some old hippies who liked the movie and wanted to capitalize on that ambience. But the place had too much skid row history. I went in for the history. The old skid row contingent was there. So were the new urban pioneers. There was tension in the place between the old and the new, especially between the older wives and the younger women their husbands were dogging around.

The bartender was from the old days, a bearded, large-boned, but mostly beaten man. He had that combination of frailty and confusion mixed with a very real potential for brutality that makes a good bartender. Except he wasn't one. He could throw a guy on his can but he couldn't see a guy waiting to order a drink if that guy was sitting in front of his face. I was. He walked away. I gestured several times. I snapped a fin in the air. He stared at the speed rack. Finally some woman brought me a Bud.

I turned my attention to the TV. But the same thing was happening there. It was a comedy about drunks in a bar trying to get a drink. Outside the door, Old Town went on almost as city planners had wanted. Artists roamed the streets looking for experience. Couples were holding hands as they entered Thai restaurants. Drunks were pissing on the sidewalk. Suddenly I felt a familiar presence, the *odeur* of Ogden, Utah.

"There's something out there," the voice whispered, "something sinister."

"What?"

"You know . . . you know what I mean, something we've forgotten."

"Okay, okay," I said. I didn't look at him.

"I was once like you, son, didn't have to listen to anybody, yes, I was a pure spirit, righteous and uncorrupt just like you, then I took a fall. You're not so special."

There was something gravelly about his voice that seemed familiar. Like I should remember. Then he read my thought.

"It's an old tradition, my friend—we don't invent, we only remember. It's an old alcoholic tradition that we don't even remember. Buy me a drink and I'll tell you a story you can repeat to your children."

Then it hit me. I turned to look at him—a thinnish man, medium height, dressed in a grungy trenchcoat, bum leg, a cane with a carved clown-head and a shopping bag. He wasn't as old as he appeared, though. I ran down my list of premature aging possibilities: stroke, LSD, hard women. I couldn't account for the changes, but it was definitely Walker

Birdsong—from the "old days." He was clean-shaven now and the haircut was shorter, but I recognized the glittering eye, the pompous overblown banter.

"Are you Walker?" I asked.

"That's Walker to you, my friend, more miles than you have minutes in your life."

"Jesus. What's up? Remember me?" I realized this was a stupid question. "Frank? Luc?" I tried to remember the name I used back then. Then I remembered what he called me—"Pilgrim?"

He answered with a waffling glare, took a drag of his cigarette and let the smoke form Arabic letters around his head. He seemed to read them then batted them away. He'd been cruising stool to stool to score a drink. I bought him one. He sat two stools down. I wanted to tell him about his brother Hollis, about everything that had happened in the last eight years. But he didn't seem receptive.

He waved his hand across the scene we were in. "Think you can shed all this, Pilgrim, that there's some throne of glory waiting for you. Well I've got news. I've wandered the roads for years, friend, and when I came home, this is all I found." He pointed to the TV. "There's your shining robe, your fountain of light. By God, Joan of Arc's heart never burned in her fire like mine does in this fever of consumption."

I looked up at the TV. Someone had changed the channel. It was a snappy sentimental drama about a family who had lost their faith in God. Some bohemians came in the bar—they were dressed like bums. A motorcycle pulled up outside, a Honda 750. The girl looked like Tanya, only several years younger. I'd rather not say what the guy looked like. They went to the pool table.

I was feeling less solid by the minute. "Still it's good to be back," I said to myself, raising my glass to toast the indifferent universe, and Tanya, too. The jukebox helped me out by playing an appropriate pop song about the indifferent universe. A thin sheet of light cracked the afternoon dust. The light spread out into a greenish fan. A silhouette broke across it.

(26)

SHE WANDERED TO THE BACK OF THE BAR AS IF LOOKING FOR someone, half-heartedly greeting a couple of people who didn't seem to know her. She said a few words to Walker, moved toward the door, then turned, came back and stood behind the empty stool beside me.

"Anyone sitting here?"

"No . . . no, go ahead."

She was wearing a muted green zippered sweater, one of those euro things, with jeans, a beret, and a scarf tied around her neck. She had short reddish hair dulled to brown by age and flecked with grey, but you could still see embers when the light nicked it. She was handsome, self-possessed, with metallic blue eyes that could hide whatever she wanted. Alive but not overbearing, confident—I put her in her mid- to late forties. Glasses, fake pearl earrings and some kind of little Hindu-style broach completed the ensemble. In the dusty light she had the grainy look of an old photograph. But that could have been me. I hadn't had much sleep. She sat down.

"You from around here?" she asked. She studied me closely.

"No," I said, avoiding any show of interest. Too much of my life had already been guided by who I happened to be sitting next to in places like this.

She ordered a gin and tonic. "I'm not either." She kept looking around the bar. "I mean, from Portland. A little town called Mount Angel, if you know where that is, north of Salem."

I nodded. Down the bar, a man nodded with me. His head was large enough that I felt a small refreshing breeze. The news on TV was about a revolution in some third-world country.

"You know, I was thinking . . ." She was ready to tell me, too, when Walker got up and made for the street. He needed some air. He was tapping the bottom of the barstools with his clown-head cane, obviously to annoy the patrons. He gave the redhead a look that had some mileage behind it.

"Careful of wanting what you don't really want," he said, pretending to direct the statement at me. The woman smirked.

"What was that about?" I asked.

"Who knows?" She paused. "Ninety-five percent of human behavior comes from the stone age." She paused, smiled. It was a good smile, self-conscious, knowing, a bit off-balance and it showed a sense of humor, if a wry one. "You can't expect a lot of sophistication these days."

But if her smile was younger than she was, her voice was old enough, weighted with a measured surety. There was temper to it, too, and you could feel it. You could feel her controlling it.

"Some things come with age I guess. But everyone is searching for youth."

"That and their mothers." She added. "But you know something, my friend, you might as well become an adult. We're alone no matter what." Her drink came and she raised her glass. "*A votre sante.*"

"Glad to meet you," I said, "even though I have no idea what you're talking about."

"Don't worry, no one does."

I didn't know if I should be offended, so I let it go. She was looking out the window to where Walker Birdsong was holding onto a lamppost, engaged in the timeless effort of standing up. "Friend of yours?" I asked.

She clinked the ice in her glass. "I know him. But then I've known little men clinging to lampposts all my life. They think the world revolves around them. Believe me it's only the alcohol—it makes everything spin around, like a whirlpool."

I wasn't going to let her get to me with pessimism. But then again, the moment had long passed when I could have blown her off. I watched Walker out there clinging to his lamppost. Then I saw myself in the window's reflection. I didn't look so good myself, so I turned to the bar mirror, pushed my hair back and tried to look like a character. I failed.

"Well, we've all been there," I said.

"Really? Have we? Are you always posing for the camera?"

"No."

"Who's it for then? A girl? God? Don't tell me you're posing for God?"

"Huh?" She was moving too fast. The situation should not have been so sarcastic so soon.

"And what about that jacket, the boots, the whole on-the-road look? Read a little too much Kerouac in our wonder years, have we?" She laughed.

Now I *was* offended. "I'm not *trying* to look like anything. A lot of people dress like this."

"C'mon. You know what I mean—that whole *homme fatal*, heart-breaking, carny-working, folksinging, cowboy-who-wanders-into-town-in-a-snakeskin-jacket-and-all-the-lonely-women-want-to-blow-him-in-the-cemetery look."

"That's in your head, not mine," I said.

"Doesn't matter whose head. I bet you even got a harmonica in your pocket."

"No way." I was lying. I did have a harmonica, key of A. I never used it, but I had it. And now I was embarrassed because of it.

"You know you on-the-road guys crack me up—you think there's some reality out there."

"There isn't?"

"In my opinion, reality is a negotiation. You make it up as you go along."

"Okay. But if you know the answers, why do you ask the questions? I was just sitting here minding my own business, watching TV—just like I'm supposed to do. You started this, remember."

"TV, it figures."

"I like it. It keeps me from thinking."

"I'm sure it does. You grew up on it, I suppose. TV was the collective Mother-conscious for your generation, right?"

"Men do love their mothers," I said.

"Or they don't." She tried to act nonchalant.

"I don't know what you're getting at."

"And, I suppose it's quite possible their mothers love them. But I'm telling you, that look you're after, it was the very death of the world you're looking for."

"You don't know what I'm looking for or why I'm here. Stop acting like you do."

"Okay. Why *are* you here then, getting drunk in the middle of the afternoon? No TV at the SRO?"

"Actually I came here looking for someone," I said.

"Who you looking for? Oh, don't tell me—the girl. Right?" She took a drink and turned slowly toward me. I had the strange feeling she knew me and that I was playing a part I hadn't been informed about.

"It's a long story," I said, "and not that interesting."

"They're all long, and none are interesting, so what?"

"No, I mean really, long and really boring."

"C'mon. You in a rush or something? We're in a bar. The world grinds on. Let's talk the talk."

"You're not exactly inspiring me, lady. You got to ease into these things."

"I'm not trying to inspire you. I'm not trying to tell you anything. The world changes too easily. Too fast. It makes people sick, it's so fast."

There was a sound of retching from the bathroom. "See what I mean?" She laughed at her own joke. "God, I hate synchronicity."

"This conversation is a little deep," I said, "considering our environment, don't you think?"

"Actually, I think the environment is deeper than our conversation. But then I *am* a Romantic. I suppose you're a cynic. Most people are, young people anyway. Or are they the same thing—Romantic and Cynic? I don't know."

The retching stopped. Then I heard the toilet flushing. "How so?"

"There's more to be learned by watching than listening. Events just happen. There was a poet once, I forget who, Rilke maybe, no it was Novalis—he said philosophy is just homesickness, trying to feel at home everywhere. That's why people hang out in bars like this. Everyone's trying to feel at home."

"So, that guy puking in the john, all these people, you, me, we are philosophers?"

"By my definition, I guess we are." She gestured out the window. "See Walker there? He used to have a good mind, an appetite for life. Like you, probably. Young men think they know the world. The world always proves them wrong."

I noticed her empty glass. She was rolling it in her hands, making sure I would notice. "Can I buy you a drink?" I asked.

She started slightly. "What? Why? Why would you want to?"

"You know, to keep up the conversation. Think of it as tuition." I was being sarcastic only because I felt she could handle it. She didn't disappoint me. Besides she already expected it. She faked some offense.

"Why not? You know I have a daughter. She's cocky as you. She's also in trouble a lot, because of it."

"Kids these days, huh?" I was trying to be funny. It didn't register.

"She hates me."

"Who?"

"My daughter, she hates me because she doesn't understand me. She thinks life is a movie you can go see again, think things over, reinterpret scenes, maybe change the meaning. People appear, but you can turn them on or off—the show's always there. It's like the subconscious or something. But dumber." She looked at me. "You know what I mean?"

"No. You said she hates you. Why? How do you know?"

"She hates me? Yeah, I guess she does. She thinks I abandoned her. But I didn't, not really. I left her with her father. Sometimes I had to. Of course, I don't know why I thought I could trust *him*. I don't think she likes her father. I know she doesn't like me. She loves me, maybe. But loving ain't liking. Like you said, people have to love their mothers, but they don't have to like them. That's what I mean, she might be like you. You know, kind of between emotions all the time."

"You asked why I'm here. Why are *you* here?" I asked. "This doesn't seem like your kind of place."

"Yeah, well. Looks like we both got stood up. See, I'm looking for someone myself. But of course, she's not around either. Teresa never was very reliable. She likes to pretend she's, oh, I don't know, living the way she wants. But when the moment comes to fully engage the fantasy, she backs down. Still, we didn't really have a plan or anything, so I can't complain. I'll see her sooner or later. I'm gonna be around until I do."

I'd already stopped listening. The game-show buzzer had gone off in my head. The beret, the scarf. The image of the man-eating insect which had visited my dreams. It was here.

"Tell me why I should know you?" I asked.

She lit a cigarette. "You know. You just don't know you know. I mean you know me through *her*."

A picture was coming into focus in my brain, a grainy photo of a New Orleans street. A woman in a beret. A radical baby named Tanya. The closest I had ever been to the famous mother was that photo. But this woman couldn't be her. She was too cynical for the optimistic progressive force called Naomi McCoy.

"*Her!?*"

"My daughter. Yeah. I think you know her."

"Jesus."

"Teresa."

"Tanya?"

"Is she still calling herself Tanya?" Her eyes narrowed. She took a drag of her cigarette, "Well then I'm Naomi, Tanya's mom. Naomi O'Connell. You'd be Luc. Or is it Frank?" She swept her arm across the confines of the bar then laughed. "Alas the traveler always finds his way back to where he began, only to recognize it for the first time. Welcome home, Luc."

"Frank's fine. But how'd you know me?"

"I've seen your picture."

"Christ." But of course Tanya probably would have sent her one.

"I'm sorry Luc, but I forgot your last name."

"Payne. And it's Frank. Wow. Tanya's mom." I snickered to myself. "The famous Naomi."

"Is it funny?"

She did look the part. But she looked ten years younger than she should have been. Of course Harry had said she never seemed to age. I rummaged through my file cabinet of Naomi facts, cross-referencing, as if this could be somebody *pretending* to be her. I can get pretty absurd. Still after all these years—meeting Tanya's mom. I ordered another drink.

"I can't believe this," I said.

"What, you think I sat here because I was trying to pick you up?"

"You know, I came here looking for Tanya. She called me, said she wanted to meet, that she might be in Portland. But she's not, I don't think. Actually, maybe she is. I don't know. Where do you think she is?"

"She *should* be here," Naomi added, a bit concerned.

"She was up in Washington with that guy Paulie Manzoni. You know that, right? I mean, when she called me, that's where she was."

"Yes, no, I know. When did she call you?" She was sliding her glass back and forth between her hands. It was a nervous gesture that didn't fit the scene.

"A couple weeks ago, maybe a month. But I thought she might be down here by now. She said she was moving to Portland again. But we didn't really have any plans, like I said. But we used to hang out here."

"Well she told me something similar, must have been after she talked to you, a few weeks ago. Anyway, I sent her some money, you know—so she could move. I didn't want her staying with that meth dealer." She paused. "You know she was in that accident right?"

"She told me a little bit about it. Not much, as I remember."

"I'm sure she was drunk or high or something. I've been concerned about her. Especially the drinking. I don't need to worry about her getting strung out on speed, too."

"What about the arrest she talked about?"

"As far as I know she's cleared on that. Another dumb move on her part, being with the wrong people at the wrong time."

This crazy idea came into my head that Tanya had no intention of showing up in Portland. "Do you think this is a setup? It would explain all the coincidences."

"Oh God. You're a conspiracy theorist." She rolled her eyes, which for a second looked like strained eggs.

"No I mean—you, the bar, the picture. She sent it."

"What?"

"She sent me that picture of you and her in New Orleans when she was a kid. Probably so I would recognize you."

"But . . . you didn't recognize me."

"Well it's an old picture. And I wasn't paying attention. I'm just saying, maybe that was part of it. A test. Maybe she wanted us to meet."

"Yeah, maybe. And did you know JFK is still alive? And that aliens are living in Area 51?"

"No wait! See, she would have had to send the pictures *after* she talked to you. When I talked to her, she said she wanted me to find you, but I guess she did on her own."

"Want to do yourself a favor, Frank Payne?"

"What?"

"Stop writing the book."

"What do you mean?"

"All this detective crap. People don't talk like that in real life. They don't even think like that."

"Like what?"

"Like there's some big mystery to solve. I mean it works in books, where there's a limited amount of, you know, information that matters. But in life everything matters, the details get overwhelming, you end up talking in circles, kind of like you're doing."

"I don't know. It just seems right to me. It's like a metaphor—detective work, crime. It's a frame. You know what I mean? It works as well as anything."

"Yeah, but . . . don't you think people are laughing at you?"

"What do you mean?"

"Well, it's kind of silly. But anyway, listen, I mean, if there's a clue in everything, right, if every inanimate object has some moral significance, it can get pretty busy out there. I mean, there's always the danger the world might actually start living up to your paranoid descriptions. Or not. You don't know whether to be disappointed or glad. Besides you can't keep it all straight, anyway. How can you be sure you didn't slip up?"

"So you think I'm paranoid?" I said, jerking my head around a little just to act the part.

"That's not funny. Look, it's not criticism. There's nothing wrong with it. But you have to have certainty and control." She looked wistful. "To know exactly what people are going to do, and who they are, even before you know them. Or anything about them."

"But that's what I'm saying. Sometimes it even makes it seem like there's a plot to all this."

"Maybe. But you can't get there just by talking that way, using the voice. You can't make a plot by stringing together a bunch of aphorisms and non-sequiturs. You can't make characters out of your desire to hear someone speak."

"I've lived a good part of my life doing just that," I said. "At least I think I have."

"See, you don't even know. Besides, you don't have the empathy for it. Compassion doesn't come from innocence and that's your problem—innocence. But you don't want to own up to it. You want to be jaded and worldly. You size people up, only to dismiss them. You like to define them, but you don't engage them."

"That sounds like something Tanya said to me once."

"That sizing up stuff didn't work on her did it?"

"Not really. I knew her too well. At least I thought I did."

"Well, maybe she mattered to you."

"Lots of people have mattered to me," I insisted. I ordered another drink.

"Look, what if I turn it around? Two can play that game, you know." She started looking me up and down in an exaggerated manner. "Let me guess. I'm pretty good at this, you'll see."

"Okay."

"Okay then. You came from the middle-class. But you don't talk about it. You never talk about your parents. You act like you came from nowhere. Perhaps it gives you an excuse for feeling invisible. You bought into the "on the road" thing big-time, figuring it was a way to make sense of life. I know Teresa thought the same thing. You met her. You clicked. One day it hit you that it wasn't working. She was more of a problem than you bargained for."

"You got that right."

"Yeah, well, real people are way more complicated and a lot vaguer than people in books. But by then it was too late to stop, because if you did, things stopped making sense. Your life was half over and you hadn't arrived anywhere. The road didn't make you anything but confused. It made you feel old before you were old. It made you feel impotent before you were creative. Your dreams were defeated by circumstances. The future seems like an accident now, not an act of will. As hard as you try to stay ahead of it, you lose."

She was good and I was properly chastised. I'd lost the habit of being around women like her—women who were one step ahead of me. I hadn't been in an abstract conversation like this since my college days, talking to pretentious existential girls. At least this conversation seemed to have a point, or at least a different point. I nodded to the mirror. Even the mirror was in on it. The jukebox was telling me what a failure I was. Some Flat & Scruggs thing—a banjo and fiddle tune about failure and how funny it is.

"God, I hate hillbilly music. Why do they play hillbilly music in Portland?"

I thought this was an odd comment for her to make. The music *was* fast, but my paranoia combined with the alcohol slowed it down enough.

196

And I knew it was about me, not her. You see, I was in the swamp again, back outside Houma, with Tanya. I could hear the sawing of the insects. I looked at Naomi talking about me to me. Then I saw the mandibles of her mouth reaching for my neck. I pulled back. I was floating. It was one of those moments when the drink catches up to you, washes over you like a wave.

"What's wrong? Lost count?"

"Nothing," I said. I laughed. But the laugh sounded stupid. People in the bar looked at me. Then they looked away. I looked down at the floor. The puddle of beer on the floor was starting to look a lot like my personality. Apparently some of it had leaked out through the nail holes in my hands. It was slippery and vile, and now it was oozing slowly toward the center of the floor. "Stand up for yourself," I said to myself. And so I did—I lashed back, awkwardly, without sophistication.

"Okay, okay. So the mighty Naomi. Ha! If you really were her, you wouldn't even be here. Shouldn't you be out changing the world?"

"The world is changed already, or haven't you noticed? Everything is. It never changes back."

"That's good, though, right?"

"You don't know how good it is. Besides, I've had my fights. I never pretended to be anything really. Maybe I threw a bottle at a patrol car or marched against the war. Does it matter? Lots of people did those things."

"What? Is this modesty? Or is there a point?"

"I was out there. I could see myself. A lot of times you're just doing what you think you have to do, playing a role, following some dictate, you may well believe in it, even passionately, God knows, but you can't escape the feeling that in some way a script has imposed itself on your life, depleting it. You don't know where it comes from, but you do. The scary thing is that you yourself are writing it."

"Soooo what?" I tried to look more disillusioned than I was.

"Listen. Whatever history is, it most often isn't anything but the accumulated selfish decisions of numerous fools trying to get by and draw a little attention to themselves in the process, trying to climb that social ladder, find a little pleasure in the politics. It all boils down to hedonism. It may be for the greater good, but it's all still vanity and sex. If you're truthful, you face up to that. There's nothing so wrong with it. A lot of so-called history is made by bit players, people hanging around the scene, oiling the gears, taking a spine from the crowd. So here we are in this bar, so what. It keeps things moving. It's not a failure of the script, it's only part of it."

This was true, I thought. And everybody in the bar knew it. But no one was looking at us. They were watching us on TV. It was a TV show about people like us trying to figure out what went wrong—some sincere daytime drama.

"At least I'm young," I said. "My time is still ahead."

"That's what you think. You're not young. Ask yourself, why are you really here then, in this neighborhood? Maybe you identify with it, with failure. After all, you're alone. You left Teresa because she was holding you back. Now you want to find her, because you realized you weren't going anywhere anyway. You need comfort. You need to be rescued."

"Oh, c'mon. That's not it. I don't want to be involved with her again. Not that way."

"I'm not defending my daughter. I'm just asking you what you really want. How do you intend to escape the face you see in the mirror?"

"Is that even possible?"

"Everything is possible. If things don't fit your definition, you change the definition. Genet thought 'saint' was the most beautiful word in the French language. For him the saint was a murderer. But he himself could never murder. Sartre thought Genet was a saint. But he could never be Genet. See where this is going? The path to beatitude is the violation of a boundary—it's the thing you can't do, the line you can't cross. That's what people care about. And they don't even care about it that much."

"Hey, I read Genet, I read *Thief's Journal*."

"You and everybody else. So what? It was the trendy book for a while. You want to be St. Brando or St. Marlowe or something. But you're not, are you? Saints have humility. You're just little Frank Payne, all adrift in a world that doesn't care about you, and you don't know how to deal with it. Always looking out the corner of your eye at yourself. Trying to trap yourself in an interesting pose, trying to catch yourself existing."

"Well, you're no Jenny Fields, either. You dropped off the map yourself." The *Garp* joke rang hollow, but I couldn't take it back. Still, she laughed, she got it.

"John Irving was an opportunist and Jenny Fields was a cartoon." Naomi pulled a copy of Proust from her bag— *À la recherche du temps perdu*. "Maybe you should read this. It might be closer to where you're at in your head."

"I don't read French," I said.

Pointing to Walker outside, she continued. "Look at him. He was going to change the world, but couldn't even change his own life. He *was* a poet when he was younger. He was like you, a romantic, and now he's a bum."

"What happened to him?"

"Bone cancer. Arthritis. Alcoholism. A busted kidney. A bad leg. A motorcycle accident. It's a long list."

"Jesus. All that?"

"Not all at once, but they add up. Oh. And did I mention disillusion, despair? Want me to go on? No nirvana. No autonomy. No purpose. No sainthood. Everybody's just another body. Another bag of chemical clocks ticking down, ticking down." She was moving her index figure back and forth like a metronome. "I'm tired of the body. I'm tired of clock-like men. I feel let down." She was on her fourth gin and tonic and she was getting a little resentful. She raised her glass. "Say no to sainthood, Frank Payne. Like the man says. Fuck everything. And I don't even know who that man is."

"Where did you get that phrase?"

"C'mon, how old are you?"

"Nearly thirty. And not that. I mean where did you get that 'Say no to sainthood' thing?"

"It's a toast. I don't know its origin. They say it in taverns of the damned, I've heard—where free thought is locked and love shows its roots in deepest hell. Why do you care?"

"I saw it—written on a hotel wall, in New Orleans. Just a week ago, actually. But the writing was old. I don't even know why I remember it, but I do. It's odd too . . . because."

"Because how?"

"Because it keeps coming up. I mean like I'd heard it before, in different ways. I thought it must come from somewhere."

"Yeah, well. Don't try to make it mean something—it probably doesn't."

But I wanted it to, so I said the name. "The Hummingbird Hotel. That's it."

"You saw it there?" Her face went slightly pale like a leaf turned up in the wind. She pulled back slightly.

"Yeah. Written inside the closet no less. Like it had been there for twenty or thirty years years."

She paused, considering, weighing some outcome. Then whatever was stopping her, gave way. I could hear it. A bottle broke somewhere. "Room 33?"

"Yeah. How did you know?"

"Well, now I'm going to tell you something. That was the room where Tanya was conceived. Walker wrote that there. Something like 27 years ago. Indeed. 27 years, I guess," she said, musing. "I can't believe they haven't painted the walls in all that time. But that place always was a dump."

(27)

"**T**hat's TANYA'S FATHER?"

"Makes life interesting, huh?"

"I don't get it. I mean, now I do get it, but . . ." Actually I couldn't believe it, still I had no choice but to play along with it. "Why doesn't she know?"

"Maybe because Walker makes a modest living by not telling her."

"Blackmail?"

"It's not much, besides, he needs it. Actually, I'm happy to give it to him."

"You're kidding, aren't you?"

"It's a good story, though, isn't it? And that's all we can ask, really. Kind of like the story you're telling yourself."

I did the math in my head. Say Naomi met Birdsong in the Portland beatnik scene. He'd been younger than Naomi by several years. If he was ten, twelve years older than me, and Tanya was four years younger than me, and Naomi was around fifty—it could work. I'd seen it in movies—though I couldn't think of one off-hand. Anyway, it would place them in New Orleans in 1961. Tanya would have been five or six years old the year the picture was taken. But I didn't recognize Birdsong in the picture. But then of course he would look completely different. Besides he was in the background.

"God, no wonder she's so fucked up," I said.

"Hey, a lot of that has to do with her, she doesn't want to know. She wants to see what she wants to see. I mean you can't just tell someone something like that—the timing has to be right."

"And?"

"And . . . it never was. You can't replay life."

"But you know, she's always suspected something."

"I know. Part of the reason I wanted to see her was to tell her, you know, get that cleared up at least. I think Tanya in her own way is reaching out a little."

"It certainly seems to explain a few things."

"It does? I suppose it does, for you. I don't know what it will do for her."

"So what does the 'Say no to Sainthood' thing mean to you?"

"It was something in the news, some debate over canonization. I don't even remember who it was, Pope Innocent, maybe. And back then, Sartre had written that book on Genet. It hadn't been translated yet, but we knew about it; people were talking about it. Especially the idea that you had to violate society, do everything you could to undermine the value system. Anyway, Walker picked up on it, tried to turn it around, made it a slogan of sorts for one of his 'plays.' He said it was wrong to put people on pedestals they could never live up to. It changed the way they acted and the way people reacted to them, besides making all parties morally suspect. But anyway, New Orleans, yeah, well we were pretty wasted that night as I recall. He figured if he wrote it in the closet they wouldn't paint over it right away. Don't ask me. He really did have a theory about it, that's what's so funny. He always had theories back then."

"And so, what about him?"

"Walker? What about him?"

"How did you get together with him in the first place?"

"We met when I was a student at Reed, in the early '50s—he was still a kid, but he was on his own, hanging out with his brother. They were from a kind of migrant family, I think. Those were crazy times. We didn't get together right away. It was an on-and-off kind of thing. Teresa wasn't born till a several years later. I was already married to Harry. I never told Walker she was his kid. I told Harry she was his. But you know everybody sort of suspects these things."

"Oh God, so Tanya was really the hippie love child she always feared she was."

"I was twenty-four when I had her. Steven is two years older. He *is* Harry's all the way."

"I don't know, Walker doesn't seem your type," I said with a note of aspersion.

"Like Theresa is *your* type. What does 'type' have to do with it? Besides, he was a poet, he was doing a lot of shit, and he was young, charismatic, brilliant. I thought so anyway. A man of the people, I thought."

"What about Harry?"

"I married him when I got pregnant with Steven. I was still in school. Harry was against marriage, politically, but he did it for the kid. He had no way of knowing about Teresa but, like I said, I think he suspected. Anyway, what could he say? He was a free-love advocate, at least in word. God knows how many kids he has that I don't know about. If I ever knew, I probably would have left him. I left him anyway."

"Why didn't you just tell everybody the truth? You were all

liberals, right?"

"Somehow that doesn't work in the real world. Anyway, I suppose I had this idea—a little plot of mine that failed. That's why I'm telling you—don't make plots, life doesn't fit into them. Anyway, Harry was something of a freak himself. But he was conservative compared to Walker. I mean, he had that book out and people respected him, and he had some money, or at least I thought he did. And he was a teacher. I thought he was going somewhere. He never wrote another book.

"Anyway, we had already had Steven, and I really needed someone to stick by the kids. Walker might have pretended he wanted to raise Teresa, but he would have split eventually, the way he was. I couldn't risk it. I had to lie to Harry. It's one of those things only women understand."

"So your plot failed?"

She snarled a little. "I figured Teresa would probably hate me, when she got older. I mean, I hated my mother. But, I mean, imagine, if Teresa knew Walker was her dad, hell, she might be a young republican now. You certainly wouldn't have met her."

I wasn't sure about that. "Sounds to me like you didn't have much faith in your beliefs," I said.

"There's faith, and then there's statistics. Human beings use 15% of their brains. Over 60% of Americans believe the Bible is true, the literal word of some sky-daddy. These are statistics. That passion will mean something in this world—that's faith. That people will act logically or in their best interests—that's just foolish. Statistics always win, if only because once they exist, people have to live up to them.

"And so you left her with Harry?"

"Not as much as she thinks. We actually traveled quite a bit together. I knew she resented me, though. But Harry was teaching, he couldn't travel. Besides, I always came back. Actually, Harry resented me more than Teresa did. Still, I mean the three of us were together for years. But it was hard for a while. There was just too much going on. And Harry changed—first he got weird, then outright bitter at the way his ideas were used, sometimes even turned around to mean something opposite. He just couldn't see feeding the fire. It's funny looking back—he was more like Walker than it would seem. They both got depressed watching everything go sour, seeing everything get swallowed up by commercialism. Men don't hold up well. They believe in free will, and then they feel impotent when things don't go their way. Women aren't deluded by free will."

"I would think Tanya could handle all this. She'd probably dig it." Indeed, she might have *preferred* Walker as a father. But maybe that's because she didn't think Walker *was* her father, so the relationship could be vicarious. It would also mean she was at least one-eighth Native American, a trait she would not have failed to exploit. But there was no sense in going down that path.

"Yeah, well, then there's the small matter, maybe she told you, of Harry screwing the babysitter. What a cliché. The holy grail of middle-aged men. Hard as you try to avoid them, the clichés are there anyway. I actually caught them, *in flagrante*, as they say. Harry thought I was in Portland, probably with Walker. Maybe he thought of it as revenge. Anyway, I think that's what started Tanya on the road she's on. The primal scene, as they say."

"Wow. You know she turned twenty-seven this year."

"I know. We used to say if you lived to twenty-seven, you'd probably live longer than you wanted to. So I figure it's time. Somehow I have to reconcile with her."

"Reconcile what? I don't think she hates you or anything. Living up to your image is the focus of her life."

"I don't know if that's true."

"I was going to add . . . in some convoluted way."

"Right. I don't know if she respects me, or if she's just using me for her own purposes. As you probably know, Teresa lies. She gets in a jam. Old Naomi to the rescue. I don't even have to be there."

"But wait. If all this is true, then Tanya was rebelling against a false identity, you know, being Harry's daughter, like you wanted, but different."

"Ironic, isn't it?"

"I don't know irony from Adam," I said, "but I do know life isn't that simple. People never live up to the manipulation. They always fall short."

"That's what I mean. You can't second-guess it, it's just going to happen the way it's going to happen."

That was true. But then I got to thinking about how it affected me. Because if Naomi's story falsified the story Tanya thought she was living, and which I was reacting to, then it also falsified my story. That pissed me off. But I was being selfish. I may be a cynic. I may always assume everyone is lying. It works for me. But I don't like lying to myself. Even though I do it. Besides, it bothered me that Tanya's persona had something to do with this conniving mother. But then I also felt sorry for her. But there was also a bonus in all this complexity. It relieved everyone of responsibility, like an intricate bureaucracy of alibis in the invisible corporate structure of random life. And they were all in on it—Walker, Naomi, Tanya, Harry, Hollis, me—all buoyed into existence on the gossip they told each other. In fact, it just made them more of what they were or wanted to be, which was oddly comforting, if self-perpetuating.

It seemed the more I thought about these things, the shallower I felt. A strange inversion was taking place. I looked at my hand—flat as a movie screen. I looked around the bar. Flat. Everyone had an alibi, and we had to keep stating it so we wouldn't disappear. It was a sick way to look at life. Especially because the drama we relished was only achieved by editing out the hours of indecision, boredom, doubt, failure and biological necessity. You had to sort of become a logo of your own life. What was edited out was important only to your biographer, or as the unspoken back-story.

And Tanya was the center of the whole thing, even in her absence. I don't know how to explain it—her moral ambiguity maybe—it acted as a gravitational force. They resented her and they needed her like they needed Naomi. Or someone like her. Just as I did. Indeed, Tanya was the hub of a wheel on a wagonload of lost souls rolling downhill, and she knew it, and she played on it.

And that's how the spectator influences the game; that's the foundation of the passive-aggressive power structure. I started to understand her better than I ever had, if you could call my thinking some kind of understanding. Just then "Piece of My Heart" came on the jukebox. The song had a habit of acting as an inopportune punctuation in my life. We paused.

I changed the subject. "You know me and Tan met Walker's brother, Hollis, out in Hood River. He told me a little about Walker. Said his real name was Seth or something like that."

Naomi drew on her cigarette. "Hollis, now that guy, he's a real freak."

"I don't know. I liked him. He doesn't seem to like you, though."

"Well, there's more there than I want to get into. I don't know how much he knew about us. We kept it from him. He would have thought I was corrupting Walker. Hollis had his own idea of the Righteous Path. I suppose you heard that wolf-heart story of theirs?"

"Yeah, pretty amazing. Is that true?"

"I guess. Who knows? Personally, I doubt it."

"But I seen the scars."

"Everyone has scars."

"And what about these guys, Jack Starkweather and Ruby Beauvoir?"

She thought for a second. "Yeah. Yeah. The filmmaker, Jack Algiers. Fancies himself a Blakeophile or something." She laughed.

"You didn't like them? They acted like you guys were friends."

"Oh, we were. For a while. They were nice enough people, good hearts. Ruby was cool, as I remember. But that guy used to bug me. Him and his anarchist documentaries—always trying to stick a camera in your face. How do you know them?"

"This is crazy. Tanya and me met them in Chicago. When we found out they knew you, that was part of what set her off—that and Steven coming to visit."

"There's another ungrateful child angry at me. Don't have kids, Frank. You don't, do you?"

"No. But Steven, he seemed to want to be the Great Reconciler around us."

"Let him think what he wants. Ever since he got in AA he's always trying to solve other people's problems." She paused to polish off her drink before changing the subject. "That Starkweather guy, there was something sinister about him, you know, he could get into people's heads. I actually think it was Jack's bullshit that turned Walker around, all that crap about ego appropriation. I mean it really got Walker depressed, like there was nothing anyone could do."

"How did you meet them in the first place?"

"Madison. Me, Harry and Teresa were in Detroit at the time. Harry was from there. That was before we moved to Eugene. I hooked up with Walker in Chicago. He stayed there and I went to Madison. Then when we were all out in Frisco, Jack came out too. Don't think Ruby was there then. Jack ended up living a few doors down from Janis, actually," she said, pointing to the jukebox, because the Joplin song was playing, "if you can believe that."

"So you *did* hang out with her? Like they said?"

"Janis? I was actually her roommate, once, just for a few weeks, on Noe Street. In '64. You know Harry brought Teresa out there—she was really young, maybe around six, seven then. I'm sure she doesn't remember."

"She would go crazy if she knew some of this stuff. I'm kind of glad she never did, actually."

"Well, don't believe what you read. I hope she doesn't. I'll tell you one thing, too. That bitch who wrote that biography, I forget her name at the moment, she even mentions me in her book, at Woodstock, but doesn't use my name 'cause I told her I'd sue her ass. Even though I wouldn't. But writing to settle old scores isn't art. Dragging people through the gutter for money. But then she's a junky and they do anything for money."

The song on the jukebox stopped at the end of the guitar riff. The bar went briefly silent. Naomi looked briefly pensive. "Funny, I used to have that album in the old days," she said, "I had a lot of good stuff, most of which I left behind in New York, or gave away. I remember some speed freak, from Texas I think, who was crashing with us then, took off with a bunch of those albums. Maybe I gave them away. I was moving back West anyway and didn't want to carry all that stuff around. That was '69, I guess. Gave away my books, too."

Suddenly there was something bugging me. "There was something you said that I didn't get. You said I used Tanya?"

"Did I? I think we're way past that now. Whoever you use, you can bet they're using you too."

"No. I mean, what did you mean by that?"

"I didn't mean it as a criticism. I mean there was something you were getting from her; it could easily have been somebody else, but it wasn't. You know."

"No, I'm not following."

"I mean I don't believe that it's all nailed down. Some of it is accident, that's sure. But we choose to be in places where accidents easily occur."

That was true, of course. And I could see Tanya as some "accidental" messenger at my window. But I had left the window open. And I did use her. She brought me a kind of access. It's funny now to think that Tanya could have also brought me innocence. I actually feel more innocent now than when I knew her. Maybe we grow into innocence. We're not born with it. We're born with knowledge and then the angel of shame puts its finger to our lips and tells us not to tell what we know. If we don't talk about it, we forget. We grow dumb and susceptible to television. That's how the whole thing works.

I owed Tanya a great deal. And it was also she, I hoped, who would give me the way out of this. Perhaps that's why I sometimes assumed Tanya was dead, at different points—before the phone call, and after. I had no reason for it, but it was useful. It was like this thing I could "feel." I could feel sorry for myself and be free at the same time. I'd have no worry of finding her, which meant I could look for her without compunction or responsibility. It goes in circles.

And here was Mother Naomi in the flesh—less Ann Bancroft in a green sweater and more Joni Mitchell, pre-plastic surgery. Younger than when she first walked in, it seemed—decent shape, shoulders slightly rounded in a sexy librarian way. Who said the mother is the daughter in twenty years? Ben had said that. Naomi didn't really look much like Tanya, but if Tanya looked that good I'd be doing all right. But then I remembered I wasn't with Tanya anymore. I was with her mother. Not really "with" her, just drinking.

"I'll tell you something else, the older you get the less you know, and it's a good feeling. Yes it is." She stood up. "I should introduce you to Walker. But first I'm gonna take a piss."

She went back to the bathroom. I ordered a gin and tonic for her and something for myself. If only I could travel back in time and use this fact as a lever to popularity in my earlier days. "Yeah, I used to drink with Naomi McCoy," I'd say, lighting up a Camel and adjusting the bandanna around my neck, "Down on Burnside, Old Town, back in Ye Olde '80s." Somehow it didn't sound right. But it was a nice movie. I could imagine all the junkies and drunks looking at me and saying, "Wow, you used to drink with Naomi on Burnside? Cool, man."

Naomi came back and went over to Walker. She was trying to get him over to the bar, to join our conversation. This was going to be odd. "Guess what baby, this is Frank, Teresa's old boyfriend."

Walker sat down on a stool next to us. He was holding onto Naomi's arm. She slapped him lightly. Then she looked at me as she lit a cigarette. "Now Walker and you and me, we all got something in common. The symptom is different but the disease is the same, and the cure is the cause. You know the parable of the double man, Frank? Sufi thing I think, or maybe Borges."

"No. What?"

"The guy who saw his double in the street. He thought the guy was stealing his life. So one day he follows him and kills him. Then he realized he had killed himself and only his double was left."

"Oh wait. I heard that. Someone told me. In fact, I think it was Hollis told me."

"Maybe I got it from him. The point is that's exactly what happened."

"Still, I don't get it."

"You think about it awhile. Or don't. It doesn't matter."

Walker added, "Expect poison from standing water, Pilgrim. Don't love the poison."

I let that pass. "All right, but there's something else I want to know. First, about the rumor that you were having, shall we say, 'mental problems,' and second, what were you doing in Calcutta?"

"Let people think what they want."

"But what about Calcutta?"

"It's a long story. See it all started with an article for the *Voice*. They were actually going to do a photo spread of '50s and '60s people, one of those 'What are they doing now?' stories. We were all supposed to sit on a couch. They put all these books on the coffee table. I remember some of them—*Tarantula, The Electric Kool-Aid Acid Test, Soul on Ice, Really the Blues*. The writer called them "iconic" books. What an ass. *Steal This Book* was one of them. I mean, here's something that's a fake "cultural product" already, and they were using it like it was "real" in order to simulate another faked reality, all of which had no other purpose than to sell ads to an ad-created subculture so that they would gain a sense of community from owning the same stuff, *and then* start to think they were better than everybody else.

"God, I don't know how, but the working-class got left behind long ago in this; the old left, any real affiliation with ideas, the thing just went all wrong, it was all about fashion, radical politics as fashion choice, a form of segregation. Anybody that had any dignity got out of it, started working off the air—it was the only way you could escape being used. But if you didn't let yourself be used you were condemned as a traitor, you know, not being public enough, not promoting your ideas, like it was your duty. What we thought was our power was actually our worst enemy. I couldn't take it anymore, I thought maybe religion was the way back. I went down to the Lower East Side and hooked up with Dorothy Day. She was still there at the time. It was she who suggested going to India, somewhere where the cameras and the consumerism of the *Voice* and the all-seeing eye of the market was not. She said I could hook up with Mother Teresa. You probably didn't know but Teresa is named for her. Well, her and Teresa of Avila. Anyway that's what I did."

"What is the price of experience?" Walker asked. "Do men buy it for a song?" He shoved his face toward my face. "Or wisdom for a dance in the street?" Then he got up and stalked off.

"Don't worry about it. He does it all the time. He doesn't trust his own words anymore. He loves to quote old poets. Blake especially, picked that up from Jack, I guess. He mostly doesn't know who he's quoting, though. I feel sorry, but I can't help. You know with everything that happened to him, it made him appear a fool. In time he began to believe that he was a fool. Is Teresa still singing?"

"I doubt it. I don't actually know."

"Oh, that's right, you haven't seen her. She never put much into that, I mean I don't know if she was ever serious. You should have heard her, though, when she was a girl. She would sing to the radio. Something happened to her. But I guess kids grow up, something happens to all of them, you never know what it is."

"I don't know what she was before she met me. Her whole life was about letting go, but she never really could. She couldn't tap into it. Maybe I did teach her something. Maybe I taught her repression. Or that's what she identified in me. I don't know."

"You give yourself too much credit. She was bad for herself."

Then I remembered. "Hey, who did she marry anyway? Did you meet him?"

"No. But his name was Tony or Tom. It didn't last but a few months.

Just a desperate crazy move if you ask me, the kind of thing she is prone to."

"What do you mean?"

"I mean I think she married him 'cause she wanted to stop, you know, settle down. But apparently he didn't. I heard about it through Harry. He was extremely upset about the whole situation."

Walker was getting anxious. He came back to where we were sitting. "C'mon Nomey, I got to get something to eat."

Naomi made as if to get up for a second. "You know, you might hear from Teresa soon. You might find her, or she'll find you. I don't know what she's up to. It's hard to tell with her. Whoever she reaches first, tell her I'm available. I want you to let me know. All right? I'm going to give you my number in town. And listen, you too, I mean if you need anything, I'm available. I'll be around for two weeks. I'll give you my address and number. Call me anytime—we'll make some kind of arrangement. Tell Teresa I need to see her, that I'm not angry or whatever she thinks." Then she pulled a little notebook out of her breast pocket. She had to undo a couple buttons to get at it.

"Let's have another drink," I said, not wanting to end the encounter. I pushed the new gin and tonic toward her. She wasn't expecting it.

"Okay Frank." She was half laughing. I was looking at her perplexed. The asymmetrical smile broke. "Here, let's toast." We raised our glasses. "To anarchy, or whatever," she said. "Speaking of which," she continued, "whatever happened to that motorcycle you guys had?"

"Sold it, almost a year ago. Tanya doesn't know."

"Escapism's not what it used to be, is it?"

"Nowhere to go," I said.

"I thought it was supposed to be the journey."

"As opposed to what?"

"Didn't find yourself, eh? That's okay. Self-knowledge is usually bad news. C'mon, we'll have one more drink. Walker can wait. We'll buy him one, too. I'd really like to see Teresa. I brought pictures of her when she was a kid. If you want to see them, you can call me before the weekend. You'll see—a little freckle-faced angel. I'll tell you about the trial. Or do you know about that?"

"Something about a Teacher's Union in Eugene?"

"A lot more to it than that. I'd like to see that picture from New Orleans, maybe you could show it to me. I remember telling Harry I was taking her there for some conference. He didn't care."

"Maybe I'll send it."

Naomi was rolling her fingers on the bar. There was a documentary on the TV about insects taking over the world. Then the jukebox jumped on suddenly with that Simon and Garfunkel song, "Mrs. Robinson." It was all a little too well orchestrated. I don't like having my paranoia coddled. Even if I felt oddly comforted. Then some guy came up to us trying to sell plastic watches. "Genuine plastic," he said, seriously. We both began to laugh. The late afternoon sun was blaring through the window. My future was a blank. I ordered another round. The world is a sick place—I knew it before and I knew it again. They say you can have an opportunity twice but you can't know things twice. Well, you can. Actually, you can know things more than twice, you can know them as many times as you want, it just doesn't make any difference.

Part VI
flashback/tombstone

(28)

IT'S ODD THAT I REMEMBER THE EXACT DATE THAT ROY LATOURE died. It was October 11, 1970. A week after Janis, actually. The two events seem connected for me by more than proximity in time. Maybe Roy heard the news and took a cue. Maybe being from the same region, he moved with a similar tragic momentum to the singer. There were theories as to Roy's death: enlarged heart, alcohol, phenobarbs, speed. They found him alone with his head on the table and a broken bottle of mescal on the trailer floor. There were lipstick stains on some glasses in the sink. But Ginny Lynn was gone by then. I don't know if she left him, or he, her, or if that rupture was even the trigger. The news was already five years old when it got to me. I had known he was dead, I just didn't know exactly when it had happened or that it had been suicide. My brother told me. I was with Tanya at the time, in Chicago. That makes it around '75.

A record was skipping on the turntable in Roy's room, *Cheap Thrills*, I imagine. And that scene as I imagine it, brings into high relief another scene six years earlier, in a basement pad in Hammond—Roy and me were listening to that same record. Very clearly the image of the album cover was tied to the song. But more important is how each of these remembered scenes serves as a stepping-stone to yet another. Each is a *tableau porteau* or window through which I am able to step back, yet again, into my hometown kitchen, on the day I first heard that song, "Piece of My Heart," which would have been back in '68. I remember the voice clearly. Back then Roy would have been on the road himself probably. He may still have been in New York, because it was toward the end of '69 that he came back to "the Region" figuring to lose his speed habit and his troubled mind. But Roy had brought the music around which these scenes accrued, as if the music were a glue to disparate perceptions.

I wanted to believe Roy had handed me some legacy then, some appetite which I wouldn't be aware of until I saw it in Tanya's eyes several years later. It might even have been Ginny Lynn's similarity to Tanya that was part of my initial attraction, I mean that whole tragic package of irreverence and spirit that tumbled in through my window one October evening on SW Clay. I sensed it emotionally, even if I did not recognize it intellectually. I sensed it when I heard the bottle break in the alley below that window, seconds after she knocked it off the ledge. But I recognized it three years later, watching her guide the spike into her arm. And, of course, I only seem to be *knowing* it now. Is there a difference between recognizing and knowing, between sensation and certainty? This I can't say.

But what I am talking about is not any particular truth or kernel of wisdom, but rather the beginning of what I later came to call the Hank Williams/Patsy Cline gestalt—a certain imposition of melancholia upon hindsight, whereby I was clued-in to emotions I would not actually experience for several more years. One of them is that day-late-dollar-short, empty-dance-hall feeling a man might have who returns to marry his high-school sweetheart only to find another flawed human girl grown tired. There's a certain satisfaction to the inevitability that is not entirely unlike the satisfaction of the weary traveler who finds himself in a crumbling deserted church in a jungle or a foreign city and he hears in his brain the old serenade of windshield wipers and breaking bottles in the rain, and he wonders how he got to this point in his life, even though he really knows.

But let me go back to that morning in '68—I was sitting in the kitchen eating a bowl of Lucky Charms, or some such cereal. I heard "Piece of My Heart" on the radio. I'd never heard anything remotely like that—a voice that could split open the dead air of dance halls exposing the vast chasm and chaos beneath, and hinting there could be a thrill in looking over that edge, be it dance floor, kitchen table or end of the road. A question seemed to construct itself in the seductive abyss: Did I want to try?

And what's more incredible is that while the song played, my eye moved from the cereal box to the radio, which then became kind of animated, vibrant-like, with an aura about it, like a cartoon character. I half-expected it to sprout arms and legs, strut across the white formica and start jiving with me, telling me to "tune in, turn on, and drop out." Perhaps the seeds of my attraction to Tanya had been planted then.

Of course I was only fifteen at that time, and probably incapable of such influence or insight. But I did have a strong visual and emotional image: I imagined this woman, Janis Joplin, getting up on stage in some great auditorium in limbo. She's not the main act. Maybe people are filing out, or they're already gone. But she has to sing this story. I don't want to hear it. In fact I'm already at the door. But that voice uncoils slowly upon me anyway, like a barbed-wire serpent's tongue, and then it snaps and I am snagged in the gut, my hands up against the wall, assuming the position.

As I look back, it's funny how my image of Janis at that time was as an older woman, a blowzy somewhat broken woman, perhaps wearing a stained white wedding dress, with a cigarette and a bottle in her hand. Like I said, I was only fifteen. Then at some point, maybe twelve years later (a few of those being the years during which I knew Tanya), when I heard that song, I didn't connect to the fact that Janis Joplin would have been the same age as me, both of us in our mid-20s. And now, of course, looking back on those days, I see her as a kid, as I was a kid at her age. Truth is, she was already dead most of the time I was aware of her. She was even an archetype before I knew what that was, a martyr for desire before I knew why that mattered. She remained frozen in time, while I aged.

And, it occurs to me now, oddly enough, that the cartoon characterization that radio took on years before might actually have been a message sent back to me through time, from 1972 to 1968. The message being that my fate lay in living up to certain future images; I mean specifically those cartoon images on the album's cover. It was strange—I don't know if I needed them or they needed me, but it is quite possible that both were true, as if we were/are all buoyed up into a mutual two-dimensional reality by an unconscious yet controlling faith that existence is a fragile self-reflexive contract between ghosts (of all tenses nonetheless) agreeing to agree to agree to agree unto infinity, or at least the end of this, our mortal coil.

&

I DIDN'T MENTION the hippie farm earlier, but once, before I knew Tanya, I had spent three days on such a farm down in Wallace, Indiana. I got high and stared for a prolonged moment into the "eye of God" design of that *Cheap Thrills* album cover, while the record spun on the turntable like a black flat flying saucer with little pain-and-grace notes dancing over it. I could and did touch those notes, and I "knew" the feelings they represented. But everything we know is always something else as well, and the flying saucer of that record spinning was also the maw of a whirlpool drawing me in and onward into time and down.

The other spooky thing about the experience, and what made it truly Hank and Patsy-esque, was the fact that at some point in one of the songs—maybe it was "Turtle Blues" or maybe it was "Ball and Chain" (they become the same in the fluidity of memory), you can hear a bottle break in the background. It's very subtle, but under the influence of Windowpane, it picks up an incredible amount of significance, as if the breaking of that distant glass were a decimal point, separating my youth, from my eventual adulthood, if indeed the latter was ever achieved.

Things did seem to happen in the interim. Altamont happened. Manson happened. The first Nikes were rolling off the assembly lines. McDonalds was already planning a franchise on the moon. In 1984 the Macintosh would appear in an ominous Superbowl ad. But that record would continue to spin unchanged. Indeed, that sound and what it came to symbolize, could be replayed, and replayed endlessly. It would repeat itself in echoes throughout my life, like a psychological black hole. Past experience kept accreting to it, until over the years the memories grew so dense around it that nothing could escape, not even my so-called "personality."

The breaking bottle at the center of that whirlpool would suck up every aspect of my personality until I was little more than a blank page, what they call a *tabula rasa*, a tablet for associations, appropriations, recollections, which had already began to write themselves despite me. And they did so with a vengeance—as augmented memories, ornamented testimony. I even began to recall Bette Davis-style arguments with Tanya, complete with hi-ball glasses flying across the room and slamming doors. I suppose it was then I began to drink more to escape this weight, this force of gravity. But drinking confused the issues, causing me to remember things I actually wanted to forget. And the human need to narrate the impressions often tied things together too tightly: coincidence became plot, anarchy became obsessive compulsion, and existence became the prolonged revisitation of certainty cast into doubt.

But it wasn't all weakness or mere facility; there was a spirituality to it. After all, prolonged existence on the road allows you to short-circuit whole parts of normal life. One jumps elliptically from location to location, conveniently forgetting everything that happened in between. Hindu and Buddhist saints can do this without moving. But the talents of such holy men have been replaced and improved upon by TV. I suppose that's why modern people watch it, for the illusion of transcendence. In fact, today they actually want you to believe that everything is happening everywhere and that there are so many possibilities you can watch and shop forever and never exhaust your human potential.

&

THAT BRINGS ME back to the road. Today, when I remember that road, I remember Tanya McCoy. And I think maybe we did overplay it to compulsion. After all, we did travel with a certain amount of fury, criss-crossing the country endlessly, it seemed—New York, Chicago, Portland, New York, New Orleans, Los Angeles, Portland, New York, Chicago, New Jersey, Eugene, Ogden. We didn't just run the hitchhiking lifestyle into the ground, we stomped on it, flayed it, scraped it with stones, hung it in the wind like a Buddhist prayer flag—an offering to unknown gods. Yes, we took the kinetic call-to-arms to heart.

Sitting over cheap local brews in roadside diners, we fantasized that people wondered who we were. We let them wonder and we wondered back. For all they knew we could be heirs to the Starkweather/Fugate heritage—highway killers reborn in passive bodies, but still bearing forth the noble momentum, the past-life memories. For all we knew they could be the ones who'd gun us down on the outskirts of town. But it was that "wonder" that drove Tanya and me insanely across the landscape, thinking that, if we stopped, the world would stop making sense. Or maybe it would start making sense and then we would have to take responsibility for it. Or maybe we were just running out of piety.

And if someone pinned us down as to the meaning of our lives, we tried to give the lifestyle an esoteric twist. We'd say stuff like "The great thing is to move," or "Get complacent and you die inside," or "Movement is the opiate of the disaffected." We could keep it going—tossing off the aphorisms, stringing the clichés out like hot cheese. We'd drop names: Fitzgerald, Kerouac, Steinbeck, Kipling. We quoted people we'd never even read. "Trust no thought not born in motion," Tanya had once said. Someone told her Bob Dylan wrote that. I think it was Fred Nietzsche. No one ever called us on it. Why would they?

&

LASTLY, THERE WERE the photographs. Although I never saw Tanya again, I did have four photos. I sent the two "New Orleans" photos to Naomi in Eugene, as she had asked. The other two I kept. One is of Tanya and me, taken at the intersection of Highways 49 and 61. Mary Stone had sent it years later. Somehow Mary had tracked me down in Chicago through a mutual friend. Mary had been in the van with us that night on the way to New Orleans. It was her camera. We insisted she take the picture. The road sign reflects a sinister glare from the van headlights. Me and Tanya are shaking hands. Her expression was one of goofy enthusiasm. Mine was more puzzling, as if I were saying to the future viewer of this photo, "Don't come back here. It's not what you thought it was." But now I have to wonder "who" that was—that past "me" who had the wherewithal to send this message into the future.

And then there is the passport photo of Tanya, the one we had taken for our big Amazon adventure. I read once that all photography is actually some kind advertisement for death, a product or service that somehow makes life better by forcing a comparison. We therefore like to see them as proof or promise of a past "reality," a life lived fully without the burden of after-knowledge. I think of passport photography this way, but in a more sinister fashion. I think a passport photo is basically a lifeless set of physical data meant as evidence, a mugshot for border crossings. The irony here is that the image is supposedly a form of security. It claims that the person represented really does or did exist, and is not merely a set of contingencies, a product that varies with circumstance, untraceable from one moment to the next, something we suspect is true.

Today, I look at these two photos and I see certain emotions I never saw in real life. The immobility of the image allows me to meditate, to project, and to expand, even to construct. Often the construction dominates. But if Tanya was, and now is, primarily my construction, it does not mean I cared less for her. It doesn't matter that my memory has made her into someone she never was—made her smarter, dumber, thinner, fatter, more or less moral than she ever was. It doesn't matter who she became after I knew her. Today, I'm sure I wouldn't even recognize her: a middle-aged housewife with kids, a prison guard driving a mini-van, an unmarried woman on a barstool. She's likely someone I'd avoid.

&

WHOEVER WE THINK we are, we are only temporarily that person, and then we are someone else. Both to someone else, and to ourselves. In fact, we are never even the same person to ourselves. We are indeed wanderers without even moving, and so we might as well move. Medieval Christians had a term for this condition—*homo viator*. The phrase acknowledges that we are only passing through this evident world, and that we have no true home within it. Centuries earlier certain gnostics had said that all souls are condemned to roam the roads toward some forgotten goal—our job is to look for clues to our purpose, to remember. Various mystic sects throughout time have claimed that the human head contains a pea-sized gland evolved for this purpose (a gland perhaps bypassed by evolution), and this gland is a receiver of some sort, a radio for ethereal wisdom implanted in the fleshly body of the wanderer.

If this is true, I believe I have unwittingly condensed this "ethereal wisdom," as it were, into a single human image, something I could understand. I first saw this image on a road in Wisconsin the summer after the Speck murders. The year was 1964. There he was in the middle of the night looming up in the headlights of our family car, in his ragged overcoat. The radio slid temporarily off its station. My parents swerved temporarily out of the lane. They regained their path. But for me that swerve never ended. It repeated itself in the funhouse of my peripheral vision: the theater balconies, game arcades, bus station lobbies, and the mirrors of SROs.

It's a hard kind of condensation, as the ethereal wisdom becomes merely the image of this unwanted friend, always hanging about the outskirts of significant events, smoking his cigarette. He was the appendix to every narrative, every explanation, the discarded option at every junction. It was not a happy circumstance to see him, but perhaps a necessary or inevitable one. He's not always a guilty party either. In fact, he's often innocent, but innocent in a weird world where shame is not the end of innocence but rather its constant companion. Let the scholars talk all they want of Rousseau's natural man, Romantic orphans, Promethean shadows, Blakean spectres. Maybe that's the problem—an inability to live in the face of constantly having to mean something. That's the rub.

Thus when I think back to those flashing road seams, those ticking demarcations of time, I think back to the piercing of the darkness by the white-bolt light, I think of the tunnel experienced by the dying, and I sometimes remember how I believed that while driving down all those night highways, that Tanya and I, as participants in an evolving warp and weft, also existed in a naive sleep-like state, and that we were being solicited all the while by wiser beings. Call them what you will—the dead, the damned, ghosts or gods—maybe they were manifest wisdom, maybe they were merely messengers between our world and some more perfect mechanistic beyond, between flesh and mathematics, between the ether and the enormity of earthly desire. This is how the world rebegins. This is how things happen.

And, as I said, it does seem things happen. And we do think we remember them. Alcohol and time may blur the edges of such so-called memories. Or we might blend them with excuses and accusations. People ask questions. We make up answers. We keep the game going. Sometimes I get a glimpse of that questioning face at the edge of the campfire, beyond the crown of the headlights, in the outer dark, and it's then I realize the prosecution looks just like me, or rather some has-been version of myself with a has-been agenda.

He's got photos and fingerprints and he's also got a theory about why such-and-such a scene went down—where and when—and he's going to get a conviction if it kills us both. I can smell his breath as he says, "Listen Frank or Luc, or whatever the hell your name is, we want to know what you did, October 3rd, every detail. We want to know when you went to the toilet and when you blew your nose, what you had for lunch and who you spoke to. If there's a second unaccounted for, we will nullify your existence. Your life will disappear. No one will ever know your name." It's enough to drive you to drink.

NOW VODKA IS clear, but it can make you black out if you drink enough. Like there's a little switch somewhere in your brain, and all you have to do is find it. But mescal is golden and a shot or two can add a religious dimension to experience—a sense of fresh arrival upon a familiar scene. I've used them both according to my needs. I think it was Albert Camus who claimed that art (and perhaps, by extension, intoxication) was but a slow trek of rediscovery, the hunt for those few great and simple images in whose presence one's heart first opened. One of mine was, incidentally, a fabricated scene: Janis with her whiskey on an empty stage in an imaginary wedding dress.

Which is why, all these years later, I still can't watch the Monterey Pop Festival film and see that woman in her white outfit, singing "Ball and Chain" without grief. I hear the sound of a bottle breaking down the haunted halls of the long hotel of the mounting recollections and it makes me want to turn to whoever is nearby, grab their lapels and tell them about it—you know, how it is. I could act out all the passion I didn't have in those days. I could use that same exaggerated vocal quality Tanya herself might use. But what would I say? How would I ever explain myself? Is it a game or some kind of mystery that can be won or solved? Besides everyone's got their own problems.

And if it is true that we are only increasingly restrained by the accumulated habits or fashions of our fallen path, then it *must* be a pleasure to look back. If only you could look back far enough, to remember the world started out hard and small and so well organized there was once nothing there. There was no opposition at all. It could almost seem like freedom.

Carl Watson is a writer living in NYC. He has published some books including *Beneath the Empire of the Birds* (short stories) by Apathy Press, and *The Hotel of Irrevocable Acts* (a novel) by Autonomedia. These books have also been published in France by Vagabonde Press and Gallimard respectively. Recently Vagabonde has published *Une Vie Psychosomatique*. Watson also writes regular opinionated essays (under several names) for *The Williamsburg Observer*, an anarchist publication that originated at the Right Bank Cafe in Brooklyn. Currently he is working on a book about Henry Darger's autobiography which he hopes will dispel the myth of literature and romantic genius and condemn all writers to the category of biological machines engaged in redundant self-constitution no different than the growth of crystals, the birth of stars, or the splitting of amoebas.

"The voice is loose, jazzy and fast, the tales liquid and hot, avoiding the romance of macho drug memoirs with black humor, verisimilitude and a knack for the absurd . . ."

Kate Christensen, author of *In the Drink* and *The Astral*

"*East of Bowery* is a sharply focused, street-level view of downtown before the real-estate agents started renaming everything."

Steve Earle, author of *I'll Never Get Out of This World Alive*

"Drew Hubner's prose and Ted Barron's photos are kin, at once raw and lyrical, grit and grace, which is what the city was like back then. The combination is magic, the essence of the time and place."

Luc Sante, author of *Low Life* and *Kill All Your Darlings*

ISBN: 978-0983927105

SENSITIVE SKIN

art, literature and music by and for ne'er-do-wells, black sheep, blackguards, scoundrels and wastrels

Number 8 $24.95

Jennifer Adams
Thaddeus Rutkowski
Karen Lillis
Todd Colby
Ruby Ray
Mike Hudson
Ray Jicha
Chavisa Woods
Mark McCawley
Jim Feast
Tom McGlynn
William Lessard
Les Bridges
Su Byron
James Greer
Rob Hardin
William S. Burroughs and Allen Ginsberg
Justine Frischmann
James Romberger
New Monsters

plus: Chris Bava, David West, Ted Barron, Leslie Hardie, Charlie Homo, Jeff Spirer, Marcin Owczarek, Kym Ghee & Cédric Monot

SENSITIVE SKIN number 8 includes a rare interview of William S. Burroughs, conducted by Allen Ginsberg, with never-before published photographs of Burroughs by Ruby Ray, from the iconic *RE/Search* magazine shoot of 1981. Also from Ms. Ray, a portfolio of classic punk photographs (Flipper, Sid Vicious, X, Darby Crash, etc.) from the late '70s Bay Area scene. Also includes fiction by James Greer, Mike Hudson, Chavisa Woods, Karen Lillis and Thaddeus Rutkowski, poetry by Todd Colby, a comic by James Romberger, art by Justine Frischmann and much, much more.

ISBN: 978-09839271

Barefoot in the Heart is a collection of transcribed oral stories of the Indian saint Neem Karoli Baba (Maharaji). It includes many anecdotes and first-person retellings of stories collected in India and the in the USA over a period of 9 years, by Keshav Das, including a small selection of unpublished stories originally intended for inclusion in *Miracle Of Love* by Ram Dass.

"*Barefoot In The Heart* is a divine raft to take us across the ocean of darkness to the glorious land of light. Every page is filled with Maharajji's nectar. Profound gratitude to Keshav Das and his collaborators."

—Jai Uttal

ISBN: 978-0983927129

MUSIC

DRAWING DOWN THE MUSE

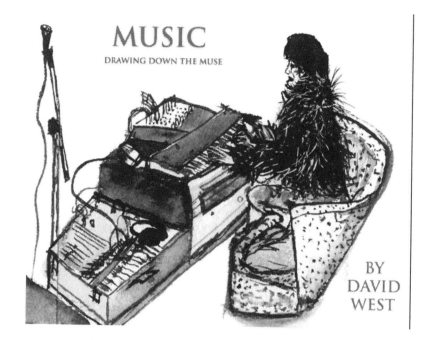

BY
DAVID
WEST

"Inside this book you get *portraiture vérité* of bands in action. Banging away in rehearsal. The appreciative eye watching the battle of the bands as they try to navigate their way through the sometimes complicated maze of illusions, delusions and solutions of grandeur before asphyxiation and evaporation of all the notes into the air. I'm the wrong person to comment on rehearsal as I work in a more backward way. I don't care if a performance is anally-retentive-perfect because a computer can do that now. I'll work hard on something to a point then I stop, as what I want surprises myself, especially in a live situation. It's a viewpoint probably not shared by most of the bands in this book but that's what makes things interesting. It's up to others to state theirs and that takes us to the artist.

David West hits the target dead center BOOM with his beautifully liquid renderings of NYC bands in rehearsal. Mr. West captures a scene in the late 1990s largely ignored. These aren't vacuous American Idols but musicians who are The Real Deal. Like a fly on the wall, David gives you an inside view from his own multifaceted eye. There is a dripping aquatic fluidity to his drawings. Mr. West is not afraid to let the ink, gouache, and watercolor run and flow never betraying the nature of his medium. That's why he's The Real Deal. If you the viewer can't understand, appreciate and see that in his work then go out and get corrective eye surgery!"

—Monte Cazazza, Psychic TV

ISBN: 978-0983927174

Shamed by your English? You can learn to speak and write like a college graduate by reading **SENSITIVE SKIN** magazine just 15 minutes a day!

www.sensitiveskinmagazine.com

To buy print versions of the magazine, and to find books, CDs, DVDs and more by our contributors, go to our store:

www.sensitiveskinmagazine.com/store

To find out more about **SENSITIVE SKIN BOOKS**, including our ever-growing catalog, go to:

www.sensitiveskinmagazine.com/books